When she was at school, An   f
PE by saying she would us   and
dedicate it to her gym teache

In the following years, she pursued a career in journalism, working for women's magazines including *That's Life*, *Cosmopolitan* and *Good Housekeeping*. Specialising in 'real life' stories, she interviews seemingly ordinary people about their extraordinary lives – most of which you wouldn't believe if you read it in a novel.

She lives on the Dorset coast with her family where she reads voraciously, watches influencers with increasing fascination and swims in the sea. She is the author of *The Girl Who . . .* published by Atom in 2021.

Also by Andreina Cordani

The Girl Who . . .

DEAD LUCKY

Andreina Cordani

ATOM

First published in Great Britain in 2022 by Atom

13 5 7 9 10 8 6 4 2

Copyright © 2022 by Andreina Cordani

The moral right of the author has been asserted.

A CIP catalogue record for this book is available from the British Library.

ISBN 978-0-349-00354-2

Typeset by Hewer Text UK Ltd, Edinburgh
Printed and bound in Great Britain by Clays Ltd, Elcograf S.p.A.

Papers used by Atom are from well-managed forests and other responsible sources.

Atom
An imprint of
Little, Brown Book Group
Carmelite House
50 Victoria Embankment
London EC4Y 0DZ

An Hachette UK Company
www.hachette.co.uk
www.atombooks.co.uk

To Yvonne Uttley-Wright and Mrs Mason,
my understanding PE teachers.

And to all the funny, fabulous, frank
and fantastically freaky people who
put their whole lives online for our
entertainment. You're braver than I am!

Author's note

The characters in this book are influencers who mainly post on the fictitious online platform, PlayMii. Over the past few years, the real-life video-sharing platforms we use have worked hard to ensure that inappropriate content – you know, things like hate, extremism and onscreen murder – is taken down as quickly as possible. Unfortunately, the programmers at PlayMii haven't quite caught up with the curve . . .

Chapter 1

By the time the video was taken down, three million people had watched Xav Bailey's murder.

The post is an unusual one for Xav these days – no stunts, no laughing hangers-on – but it's still on-brand for him. Every now and again he shares classic-style intimate chats-to-camera and they often get better views than some of his crazier ones – people like to get the feeling they are seeing the real Xav.

He's sitting at the desk in his apartment; the shelves behind him are as messy as ever with piles of graphic novels, gadgets, game packages and bits of memorabilia jammed in tight together. Chaotic mess was always Xav's style, but over the years the disorder has become staged – that bobble-head figure 'carelessly' shoved front and centre is tied into a game he's been sponsored to promote. And the coffee mug, emblazoned with the words *Ed's Tears*, is nothing less than cruel.

Xav is wearing a white T-shirt made by an edgy, cult Korean brand – the logo on it is so small and discreet you would have to know what you were looking for to see it, a dog-whistle signal for a certain kind of hipster. His shoulders look broad in it; tanned biceps strain the fabric of the sleeves ever so slightly. Xav always had the balance just right between having a tight, toned body and looking too ripped. His skin, as ever, is amazing. But the most striking thing about Xav is the aura of confidence about him, shining out brighter than his shirt. You might think it's the kind of self-assurance that comes with millions of viewers hanging on your every post, with sponsorship deals, celebrity link-ups and hot and cold Korean shirts on tap. But he's always been like this. He knows exactly who he is and where he should be and the effect pulls people towards him like iron filings to a magnet. You see that fun, laid-back smile and you want it to shine on you. Even when you know what he's really like.

There's no messing around at the beginning of Xav's videos, and he's talking fast: as we all know, those first fifteen seconds of content are everything. As he talks, reeling off a brutal review, he's waving the case of another game.

'OK, the headline is this: it's bad. Really bad. It's time we invented minus stars for games this catastrophically awful. What's the opposite of a star? Oh yes, a black hole. This piece of crap gets five black holes from me – and let's hope it gets sucked into one of them, never to return . . .'

As he throws the game case over his shoulder, there's a sound behind him, a flicker of movement, and he looks up mid-rant, a flash of confusion on his face. He leans back slightly and we can see the room behind him a little more. That's when we get our first glimpse of it. Of the face.

Oh God, that face would haunt us all, millions of us, for months to come. A rubber mask, grotesque and swollen, the mouth a twisted, red-raw grin, the skin a sick, yellowish-white colour, bulbous and knotted in some places, skull-like in others. A warped mask, horrifically unreal.

We jump from the shock but common sense tells us this is a set-up, one of Xav's acolytes winding us all up again. We wonder what Xav will say next and prepare to be entertained.

True to form, Xav's reaction is a bit more calculated now. He's not as good an actor as he thinks he is.

'Oh God,' he says. 'Oh God, no . . .'

The figure grabs him roughly, black-clad arms around his shoulders, gripping his jaw and pressing his head against its chest. Xav doesn't fight back, but a look of annoyance crosses his face.

'Hey, the hair! The hair!'

Xav doesn't see the knife until it's too late and there's no time for him to react. The sound is bad on this part; all we can hear is a grunt, a cry and then a kind of sigh.

The figure stands, and for the first time you see the knife in its gloved hand – a sharp kitchen knife, the kind that costs a fortune and goes through steak like butter. It's not a stage knife; it's very shiny and sharp and slick with red. The figure leans forward until its disgusting leer fills the entire shot, until you can almost see the glimmer of the screen reflecting in the creature's eyes, deep-set and almost completely hidden by the mask. *There is a human being inside this monster.* Then some animated text appears across the screen – the same style and font Xav always uses. But this time it's not a wise-crack or a link or a #spon alert.

The words say: *He deserved it.*
And the words say: *This is real.*

At first, nobody could quite believe what they'd seen. After all, Xav's pranks often cross the line between funny and tasteful and, a couple of months before, he'd pranked his hangers-on by faking his own kidnapping. So it's hardly surprising that the first people who watched it thought it was some kind of sick joke. They shared it anyway.

The comments below start off mildly.

Whoa . . .

Xav, mate, you've gone too far again . . .

WTF is this?!?!?!

But then the real fans, the serious fans, noticed that something was off about it. Where was Xav's usual sign-off? The end screen links? Or his cheery, ever-present: 'If you like what you see, don't forget to leave a comment, like, share and follow!' The camerawork was static, when his earlier kidnap video had been shot from several different angles and edited beautifully.

It only took a few minutes for someone, a slightly-more-awake person somewhere in the American Midwest, to write:
Holy crap. This is real.

And share it.

And the only way people could decide for themselves was to watch it again, ask their friends what they thought, share it again. PlayMii stepped in as fast as it could, took the whole thing down, but by then viewing numbers had rocketed,

4

bootlegs had been made and shared, passed around chats, message groups, schools and colleges, with fake reverence and real shock. Fans were horrified, fascinated; the mainstream media went absolutely batshit. And Xav, so famous in life, became even more famous in death. The first PlayMeep to be murdered on screen, in the most ghoulish, chilling way imaginable.

He would have loved it, but he was gone.

Chapter 2

Maxine, one day before

This is amazing. It's flipping ridiculous. I'd laugh if I wasn't so terrified because what else am I supposed to do? I'm on a stage. A freaking *stage*. Every time I do this I think there must have been some kind of mistake, this many people can't be here just for me – this is *crazy*.

I've never been in a Hollywood movie, I've never won an Olympic medal or done any whizzy, science-y thing. In fact, some days it's a struggle to tie my shoes. Should I live to be a hundred and still be posting on PlayMii, I don't think I'll get over the fact that people care enough to buy tickets to an event and travel all the way across the country, just so they can meet me.

It's an incredible feeling, but right now it's not good-incredible, it's scary as hell, because this isn't the same as when nice people sidle up to you in the supermarket and ask for a selfie. This is a crowd. I can't make out individual faces and when I look down, all I can see is a forest of raised hands holding hundreds of sparkly-covered phones pointed right up at me. Little details jump out – a rainbow-print sweater-sleeve, sequinned bangles on a masculine wrist, the light glinting off someone's incredible bejewelled nails. If I met each one of these people by themselves, I'd be totally up for a hug, a pic and a chat, but all together in one big lump they are, frankly, terrifying.

My stomach backflips – the Danish pastries from the green room are threatening to come back up again. The lights are make-up-meltingly hot and now I'm even hotter because a lava-like wave of panic is flooding through my body. *Ohcrapohcrapohcrap.*

I bite nervously at one of my cuticles, then stop myself and take an awkward step forward, tottering like that GIF of Bambi on ice. Mum was right, these heels were a mistake. Out of the corner of my eye I can see her – she is also pointing a camera at me from the wings and mouthing something like: 'Come on, Max, get it together.'

Her camera-free hand is waving at something centre-stage and for the first time I see there are two stools there. One already has a blond male interviewer in a flowered shirt sitting in it; the other one is clearly meant for me.

High stools. Another surge of dread wells up inside. When you're five-foot-nothing, a stool can be a major mountain to climb, even when you're not on a stage with hundreds of people staring up at you.

Somehow, I manage to slither my bum on to the smooth seat, but I can't fully push myself up without losing my dignity. Note to self: short dresses and high stools – not a good combo. What underwear am I wearing? I can't remember but hope it's decent, because five hundred people and their followers are all about to see it.

And as I struggle, that familiar old feeling takes over. *Stupid Maxine. Can't even get on a stool. What a moron.*

Some members of the audience are laughing awkwardly, unsure if they are supposed to – PlayMii fans really are a supportive bunch in the main.

But the sound of those giggles makes something click inside me. These people know me. They know I'm not a slick media professional. I'm the same clumsy, chaotic, leopard-print-loving idiot they see on PlayMii every day. The one who didn't realise you were supposed to take the plastic casing off the Peperami before eating it, or who genuinely thought Milton Keynes was an American soap actor. Hell, most of them have seen my underpants already – albeit drying on the radiator in one of my earlier bedroom vlogs.

Sod it.

I am stupid bloody Maxine. Take me or leave me, I'm not changing.

I drop any attempt at dignity and clamber up awkwardly until I'm on, so that when I'm finally perched up next to the interviewer, knees clamped primly together and feet crossed at the ankles, everyone in the room is laughing. In a friendly laughing-*with* rather than laughing-*at* kind of way.

Now get a grip, I tell myself. The panic has dulled to a steady thud-thud in my chest and, provided I don't lift my arms, nobody will see the stress-sweat patches under the arms of my dress. And at least now I think I can trust myself to speak without my voice going all wobbly and pathetic.

'Good old Maxine.' The presenter smirks. 'We can always trust you to make an entrance! And just to kick off . . . go on, say it!'

'Oh, I don't know . . .' I shake my head, my face flushing hot again as the interviewer begs and the audience begins to chant '*SAY IT! SAY IT! SAY IT!*'

I laugh – it's the only defence I have. There's no squirming out of this one; I'll have to say it. But I can't keep the reluctance from my voice.

'I love horror films, they're really maccabree.'

Everyone erupts into laughter and once again I wonder if I'll ever be able to live down this slip of the tongue I'd made in a video aeons ago. I'd only ever seen the word macabre written down – how was I know it was pronounced mac-aaah-ber?

As the whoops die down, flowered-shirt guy starts on the proper questions. 'So, you started out at fifteen, making prank videos with a few school friends we might possibly have heard of.' He pauses as the audience laughs knowingly. 'And now look at you! Views of your explainers are skyrocketing, you're best mates with super-successful PlayMeeps Xav Bailey and leni-loves, and rumour has it there's an exciting new merch in the pipeline. You're one lucky gal, right?'

I know what he's expecting me to say – the speech every online creator makes when we're asked about it. But it's that word, *lucky*, that grates with me.

Because yes, I am lucky. The kind of lucky that's busted my butt making a video every day for nearly three years. The kind of lucky that sleeps for five hours a night and wakes up at first light, my mind buzzing through ever-more elaborate ideas, only half of which are physically possible. Lucky that I'm so famous, people make memes about the shape of my thighs which had me shooting videos from the neck up for weeks – until the comments on my double chin started to appear. Lucky that I've forgotten what my face feels like without make-up as I can't leave my room without it. The kind of lucky where I can't relax, can't breathe, can't stop picking, picking, picking at the skin on the little finger of my right hand until it bleeds, until it scars . . .

I force back the surge of pressure and think about the good things. That dizzy, light-headed feeling when you see the views and likes start to climb on one of your videos, second by second. The ridiculous, expensive freebies that land on my doorstep every day. How it feels when people you don't even know send you birthday presents and friendly fashion advice, or hug you in the street, crying and telling you that you changed their life. Because of all this, it's worth it. It's worth the 24–7 always-switched-on madness, the late nights, the corporate PR fakery that gets thrown at you, the sheer terror of messing up, of making an army of people angry by accidentally saying something stupid and thoughtless or using the wrong tone of voice. It's worth it because this is what I always wanted to do, where I always wanted to be.

'What can I say? I'm the luckiest girl alive.' I smile, and I feel the warmth of the audience rising up, enveloping me.

'The idea that millions of people are watching my videos when I'm just chatting away to a camera in my bedroom, it's . . .' I make a little *mind: blown* gesture next to my head.

There are whoops and cheers from the crowd and I realise I'm smiling. A nervous, toothy smile, but still, the cheering helps.

'So,' flower shirt guy goes on with a knowing look, 'was this part of your all-conquering five-year plan to take over the internet?'

Everyone laughs again. If there's one thing people know about me it's that planning and smart moves are not my thing. Mum and Carl handle the business stuff; I just make goofy videos and hope for the best. I shrug in a *what can I do?* kind of way and wait for the laughter to die down. It stings a little but that's OK. Mum says ditzy is my brand, that I need to accept it and work with it.

'Well, there wasn't actually a plan,' I say. 'The people who start out wanting to make money and get loads of sponsorship deals never make it, do they? People can smell that kind of fake a mile away. But when I first started out with Leni and Ed and, yes, with Xav . . .' A small 'boo' comes from the back of the room at the sound of Xav's name. But I press on: 'When we started out, none of us expected to get this far. We were just having a laugh, like everyone else on there, and that's what makes great PlayMii content – real, normal people having fun, sharing silly things and laughing. That's why, even if I woke up tomorrow with no subscribers at all, I'll always be part of this community.'

A hungry look has appeared on the interviewer's face and there's a feeling in my stomach like a stone dropping. I've mentioned Xav, which means I've given him permission to go there – to talk about him and Ed and The Drama and everything Xav has done since.

From the corner of my eye I can see Mum shaking her head in frustration. *Easy for her. She's not sweating it out on this stage.*

When the questions come, they're fired at me like machine-gun ammo.

'And what's the deal with you and Xav? When did you last speak to him? Do you condone the way he's been acting? Would you still call him a friend?'

My first reaction is a big fat fuck-you. Is he really expecting me to spill my guts on stage? Take down a friend just because he's made a few bad decisions, and yes, OK, possibly turned into a bit of a monster?

But then, spilling my guts is what I do. My fam expects me to be honest, which is why it's easier never to say anything about Xav and Ed and the whole Drama at all. There's just too much to hide. *What to do, what to do . . .*

'I haven't seen Xav in a long while,' I say finally. 'He and Leni are so busy doing their thing – filming, feuding, whatever – they're about a million times more successful than me. I know he's been a bit of a dick lately, but I also know he's going through a bad time and . . .' *and I have no idea how to finish that sentence.*

So I don't. I leave it hanging, knowing that even those few lines will be picked up, pared down, dissected and spliced back together into a thousand memes and GIFs before I've even finished signing autographs and posing for selfies. I've just called Xav, one of my oldest, formerly closest friends, a bit of a dick in public.

I think about the last flurry of video messages from him – so many I haven't even had time to open them all – and the guilt kicks in. I told the truth: I haven't seen him face to face in a long, long time, but I still know he's in pain. Self-inflicted pain, but still, that always was Xav's thing.

I try to calm myself as I walk back down the corridor to the green room, thinking about nabbing another Danish.

But as I walk in, I can sense the atmosphere in there has changed. There's a crackle and zing in the air; people are moving and speaking like something is energising them. Then I hear his voice. A ghost of a high from the past wells up: the flutter of anxiety, the desperation to make him laugh and the brilliant high that rockets through you when you do.

And there he is, Xav Bailey, relaxing in full manspreading glory, taking up the whole of the cheap two-seater sofa. There's an adoring array of fans perched on the arms, the table and even the floor around him. I saw a TV documentary once about a pride of lions and he reminds me of this. A big alpha male lolling around, yawning and being fed by the rest of the pride, but still all muscular power, able to spring up and savage any rival who shows their face. Xav is wearing a close-fitting striped T-shirt; the ends of his exquisitely sculpted hair are highlighted in about thirty different strands of gold, but the colour peters out into brown. He likes to let his roots show. He looks relaxed, at ease, but I know he's heard what I just said. Someone would have told him.

Style it out, I tell myself. If I apologise, it'll only make him worse.

His smile is easy and broad, flashing those beautiful white teeth. He catches sight of me and suddenly his whole body is motion. He's on his feet.

'Maxi-Pad!' He smiles, arms outstretched. 'You OK, hun?'

'Dickie! I'm all good.' I smile and hold out my arms; we join in the most insincere hug in history. I know it's being filmed but what can I do about it? Everything's being filmed.

I realise I'm back to the trembling thing again and I wonder if he can feel it. He leans out of the hug, his nose wrinkled in disgust.

'Wow, Brutus Maximus, you stink of BO.'

I had forgotten the sweat patches. His acolytes cackle, all except for the shy, gawky one at the end. I've always had a soft spot for Ethan, the PlayMii superfan, even though he once confessed to going through Leni's recycling looking for 'souvenirs'.

Xav's face softens then and he laughs – he's decided to go easy on me today.

'Come, come, sit, sit! What's the crowd like out there? Are there any of those Team Ed wankers I need to look out for? What about Leni-Stans?'

'Only one boo when I said your name, you should be safe,' I say, squeezing in next to him and homing in on the pastries.

Xav makes a little pout of disappointment, as if he was looking forward to heckles and fights. He sighs and rips open a bag of M&Ms.

'Hey, Ethan, open your mouth,' Xav says. Ethan drops his jaw like an obedient lapdog and Xav starts taking pot-shots at him with the sweets.

'Your turn, Maxi,' he says, holding out the bag. I hesitate and the distaste must be showing on my face.

'I really don't mind,' Ethan's reedy voice pipes up. 'It's a laugh, isn't it?'

Xav's next M&M hits its target perfectly and, while Ethan is busy coughing and spluttering, Xav turns to me. He leans in close and I can smell coffee breath, see the tiny bit of stubble which he missed shaving this morning. And I can see his mask slip. I glimpse the tired, angry Xav who sends me messages late at night: *God, Max, this business sucks . . . I'm falling apart . . .*

Xav grabs my arm, squeezes it until it starts to hurt.

'Maxine, it's time,' he murmurs, quietly so his entourage doesn't hear. 'Time to burn it all down.'

I hesitate, flustered, not sure if this is banter, or if we've entered a whole new territory here. There's a look on his face, a fleck of bitter rage in his voice that I've never heard before. But then his eyes flit away from me and a woman with a clipboard hovers nervously into view.

'Um, Xav?' She says the name with hesitant respect, like there's an unspoken 'Mister' before it. 'You do know you're up now? They've been waiting a while.'

Xav's groan is mixed with a yawn and a stretch, then he's on his feet. 'No peace for the beautiful. See you later, Max Factor!'

He's gone, and the room is greyer and smaller without him, but I can breathe more easily.

Mum appears at my side, back from the Ladies and ready to rush me to our meeting with the stationery people. Her face has that cross look it gets whenever she sees Xav.

'Honestly, I don't know why you let him get to you,' she says, which irritates me because I thought I'd done a good job of hiding it. She looks down the corridor after him, shaking her head. 'One of these days, that boy is going to get himself in real trouble.'

Chapter 3

Maxine, one day before

My mind is still on Xav as Mum whisks me smoothly from the green room to another meeting room nearby. I swear it feels like she's holding my hand, leading me along like a toddler. But I know I'm lucky to have her. Most parents I know just yell at their kids to stop making silly videos and get on with their homework. But Mum is different. Even after what happened at school – the uproar, the fingers of blame pointed at Xav, Andy and me, her first response was: you've got something here, go with it.

And when things started to take off properly, she quit her job to help me with the boring stuff – the scheduling, working with the PlayMii algorithm, the marketing. I also have a manager, Carl at Dreams Inc, who makes deals. He greets us at the door now, looking slick in an expensively cut black suit and black shirt. He doesn't mention the whole Xav-is-a-dick thing. I'm not sure how he feels about me badmouthing one of his other clients, but he usually says anything goes as long as it 'drives fan engagement'. Which of course makes me feel awkward and strangely dirty that I mentioned it at all.

'Maxine, Giulia!' He nods at Mum. 'Ready?'

I nod and try to focus on the moment. This is it, my first proper retail merchandising line. Xav has had his own merch for ages and every time Leni launches a new make-up palette, there's a small riot in the aisles of Superdrug. But although I've been doing T-shirts and things for a few years, this is the first time I'm going to be selling something in proper shops – my very own range of Maxine Loves Leopard stationery. I am genuinely, madly excited about this. It means I've arrived.

Still, as I sit down in my leopard-print skater dress, I feel small, out of place and, despite the spritz of YSL Mum applied, still smelly.

My phone vibrates on the table in front of me. The first alerts are coming in after my talk. The backlash is already beginning. I force myself not to check it and pick at my cuticle instead. Pick. Pick. Pick. Pain blooms around the nail of my little finger. I pop it in my mouth to stem the blood.

'So, the samples are here,' one of the corporate people says, with a look of fake glee on her face. 'We think they're pretty special!'

Bzzt. My phone again. I pick it up, stupidly, and the words *bitch* and *dumb* jump out at me. I lock the screen, put it face down on the table, a new wave of heat and panic spreading through me.

There's a box on the table and the executives are unloading my new stationery range, piece by piece, out of the bubble wrap. I glimpse hot pink and leopard print. *Come on, Maxine, enjoy this moment.*

Oh.

'Hey, they look *fabulous*,' Carl croons dreamily. 'What did you say the margin was on these again?'

'Oh look, a furry pencil case!' Mum says, waving something that looks like a dead spotty rat in my face.

My heart is sinking further and further. Can't they see this stuff is crap?

Yes, leopard print has been my thing for ever and, OK, I know it's sometimes tacky. In fact, the tackiness is part of what I love about it. But this stuff is just ... a bit shit. The pencil case looks like it's been mass-produced in the worst, most unethical kind of sweatshop, and the zip would probably break in about five minutes. As for the notepad, I wouldn't pay £1.50 for it, let alone RRP £10.99.

I have to say something, I have to. But I'm still shaky from the speech and then talking to Xav, from the words on my phone. I can't think of what to say.

What if they laugh? What if they tell me I haven't got a say in it? What if they call off the deal entirely?

Bzzt. Another alert – maybe it's a death threat, maybe 'just' rape.

'What do you think, love?' Mum asks.

'They ... they don't look much like the original designs we saw,' I say. 'I'm not sure we've got it right yet.'

Carl repeats something about mark-ups from cost price and all the adults nod in agreement. The cheaper they are, the more money there is to be made.

'It makes sense, love,' Mum says in her most soothing voice.

'But I . . . I thought there'd be gold foil on the notebooks,' I finish lamely. I sound like the stupidest person in the room. Which I am. Exhibit A: no business degree. Exhibit B: in fact, I didn't even bother to finish my A levels. Exhibit C: the Milton Keynes incident.

Carl makes a soothing noise and reels off a bunch of percentages which I can just about follow, but part of me is aching with disappointment, desperate to speak up again.

Mum lays a gently restraining hand on my shoulder and murmurs: 'Leave this stuff to Carl and me. It'll be fine. And stop picking your fingers.'

So for the rest of the meeting I look at my phone, as if I'm a kid at an adults' dinner party. I scroll through the hate that's being thrown at me. *Dumbass . . . What does she know . . . Did you see her underpants? . . . Did you see her stupid face?* Memes, vlogs, Reddit and Tumblr posts saying I've Broken My Silence, I've thrown shade on my former best friend. #TeamXav on the attack, #TeamEd members accusing me of trivialising Xav's appalling behaviour as simply dickish. This is the flip-side of being so lucky; we get this thrown at us. Every single day.

There's one that snags on my eye, though, and chills me.

Forget Maxine. Xav is the one who deserves to die.

We get death threats a lot and this one's pretty standard – a Twitter egg with no followers – but however often it happens, my instinct always responds with a mild stab of panic every time I see one.

'Maxine?'

Oh right, the meeting. It's winding up now. I get to my feet, plaster on a smile as we leave the room but I feel sick, flooded with anxiety. If I don't get out of here this minute, I'm going to throw up all over Carl's expensive suit.

'Bathroom,' I garble, and then I just run, back along the dim corridor, ankles twisting in my silly shoes, until I see a Fire Exit sign. I push the bar – an alarm sounds but as soon as the door is closed it stops, and I am standing out on a concrete fire escape on a side street full of overflowing bins and litter. Finally, though the air reeks, I can breathe.

I sink down to the steps. It's gorgeously sunny and the warmth of it on my face is comforting somehow. There are passers-by, an elderly woman with a shopping trolley, a bald, skinny guy with earbuds and a messenger bag. I love vlogging and I love the people, but it's nice to know there's an outside world that has no idea of what we do.

There's someone else on the steps with me, too – a girl about my age reading a battered, curled paperback called *The Master and Margarita*.

Like everyone at the meet and greet earlier, she's dressed in a way that's supposed to draw attention to herself. It's like a tropical island threw up on her. She's wearing a Hawaiian shirt tied loosely over a vest, her knees are drawn up into a clashing, flowing floral skirt, there's a patterned scarf woven through her thick, dark hair (which looks almost as unmanageable as mine). A huge pair of oversize sunglasses, the kind you see Instagram fashion grannies wear, are pushed up on her forehead. No accessory has been left untouched in the

21

making of this look – there's a chunky ring on almost every finger, a clanging clutch of bangles on each wrist, mismatched earrings. She's got an image all right, but she's not a PlayMeep. I can tell that because, frankly, it's a complete mess.

She's wearing eyeliner and lipstick but not a touch of foundation or concealer, despite the white line of a scar on her temple and a mature (I want to say crusty but, ew,) zit next to her nose. And her rampaging caterpillar eyebrows are enough to make Leni throw her hands up in horror. But I can't stop looking at her because she's also beautiful. Not in a made-up way or a model way, but in a way that's real. There's something about her strong chin and her gentle, concentrating frown that draws me in.

'You're staring at me,' says the girl, her eyes flicking up from the pages. She didn't sound pissed off, just stating the fact. Even slightly surprised.

'I was looking at your book,' I lie. 'It looks weird.' That bit's true.

'I'll take that as a compliment,' she says, and with a flash of a smile she doesn't look odd or try-hard any more; she looks like someone who is completely at home with who she is and doesn't give a crap what other people think. *Oh, to be like her.*

I suddenly feel super-conscious of my bedraggled, sweat-ringed appearance.

'You're one of that lot, aren't you,' she says, nodding back towards the door I came from. 'From the creator meet-and-greet thingy.'

I nod. 'I'm Maxine,' I say, and wait for the flicker of recognition, but it doesn't come. I'm half-peeved, half-relieved.

'Frida,' she says. 'It's all a bit much in there, isn't it? I only came because my mate from college had a spare ticket, but I think you have to be a serious fan to get something out of this, and me – I don't really do online. This is more my thing.' She waves the book and her rings catch the light. Her fingers are short and strong; there's chipped dark varnish on her nails.

'I know what you mean. Meet and greets can be so . . .' I clamp my mouth shut. I don't want to say anything to diss my fam, even when all that love and expectation feels like it's going to crush me.

'It's fucking *weird*,' she says. 'So much need, so much desperation and excitement. It's like five-year-olds on Christmas morning but with people as the presents.' She stands up. 'It's sunny. I spotted an ice cream parlour nearby – want to come?'

I'm not the sort of person who trots off with someone she's just met, but this girl's confidence is so rock solid, her decision so final, I find myself standing up and following her to DiMaggio's Gelato. We pick a booth at the back – there's no way I could relax in a window seat with a huge shopping mall full of PlayMii fans just around the corner. I splurge on an extra-large tutti-frutti special because I know it'll look good on IG and try not to think about the Danishes I've already eaten.

We're just getting to the proper introductions when the youngish-looking waiter sidles into view and plonks the sundae glasses in front of us. But instead of going off, he sits down next to me.

'Having a good day? Bet you're having a better week than I had. Can you believe I got dumped?'

I sigh. This is something that happens to me a lot. Waiters tell me about their love lives, random old ladies on the bus tell me about their corns, Xav's superfan Ethan fesses up to going through people's trash. Xav himself dumps his desperate, sad secrets on to me. Mum says I just have one of those faces, something about me makes people trust me.

It certainly helps with work and some days it's fine, but right now it's really not. I go into self-defence mode, refusing to make eye contact, studying my tutti-frutti like it's got the secret to the universe inside, pressing myself into the corner of the booth. He doesn't notice. He talks about how he bets we've already got dates lined up and how girls always ditch him because he's not successful enough and . . .

'Please go away,' Frida says. 'Sorry to hear about your girlfriend, but we don't want to talk to you right now.'

The waiter's face twists into a snarl; he spits something about frigid bitches. Frida raises one incredibly bristly eyebrow and she looks at him curiously, like she's discovered a piece of chewing gum on the bottom of her bag and is trying to work out where it came from.

'As a matter of fact, you've stumbled on the annual general meeting of the micropenis appreciation society. Just let us know if you'd like to submit an image for our website.'

The guy's face goes blank, like he doesn't know how to react, then he stands up and stalks away, without another word.

We wait until he's slunk out to the back of the shop and then burst into laughter.

Oh my god, this girl is amazing.

You know when you meet someone new in the romance department and you really click, and you talk and talk, and there's this connection, this chemistry? Well, that's what it's like with Frida, minus the sexual attraction bit. She's just so funny, so easy to chat to. I feel like I could ask her anything.

'So if you hate PlayMii why did you end up coming today?'

She shrugs. 'I've no idea. It's not me at all. I mean, I used be on everything – YouTube, PlayMii, TikTok, Snapchat – but it wasn't good for my mental health, so . . .' She waves something small and grey with buttons at me. It takes a couple of seconds for me to realise it's her phone. It's *ancient*. It looks like the one my nan had, before I bought her an upgrade. Laughing, I tell her what I do for a living.

She cracks a smile, but there's a sense of hesitation now, maybe disappointment, as if she's thinking we can't be friends. For a couple of seconds, there's silence between us.

'But I'm normal,' I say. 'I promise!'

'Oh, how disappointing,' she says. 'Who wants to be normal?'

We laugh, and it's all OK again.

'Well, it's a living, I suppose.' She says. 'But isn't it full on, posting every day, performing all the time, being a *brand*?'

I open my mouth to tell her how lucky I am, but the word *brand* makes me realise something – I've eaten half my sundae without photographing it. That wave of panic rises back up inside me. I haven't posted on any platform since this morning. That's six dark hours. I should be editing my video about today right now, dealing with the reaction to what I said about Xav and ...

'Why are you crying?' Frida asks. 'Are you OK?'

That does it. The worst thing you can do when someone is starting to cry is ask if that person is OK. I cry even more, big sobbing gulps. *Where the hell did this come from?* I hide my eyes, embarrassed, wave her away. And then she pushes a slip of cloth into my hand.

Wait.

'Is this a *hankie?*' I ask in shock. 'An actual handkerchief? People still make those?'

'I'll have you know it's not a mere hankie. It's a reusable wipe made from sustainable bamboo. Totally different.'

'It's got your initial embroidered on it.'

'OK, it's a hankie. I like retro, so sue me.'

I've stopped crying now and the reusable wipe is really quite soft on my eyes – only a bit of make-up seems to have come off.

'You must think I'm some kind of diva,' I apologise.

'Of course you are, you're an influencer,' she says, and then, when she sees my face: 'Kidding! Just ... just tell me what's on your mind, it might help.'

I realise that it's been a long time since anyone asked me about myself. Technically, Leni's my best friend but she's so busy with her channel that I haven't seen her face to face for months, and most of my other friends are so busy dumping their secrets and stresses on me, they forget to ask. So I try to explain about what it's like being this lucky. About how I'm scared anything I say is going to blow up in my face. About Xav and Ed, how I've always tried to stay out of The Drama. About how it's hard to condemn someone in public when you know he's in a bad place, but it's equally hard to stick up for him when he's behaving like a complete bell-end to his lovely, sweet boyfriend.

'So let me get this straight: your friend treated his boyfriend like shit for months before publicly dumping him, and now *you're* the one being trolled for mentioning it?'

'And for not mentioning it earlier,' I add.

She shakes her head. 'I am *so* glad I signed off all this stuff.' Frida reaches out and takes my phone. 'I'll fix it for you.'

I watch, frozen in horror as she finds the power button on the side and presses it. I never turn my phone off. Never. I take it back and it's like a dead slab of nothing in my hand.

'I don't mean for ever,' Frida says. 'Just give yourself twenty-four hours off.'

I don't think that's going to work, but what I do know is that I want this girl to stay in my life. I feel nervous, like I'm about to ask her on a date or something, but I decide to risk it. And so I blurt out the question.

'How do you feel about early mornings?'

Chapter 4

Maxine

I'm up at 5 a.m. as usual, exhausted but still annoyingly wide awake. The flat is silent. We live in a modern apartment block designed for Busy Executives – there are no creaking floor-boards or clanking central heating pipes here, no noise from outside makes it through the huge plate-glass windows, just the quiet hum of top-of-the-range air conditioning. It feels like being in the cabin of a smooth, quiet luxury liner.

The apartment came with everything – the high-end furniture, the abstract sculptures and the blobby designer lamp-shade over my bed. It's as if we bought this successful lifestyle off the shelf. At first I'd unpacked all my stuff and arranged it around the bedroom but my old art projects and pinboards had looked small and tatty in this big, white-walled room, so I'd boxed them all up, replacing them with a steady trickle of freebies and high-street hauls. Now it's like the Graveyard of Trends. Rose gold here, cacti there, unicorns replaced by llamas replaced by sloths. Filmed from a distance it looks OK, though, and I'm getting used to it.

I check my phone and panic for a second when I see the blank screen, thinking it's broken. Then I remember Frida turned it off yesterday. I know what will be there when I turn it back on – stacks of notifications, a text from Leni along the lines of *WTF Maxine* and a new private video message from Xav: *I trusted you, Maxamillion.*

So I chuck it back on to the bed and prop up the GoPro on my dressing table. I always film myself doing my make-up – after I've got my base layer on, at least. It's a nice way to update my fam with what's going on, but it also helps clear my head, just like keeping a journal does.

'So it's the morning after the night before,' I tell the camera as I swoosh my eyeliner on with all the confidence of some-one who's been wearing the same stuff since she was four-teen. 'I've tried really hard not to talk about Xav's behaviour, but when someone asks you a question directly, it's hard not to answer them.

'So here's the deal. Do you remember the first band you really, really liked? For me it was One Direction. Oh my god, I had every single poster, every single picture. I had a framed photo of Harry by my bed that I used to talk to at night . . . actually, forget I said that. But I did.

'And then, I don't know what happened, but I found a different kind of music, stuff that was slightly more edgy, more meaningful to me and what I was going through. I started to think that *maaaayybe* 1D's music was a little manufactured and fake? And that *maaaayybe* I never really would run into Harry and make him fall in love with me? Basically, I grew up a bit and went off them. But the thing is: if you were to slag them off to me now, even if I agreed with what you were saying, I would defend them with my life. With. My. Actual.

29

Life. Because they're part of who I was then, they made me who I am now. And I guess that's how I feel about Xav Bailey.

'I know he's done horrible things and I'm not excusing any of them. Dumping someone live on PlayMii isn't something any human being should ever do, but the thing is, there's stuff you don't know about Xav's life – stuff hardly anyone knows. You probably look at it and think he's so lucky, he's got this perfect life but he . . . he . . .'

Oh crap. No, this won't do.

Problem one: I'll have every single 1D fan in the world shrieking for my blood. Deservedly so. I could never betray my Harry.

Problem two: Xav's private business is not mine to share. He's never spoken a word about it, and neither should I.

Stupid Max. Dodged a bullet there.

I delete the video, but just as I'm about to wipe the eyeliner off and start again I see a greyish light is coming in through my window. Oh come *on*, how can I be awake at 5 a.m. and still late? I jump up in a panic and tear the room apart looking for my yoga pants.

Of course I'm late. I always am when Mum's not around to hound me out of the door. When I get to the park, silvery shafts of sunlight are reaching over the horizon, glinting from the strange metal frames lined up on the grass. Frida is already there, wearing rose-patterned leggings and a purple man's T-shirt with a retro tequila ad printed on it. She's squinting in the light, looking a little bit hungover.

'Heavy night?' I ask.

'Nah, just didn't get much sleep. I've got a lot on my mind right now . . .' Her voice trails off, and I'm about to ask her what's up when she shrugs.'Nothing that an hour of dangling around in a giant sarong can't cure, though! Oh, the instructor looks pissed off.'

'This is sunrise aerial yoga, not five minutes after sunrise aerial yoga,' jokes the teacher, although she clearly isn't joking. She gives us the spiel about how greeting the sun in the morning sparks up oxytocin levels or removes toxins or whatever. Then there's more delay while Frida removes every bit of jewellery she's wearing, but eventually we're there, sitting in the two slings of fabric hanging from the frames.

The first few moves are stretchy and kind of nice, but then the instructor tells us to start our first inversion.

'What, upside down?' Frida asks.

The instructor acts like this isn't a big deal, so we lean back and wrap our legs around the fabric like she says and . . . *flip.*

Oh, this feels wrong. I'm upside down, wrapped tightly in fabric and swaying unnervingly in the breeze, but worst of all, I must have made some sort of mistake because I'm trapped. My arms are kind of bound up in the fabric so that when the instructor says to swing back up again I can't. I wriggle. It gets worse. I catch Frida's eye – she's stuck too. She looks like a caterpillar in a giant cocoon, swinging help-lessly, her head sticking out of the bottom of the fabric, her hair brushing the grass below and her face bright red. We both start to laugh uncontrollably, so hard that the instructor has to help us both down.

Later on, after abject apologies to the poor instructor and some filming on my part, Frida and I loll back on the grass, sharing Frida's flask of coffee. 'You really should be drinking coconut water,' the yoga lady says. We make polite noises and lie that we'll definitely do that next time.

'To be honest I only did this because I knew it would look ridiculous,' I tell Frida. 'I do these explainer videos where I give everyone the idiot's perspective on whatever the latest craze is. So, the more stupid I look in it the better, really. Xav once said it takes a special kind of genius to make money out of being thick and I guess I'm proving him right.'

'Your friend Xav sounds like a first-class knob. I've met people like him before, charming arseholes who are only in it for themselves. You should stand by what you said yesterday.'

'I know, and it's weird,' I say, shaking my head. 'Part of me is angry at Xav – really, really angry about the way he's treated Ed. But another part of me wants to defend him. Because they don't know the full story, where he's from, what he's been through . . .'

I feel a soft pressure, Frida's hand over mine, and I realise I've been picking the skin around my finger again. She doesn't say anything, though, just keeps her hand there until I feel calmer and my fingers grow still. It's just the kind of comfort I need right now – strong, unspoken. It's then that I notice them, the faint white tracery of scars on the inside of her forearms. Scars of deep, deep cuts far worse than my finger-picking. *Oh, Frida . . .*

'You can tell me,' she says, pulling her arms back, folding them across her chest. 'If it helps to offload.'

I hesitate. I don't want to break Xav's confidence, but it would be so nice to share it all with someone who's not involved, weigh things up and decide what to do, what to say to make life better for everyone.

I open my mouth to speak, but then I catch sight of something really strange. Mum, running frantically across the grass towards us. She's not wearing her posh running gear but the ancient leggings and hoodie she keeps for hanging around the house in the mornings. Her black, unstraightened hair is streaming out as she tears along. My stomach twists with a sudden insight that something is wrong. As she gets closer there's an expression on her face I haven't seen before. Shock, disbelief and . . . is that fear?

'Maxine,' she says. 'Turn on your phone.'

And that's how I find out that Xav has been murdered and see that nightmare face for the first time.

Chapter 5

Sam, three years ago

In my mind there are two kinds of hatred – first the pure, simple hate that we reserve for out-and-out villains: Nazis, politicians, a certain bitter-and-twisted breed of teacher or any other unadulterated bastard you might come across.

Then there's the other kind, the destructive and addictive poison that started out as longing, as love. That started out as me and Xav, running around the playground as children, playing football, playing pranks. Or us as fifteen-year-olds lying sprawled in the hideout behind my back garden, so close that our short, spiky hairstyles almost touched as we rested our heads on the ancient knitted cushion, looking up at the sky through the holes in the corrugated-iron ceiling. I never thought I'd hate him then.

'Tell me this isn't all there is to life, Samalam?' he said. 'It's going to get better, right?'

I was afraid to move, in case I caused a shift in the air which would change this moment and make him pull away from me. But, slowly, I reached out and hooked my little finger into his – the secret handshake we'd had since childhood. He linked his finger into mine and the thrill of the contact sent a slow, warm feeling flowing through my body. Just one touch, that's all it took.

'Come on, Xav,' I said using my straight-talking best mate tone to hide the fast beating of my heart. 'You were meant for bigger things than this, and you know it. Just you wait.'

Xav took a deep breath in and blew it outwards; the steam of it curled through the cold air. I could feel the strength coming back to his body and prepared myself, knowing that any second now he would ...

Xav let go of my hand and jumped up to a sitting position. 'Enough of this. The old bastard can't control me for ever. The second I'm sixteen, I'm outta here – and you're coming too.'

'India?' I suggested.

'Yeah, maybe. Via New York. Then we'll stop by Indonesia to save the orangutans. I love those wrinkly orange dudes.'

'Let's do it,' I said. At that moment, in our scrappy little shelter made of old plastic sheeting, half bricks and wooden pallets, it still felt entirely possible because Xav had made it so.

'Yup. You and me. SFF.' He held out his finger again and I shook it with mine – firmly this time, like we were making a deal.

'Secret friends forever.'

For a moment, the vow hung in the air, then a train rumbled past outside, shaking the walls as it went. The 10.57 – it was getting late.

Xav clambered his way to the rotting plank that served as our door.

'Oh, almost forgot,' he said, grabbing a bulging Tesco bag and chucking it at me. 'All done. Sorry about the funny scent – Mum's got this new fabric conditioner. Also, could you maybe give me just one or two shirts next time? She's sort of starting to notice the excess laundry.'

I nodded my agreement, and then he was gone, out into the railway siding, then squeezing his lithe body through the missing plank in his back fence.

I lay there for a couple of minutes, just enjoying the fizzing feeling in my belly a little more, before grabbing my laundry and heading back.

My own back fence had long since disintegrated, but getting through the garden still wasn't easy. I could have cut a path through all the mess – the tangled brambles, the rotting trellis, the crumbled chicken coops and garden sheds that Dad had once used to house his hobbies. But I didn't want to make it obvious, to lead Dad's eye down towards the makeshift den at the back. The hideout was our secret, mine and Xav's. So instead I scrambled over, under, through – a torturous maze of a route which left my hands scratched and the carrier bag torn. I opened the back door and squeezed through the narrow gap – it hadn't opened all the way since primary school – and into the kitchen.

I knew the kitchen smelled bad. I had eyes – I could see the teetering tower of ancient, unwashed takeaway boxes, the brownish liquid oozing out of the bottom of the fruit basket. But I'd long since stopped being able to smell it. Call it a super-power if you will; it was the only way to survive around here.

I could hear the TV – Dad was already well into that evening's *NCIS* marathon. He'd be busy for a while. I still had time.

Crouching down, I reached inside our long-since-broken washing machine, closed my fingers around the handle of my steam iron and pulled it out. The ironing board was tucked in a hollowed-out space behind a pile of tattered gardening magazines that was taller than me. Quietly, with only the light from the bare bulb above to help me, I started to press my school shirts.

My home might be a dump and my dad might be a mess, but the bullies were wrong. I did not smell. My uniform was clean. I bathed, I brushed my teeth and washed my hair. I was not That Kid.

Oh, who was I fooling? I was totally That Kid. The weirdo, the outsider who never invited anyone home. That kind of oddness is hard to hide. Why else would Xav prefer to be Secret Friends?

We both had crap lives, but for him school was an escape, and he soared through classes on the back of a multicoloured rainbow of charm. Half the straight girls and all the gay boys – plus one especially gullible drama teacher – hung adoringly on his every word. As for me, I slimed around, slug-like, at the bottom of the food chain and tried to avoid being noticed as much as possible. I was a loser, from the top of my cut-with-Dad's-clippers hair to the tips of my cheap-trainered toes. The last thing he needed was dorky gawky me shadowing him, reminding him just how horrible his home life was.

But although Xav might sail past me in the canteen as if he'd never seen me in his life, I wasn't worried about losing him. The crappiness of our lives had bound us together. As geeky kids we'd binge-watched *Harry Potter* and *Lord of the Rings* and re-enacted epic scenes in the confines of our hide-out. When the geekiness wore off (him at least), we'd gone shoplifting together, got drunk for the first time together. I'd known Xav was bi before anyone else – perhaps even before he did. He'd come out to me first, and years ago, in total secrecy and 'just to see what it felt like', we'd kissed. I knew about his horrible father and weak-willed mother; when he wore a long-sleeved shirt to school in summer, I knew it meant he was hiding bruises. I knew all his secrets, all his weaknesses. He would always come back to me.

Mr Kline's lessons were the easiest. Teachers have two ways of dealing with phones. They're either Nazis about it, enforcing the head's strict leave-it-in-your-bag rule and giving you detention, or they choose to turn a blind eye to it and only teach the kids who can be bothered to listen. Kliney was the latter. He didn't care that I had my earbuds in and my phone under my desk. And I could learn more from PlayMii than I could from him, anyway.

I'd worked my way through several videos, when I noticed the girl next to me was looking at me. This never usually happened, and I felt a prickle of unease, like her gaze was burning me where it touched. *A girl is looking at me. What did this mean? What should I do?*

I decided to glare at her. The best thing about being the class weirdo was that nobody liked to meet my eye and people generally backed off after a couple of seconds' unblinking stare.

But Eleanore Grange-Fuller stared back. Her eyes were the oddest colour – not blue or brown, but violet – and wide. Even then, with hardly any make-up and her natural flat-brown hair colour, she had that magical anime-girl quality that later won her millions of views in Japan. And there was something about the way she stared at you, steady and gentle, that made you give in to her. Fighting Eleanore was like trying to punch water.

She held out one hand, pointing at her ear with the other and I handed her my left earbud. She wiped it daintily with a smiley-face tissue, before popping it in and peering over the gap between our desks so she could just about see what I was watching. A Russian dude was in a shopping mall, balancing on the moving handrails of two escalators, trying to run up and away from the security staff. It was kind of simple slap-stick but Eleanore giggled, placing one dainty hand over her mouth, and I felt a rush of happiness that I'd made her laugh, even though the Russian guy had done all the actual work.

Let's be clear on this: it wasn't a life-changing romantic moment – we weren't interested in each other in that way. I wouldn't say we became friends, either. But it was nice to spend an hour a week sitting next to someone who didn't deliberately spill their water in my lap, or WhatsApp all their friends saying *OMG this kid is beyond weird!!!* From then on,

Eleanore always sat next to me in Kline's class, and I found myself making playlists of videos for her. I sought out the weird stuff we both seemed to love – teenage girls obsessed with the supernatural, creepy animations, twisted versions of children's TV characters. And the stunts. Always the stunts. The more random and attention seeking the better. It worked for us.

Until the day she found somewhere else to sit.

That day I slid into my usual spot near the back, trying not to glance expectantly at Eleanore as she came in. I'd learned that it wasn't good to look directly at people I want to like me – they got a full blast of my desperation and ran a mile. Instead, I looked up out of the corner of my eye and saw her sitting down at the front of the class with Maxine, the new girl. She was curvy, and Spanish- or Italian-looking, wearing not quite the right uniform and a leopard-print scarf in her wavy dark hair.

Eleanore glanced up and caught me looking. She shrugged, pointing at the girl and rolling her eyes. Immediately I understood: *I'm being forced to show the new girl around. What a drag. Rain check until next week?*

I smiled at her and she turned back to her charge, pointing at something at the front of the classroom. I felt a flush of sympathy for the new girl: poor Maxine, friendless and alone. That sympathy disappeared within minutes, as she and Eleanore giggled together. Eleanore shuffled her chair to get closer as they chatted. Their shoulders hunched together, closing out the rest of the world in a way she wouldn't dream of doing with me. I knew then that she'd never sit next to me again.

How do people do it? How do they do this friends thing? What is this magic that sparks between people that makes them instant BFFs? How do they know what to say, or get the courage to put their whole self out there for this new, scary potential friend to pick over? I had to accept I'd been born without the friend-making gene – an invisible wall between me and the world for ever. But as long as I had Xav, nothing else mattered.

I lowered my head, slipping my earbuds in, and pulled up my latest weird video playlist.

Like I said, I take credit for most of the whole PlayMii phenomenon, but it also helped that a vomiting bug had brought down half the teaching population of our school. Xav and his best (non-secret) friend Andy Duncan were supposed to be in maths, Ed Adewumi was scheduled to be in art, Eleanore and Maxine were meant to be in geography ignoring me.

But the lack of staff meant the whole of year ten had been herded into the school hall and were being supervised by a doddery supply teacher, visibly terrified and hiding behind a word-search magazine at the front of the room. In an extra-torturous move, they had us all sitting on the floor because there weren't enough chairs and they'd made us take our shoes off to protect the new flooring. Our eyes were watering from the reek of two hundred-plus teenage feet.

My back was aching within minutes, a dull throb from the base of my spine to my shoulders. The doctor said it was caused by poor posture – hunching over and curling in on myself in a desperate desire to make myself smaller and less visible.

'Social phobia,' he had told Dad, who had just rolled his eyes.

'We used to just call it shyness,' he'd said. He'd signed me up for a martial arts class to 'build my confidence' but luckily, after three weeks, he'd decided it was too expensive and we went back to nightly *CSI* reruns surrounded by old pizza boxes.

I had found myself a spot near the wall, drawn my knees up protectively in front of me and stared at my phone when suddenly I sensed movement nearby, smelled a familiar waft of knock-off designer scent.

'Xav?' I looked up, shocked to see my SFF sitting down next to me, with Andy close by.

'Fuck, I'm bored, Samster,' he said. I froze, not sure how I was supposed to respond. I looked up at him, nodded towards Andy, my eyes sending the message: *Are you sure you want to talk to me?* I wasn't sure if Andy knew about the SFF thing.

He nodded faintly, encouragingly. He must have been in a good mood that day, or perhaps he was just really, really bored.

My mind scrambled about, desperate for something to say to keep him interested. At home, I could say anything to him, mock him, laugh at him, the conversation just flowed between us, but here at school I didn't know what he wanted from me. I looked down at the phone in my hand – I'd been watching an LA goth PlayMeep exploring a cemetery at midnight – and shoved it in his direction.

'This girl reckons her sneakers are haunted,' I said lamely.

I went hot, skin prickling with embarrassment, kicking myself for saying something so random. But then Xav laughed and I started laughing too. Andy drew closer and watched as I cued up another video, one of a Russian guy (yes, another one, those dudes are *insane*) setting fire to his legs then jumping into a snowdrift. This was before the online platforms started banning dangerous stunts, so they were easy to find, and there were hundreds of them.

'Whoa,' Xav said. So I brought up another one, a woman doing a glamour pose on the edge of a skyscraper, then another of a guy skiing off the edge of a pitched roof, before moving on to that classic piece of near-death comedy: *Man Cements Head In Microwave*.

'I cannot believe you've never seen this stuff before.' I laughed. 'Dude, you've been missing out.'

So, let the record show this. Before I came along, Xav Bailey, god of pranks, had barely watched any. But now he and Andy were pulling closer, craning to get a view of my phone.

'What are you watching?' said a voice next to me. Eleanore was leaning over my shoulder, brown hair falling over one eye, braces glinting through her shy smile. Maxine jostled next to her, desperate to see, reaching out for my phone with one nail-bitten hand, but smiling at me as she did.

Xav budged up a little to let them sit down next to him.

'What? You've never seen the microwave cement guy?' Maxine howled, making Xav blush. 'Hang on, I'll show you the one that came after that . . .'

Before I knew it, phones were being swapped, videos shared and laughed over. Ed, who I vaguely knew from our form, shuffled over too and I felt a prickle of antagonism. Ed was the only kid I really felt threatened by because he was gay and out and I knew Xav had a bit of a thing for him. And bloody hell he was handsome – dark eyes, strong jaw, skinny but fit body. It was as if he'd been scalpel-sliced clean from the pages of a superhero comic book. Miles Morales without the Spider-Man mask. Maxine and Andy seemed to know a little bit about the filming side of things – they talked about the kind of cameras people used, and how clever some of the editing was. Eleanore chipped in with comments about styling and Xav glued the whole thing together with witty asides and critiques. These five people were the best fucking thing ever to happen to me and I wanted them all in my life. I wanted every school day to be like this.

As we talked, my mind raced ahead. Maybe we would all become friends after this, maybe Xav would hang around with me more, maybe we'd get closer. *Maybe, maybe . . .*

'We should all start a PlayMii channel together!' I blurted out. The others stopped watching and turned to me.

Oh shit. What an idiot thing to say; how stupid to assume that just because we'd spent half an hour chatting and sharing videos, we could all be friends. My heart thudded, my whole body went clammy and sweaty, as I waited for the laughter to start. I could feel my face blushing hotter and hotter as my hands began to shake.

Run away, my instincts were screaming. But my legs were dead. I was surrounded by people and there was nowhere to escape to. I squeezed my eyes shut, and for the millionth time in my life I wished I could rewind time.

'That's a brilliant idea,' Maxine said. I couldn't quite believe she'd said it. I felt a rush of warm feeling towards her.

'Genius, actually,' Xav agreed. 'We could share our skills. Any of you any good with a camera?'

I was working up the courage to speak up when Andy cut in.

'I got a GoPro for my birthday,' he said. 'I haven't really had a chance to use it.'

I saw Xav wince slightly at that. Andy's family were stinking, revoltingly rich (at least by our standards) and Andy seemed to have zero awareness of his best friend's lack of funds. But the awkward moment quickly passed as they came up with more and more outrageous ideas. I mostly watched in awe, too scared to speak again and break the spell.

'What about calling it Xav Live?' Xav said with a cheeky grin. He knew he was pushing his luck.

Maxine threw a screwed-up ball of chewing gum wrapper at him. 'This isn't going to be the Xav Bailey channel,' she said.

'Maxine's right,' Eleanore put in. 'We're all in it together, or not at all.'

I thought Xav would be put out about this, but he just laughed his relaxed alpha-male laugh that fooled everyone but me.

'Of course, darling Eleanore . . . Ellie . . . Nellie . . . no, Leni! It should have a bit of all of us in it.' With a dramatic flourish he added, 'This channel will be bigger than all of us!'

By the time the bell rang and we all staggered to our feet, shaking the pins and needles out, I was dizzy with excitement. It was as if my entire future had shifted and realigned itself in the space of an afternoon and I realised something really important about myself. All these years I'd been hiding away at school, but what I'd actually been desperate for was to be noticed. For one person to look at me and say, *You're special. You can be part of something special.*

And now it had happened. This was going to be big. Nothing was ever going to be the same again.

Chapter 6

Maxine, present day

Xav is gone. No more Xav. It seems impossible that the world could exist without him in it. I realise that for years I've been thinking about him constantly: every time I drop a video, I wonder what Xav would think. Christ, every time I choose a new pair of shoes, I wonder what Xav would think. Xav is – *was* – one of those people who just gets under your skin, makes you desperate to impress them even when you know it's not good for you.

Images keep flashing through my head – Xav in his school uniform, laughing and running his fingers through his thick hair. Xav talking us into doing ever-more crazy things for the channel, Xav's soppy-happy grin the morning after he kissed Ed for the first time. His tearful, tormented face on a late-night video message at the height of The Drama. Xav and his jokes, his stunts, his ridiculous variety of nicknames for everyone. The way he could look at you and make you feel like the most special person in the world.

I'd been floundering when I met him. Mum had gone to America for a year for some big work thing and instead of taking me, she'd transferred me to a new school because she didn't want me to miss my GCSEs and now I was stuck living with Dad and Glenys. They were both university lecturers who thought screens had a disastrous effect on the young mind. Her kids were banned from having a phone until they were sixteen and were always rushing between Mandarin lessons and cello practice. At the breakfast table, they'd make jokes about me in French. I tripped over, I broke things, I lost my keys constantly, I disrupted the house by playing TikToks at top volume, rearranging the furniture for Instagram shots. Dad gave up defending me. Every day, I'd felt shaky and stupid and insecure.

But making videos with Xav and the others, I felt like I belonged. He got what I was trying to do, helped me hone my comic timing and, despite the fact he could sometimes cut you down with a few scathing words, when he liked something he said so – and his praise meant so much. I never joined the Xav groupie club, I don't go for dangerous types, but he was still my friend. Whatever happened afterwards, however badly he behaved, Xav was the reason I didn't spend year ten as a social outcast. His was the attitude I channelled when my nerves got the better of me, the reason I ended up on PlayMii.

'I made you who you are, Maxamillion,' he'd said once. I'd been incredibly pissed off at the time, but he was right – he had.

I don't cry there in the park in front of the yoga instructor. I want to, but the tears just aren't there. Instead, I feel numb shock overtaking me. My phone slithers from my fingers and I'm vaguely aware of Frida gripping my arm, her face

48

completely drained of colour – she must be freaking out seeing me like this. She and Mum help me to the car. I can't walk by myself; it feels like my whole body has turned to jelly.

But here's the worst thing of all. Deep under the layers of shock and grief, another thought pipes up. One I'd never admit to, not to my friends, my online fam, and especially not to Frida. It's wrong, but it's there.

What should I share about this?

That makes me a horrible person, I know it, but for years I've lived online. Sifting through what I can and can't post is second nature to me. There's online breakfast (blueberry pancakes with Greek yoghurt) and offline breakfast (a bowl of dry Cheerios when the milk's gone off); online shopping (racing through H&M grabbing bargains from the latest drop) and offline shopping (riddled with a cold and nipping to Superdrug for tissues and Vicks VapoRub). People will be expecting it, people will want to know how I feel, what I think.

But what do I feel? What DO I think?

Back at the flat Mum sits beside me, her arm around me, trying to hide the fact that she's shaking too. Frida makes tea, moving mechanically through our sterile, white-tiled kitchen and pushing mugs into our deadened hands, our shock reflected in her eyes. I just scroll through the alerts on my phone, looking at endless reproductions of that face.

That horrible face – on every newsfeed, every social update, every online article, even on TV – the face was everywhere. I can't imagine that there's a real human beneath it, a horrific, twisted person who did this to my friend and then bragged about it online.

I know people will say Xav had it coming. I know he has enemies, but how could anyone hate him this much and still be sane?

I turn off all my social media alerts, just leaving texts: a few anxious friends checking that I'm OK, one from Nonna in Italy which makes it clear she doesn't quite understand what happened but she's praying for my friend. A short message from Dad, saying he and Glenys are thinking of me.

And one from Leni. I don't know why I'm surprised – we're supposed to be friends – but I haven't heard from her in ages. Her channel keeps her busy, rocketing from launch, to public appearance, to photo-shoot – then, of course, she and Andy need time together too. But she's messaging me now, and it's the most un-Leni-like message I could possibly imagine.

Oh shit oh shit oh shit. Oh God, Maxine, are you all right?

Just the jarring sight of swearwords next to Leni's violet unicorn thumbnail feels so wrong and so shocking that it tips me over into messy, noisy and overwhelming tears at last.

The cafe isn't Leni's usual choice. I've grown used to the fact that under normal circumstances Leni can't just meet up and chat, she has to tick things off her to-do list as well. So usually; when we meet, it's somewhere filmable. Last time, it was at a vintage tea emporium which involved weak Earl Grey served in old, delicate Royal Doulton cups and doilies on the table. The time before that had been during the Great Bubble Tea Mania and we'd slurped our way through colourful vats of delicious frogspawn with attentive staff hovering over us.

This time is different, though. We're at a bog-standard cafe chain near Waterloo station. I push in through the door and find her already waiting in a booth at the back.

She's easy to spot. Even when she's trying to be discreet, Leni attracts attention just by being Leni. Today, her blunt-cut hair is a delicate lemony yellow with blue ends, her clear smooth skin enhanced with exactly the right foundation and touches of blusher. Her eye make-up and lashes are a work of art. I instantly feel painfully conscious of my red-rimmed eyes, rumpled dress and un-contoured face. But underneath her astonishing look, Leni's eyes are as full of shock and sadness as mine.

We hug. Her flowered silk jacket smells of a hundred different types of make-up, overlaid with her own specially created signature scent. The smell makes me want to cry again. I squeeze her tight, as if losing one school friend has made it hard to let go of the others.

'I . . . I can't even . . .' I say finally.

'I know.' There aren't any words for how we're feeling. I'm not even sure why we're here – I just know that we have to be together.

Finally, Leni speaks. 'Did you post?'

Only another PlayMeep would ask that. I nod. 'Not a video. Just something on Instagram saying I was utterly shocked and sad.' I rejigged it about a hundred times, which made whatever I shared feel completely fake. 'How about you?'

'No.' Leni looks down at her coffee. 'I haven't done any social since it happened. I've put the launch of my Crimson Rush palette on hold for now. Thankfully Carl sorted it – I just couldn't face it. And Andy's devastated, of course.' Leni's boyfriend was best mates with Xav at school, a founder member of our PlayMii team.

'I can't stop thinking about that mask thing,' I say.

'Me neither. God, on the night it happened, me and Andy were doing this live Q&A thing, just chatting away. It wasn't until after we'd finished that the alerts started coming in.' There's a tremor in her voice as she speaks, and I think for a moment that she's going to cry. We've been friends through all our greatest teenage dramas, heartbreaks and crushes, and I've never seen her shed a tear before. Leni crying feels like the end of the world.

But that face could bring anyone to tears. I shut my eyes and, for a moment, all I can see is its glistening red maw grinning at me.

'I can't believe he's gone,' I say hastily, and we try to push the image from our minds with stories about the Xav we knew, the crazy one who fired us all up and set us off on this non-stop adrenaline-filled life. *Do you remember ... do you remember?*

'What about the time he duct-taped that air horn under Kliney's chair?'

'That time he made a full-sized papier-mâché Xav to sit through lessons instead of him.'

'And the cling film. How many cling film-based pranks did he pull? Cling film over the lab sinks, the boys' toilet seats, over an open doorway . . .'

We're smiling now, shaking our heads at the sheer audacity of the guy. Back at school, we'd all thought about doing this stuff, laughed about it or watched videos of other people doing it, but it takes a special kind of personality to actually *do* it.

'What was the worst nickname he ever called you?' I ask.

Her eyes flicker downwards for a moment. 'He used to call me Ele-*snore*,' she says. 'I know that doesn't sound that bad, but it was the *way* he said it. Like I was bland and boring, not worth knowing.' There's a new tone in her voice, a don't-go-there note of vulnerability I've never heard before. Leni is the most generous-hearted person I know, but you don't get to her level of success without also being hard as nails. And surely Leni would never believe that she was *bland*? Still, Xav had a way of figuring out our weaknesses and pushing our buttons. He got to us all.

'Mine got really elaborate,' I say. 'It started off as Maxi-Pad and got really gross – Jamrag was a particular low point. At best I was just Paddy or Lily Pad.'

'No wonder we used to do the psychopath test on him,' Leni said.

Oh God, yes, I remember that now. Leni had read some-where that psychopaths can't 'catch' yawns the way the rest of us do. According to the theory, if one person in a group yawns, the rest of us usually yawn too as an instinctive reaction, but psychopaths don't have the necessary empathy to pick up on the signal. We'd spent one afternoon yawning and stretching so elaborately that eventually he'd snapped at us to go get some rest.

'Didn't yawn once though, did he?' Leni said, smiling.

I yawn. She yawns too. And suddenly, even though the yawn was fake, I'm so tired again.

'Have you spoken to Ed?' I ask, changing the subject. 'Is he OK?'

And there it is, the familiar rumble of guilt that I get when I think about Ed. Leni has been much more openly #TeamEd throughout Xav's douchey behaviour – she's been graceful about it, even when Xav called her an interfering manga pixie. But then pretty much everything Leni does is graceful.

Leni takes a delicate sip of her coffee and shakes her head. 'I don't know what to say. I mean, did you read his tweet?'

She fiddles with her phone for a moment and then brings up Ed's Twitter feed. I'd muted him recently as his tweets were getting more angry, bitter and uncomfortable to read. I looked at Leni's phone, a sense of dread stirring in me as I read the words.

Something in me always knew he'd come to this.

It sounds so stark, so cruel that suddenly a horrific thought pops into my head and I speak before I even have a chance to filter it.

'Do you think . . . ' I say. 'Would Ed ever . . .?'

Leni looks shocked; her eyes widen even more. 'You don't think he did it, do you?' she asks.

There. She's said it and now it hangs in the air between us, a sick suspicion.

No, no, no. Maybe?

The world has become so warped and strange over the last forty-eight hours, I could believe anything.

When Xav dumped Ed in the middle of a live feed, he wasn't just humiliating him and breaking his heart, he was taking away his home, his job and his identity. Every day, Ed had appeared in Xav's videos, setting up his jokes, falling for his pranks, following him on his adventures. Now, Ed works at Starbucks and lives in his parents' loft conversion. No wonder he's angry.

'I don't think it can be,' Leni says. 'There are rumours going around – people are saying that Xav had dirt on us all and was going to release it. He wanted to get us all cancelled.'

'But why would he want to do that?' I'm shocked. Xav loved nothing more than dissing other influencers in his videos, but dragging everyone's secrets out would backfire on him, big time. He'd have had armies of fans screaming for his . . . blood. *Wrong metaphor, Maxine.*

Leni shrugs, trying to look casual, but her fingers are

gripping the coffee cup tightly. 'You know Xav, he just likes smashing things up to see what happens next.'

I remember Xav's words last week, *Time to burn it all down*, and I feel a chill. Yes, that's exactly what Xav would do. And part of me is wondering, worrying – what have I said, what have I done over the past few years that Xav could use against me?

Just at that moment we both become aware of someone standing near our table. We look up to see two girls hovering nervously. One is waving at us hesitantly with an expression we both recognise straight away: *I don't want to bother you, but I love your channel . . .*

'We don't want selfies or anything, don't worry,' one of the girls says. 'We just wanted to say how sorry we are.'

'Thank you,' Leni says graciously, while I stand up awkwardly, holding out my hand like a dork for them to shake it, not sure if they recognise me or if they're just here for Leni, the main attraction.

'Honestly it must be so scary,' the girl carries on. 'I mean, he's still out there.'

Her friend nudges her hard, growling at her through gritted teeth, 'Shut *up*, Poppy!'

Poppy isn't listening. 'You know what I mean, though. What if it happens again? No one's safe . . .'

Noticing our horrified faces, Poppy stops, her face flushing bright red under her superb make-up. Gulping for air, she rushes out of the cafe, her friend trailing in her wake, phone already in her hand, ready to update everyone she knows about Poppy's latest fuck-up.

I look at Leni, feeling a prickle of fear. Up until that point, neither of us has thought about it; we've just assumed that whoever did this had beef with Xav. But what happened was so sick, so extreme. What if Poppy's right? What if this person is a serial killer? What if one of us is next?

Chapter 7

Maxine

Leni posts a selfie of us on her IG at precisely midday the next day – bang on nine a.m. Eastern Standard Time in the US and just right for Brits about to start their lunch breaks. So, the optimal time for global social media pickup. There's a gentle, but not in-your-face filter and her face glows with serene sorrow as she hugs me tight. I look like a chipmunk that hasn't slept in seven days, then got into a fight with a badger.

The caption makes my eyes sting with tears: *We have lost our friend, but we still have each other. Xav would not want us to give in to fear. #Sisterhood #Solidarity #Nevergivingup #Hewillnotbreakus #TheFace*

Oh. The Face is a hashtag now. Of course it is.

'Miss Fernando, would you put your phone down please?'

I look up at the jowly, cushion-like features of Detective Constable John Riley. His face is grey under the buzzing fluorescent lights of the police interview room and his voice is weary. I can tell he has already put me into the 'stupid airhead who can't leave her phone alone' pigeonhole. I lay it out in front of me, straightening the case nervously against the chipped edges of the grey table. Without my phone to hold, I start to pick at my fingers again.

'As I was saying,' he goes on, 'you're not in any trouble. We are just interviewing all Xavier's friends and associates so that we can build up a good picture of his life, and the events which led to his death.'

The phrase *you're not in any trouble* instantly makes me imagine a million ways that I could be in trouble. You know that thing where you go through customs at an airport and even though you haven't done anything wrong, you suddenly start behaving like there's a kilo of cocaine stuffed in your bra? That's how I feel at the moment. It doesn't help that the chair they have given me is slightly too high and my legs are swinging like a child's, or that I have a photo-shoot after this, so I am in full Maxine-mode, wearing leopard-print shortie dungarees and too much eye make-up.

DC Riley looks me up and down and rolls out his first question. 'When did you first meet Xavier Bailey?'

I relax a little. I've told this story a lot at meet and greets and can do it on autopilot.

'At school. We came up with the idea of setting up our own channel, along with Leni and Ed, and Leni's boyfriend Andy, and we made some brilliant videos together. The problem was that Xav and Ed wanted to do stunts and pranks, Leni wanted to do beauty stuff, then Andy hooked up with Leni and lost interest in making videos, and I just loved talking nonsense at the camera. So eventually we all went off and did our own thing. But we'll still pop up in each other's videos all the time and we'll always be friends . . .'

I stop short there because, I realise, I'm no longer telling the whole truth.

'We're not, though. To be honest we don't see much of each other any more. Xav only gets in touch when he needs to vent about something. And he and Leni have beef. Like, serious beef. Oh God, not that she would have done anything to him! I just mean he dissed her Luminescent range when it came out last year, and she dissed him back when he split up with Ed. But everyone had beef with Xav, it was like . . . so much beef he could open his own branch of Burger King. In the last six months he's probably offended half the creators in the country, and some in the States, too.'

Oh shut up, I tell myself. I'm blabbing, talking in the Maxine-speak I use on my channel – bright, airy, garbled. But somehow I can't seem to switch it off. I guess I'm nervous. Why should I be nervous?

'And did you and Xav have "beef"?' I could hear DC Riley placing sarcastic quotes around the word.

'I try to stay out of everything. I mean, the last time we met, I'd just called him a dick in front of four hundred people, but that was kind of an accident. And believe me, he deserved it.'

For a moment, DC Riley's face hardens, and a hot, uncomfortable feeling is spreading over me.

'I mean, he deserved to be called a dick, not . . . what happened after.'

'When you called him that, were you referring to Xavier's . . . um . . . *beef* with Edwin Adewumi?'

There's a note in his voice, an intense interest that makes me uneasy.

'Yes,' I say. And suddenly I can't say any more. The whole world knows how Xav humiliated Ed onscreen, how he cheated on him, but I know about the tiny, everyday put-downs, remarks about his body, dress sense or musical taste that sliced off little slivers of Ed's confidence. I saw Ed change his hair, his clothes, his mannerisms until he'd more or less become a Xav clone.

And then, after Xav broke him down to nothing and dumped him, I know about Ed's rage. The time he smashed his fist through a wall during a row, and shot an arrow through a big canvas print of the two of them. How he'd stand for hours under Xav's window in the rain. I don't want to share this with DC Riley; I don't want to make things any worse for Ed than they already are.

And I don't want to suspect my friend. I can't picture him putting on a mask, stabbing Xav then calmly uploading the video to Xav's channel, and so I choose not to. After months of hovering around, trying not to take sides, I owe him this much.

It must have been someone Xav trusted, though ...

Shut up, Maxine. It wasn't Ed.

The policeman waits for me to elaborate, leaning back in his chair, his sausage-like fingers linked over his white shirt. My phone bleeps and I pick it up.

'Miss Fernando.'

I jump, drop the phone in my lap. 'Sorry.' And just then, I think of all Xav's messages that are sitting right there on my phone. Video after video slagging off rival creators, ripping into Ed and generally wailing into the night. Should I show him? *But that might cause even more trouble for Ed.*

DC Riley has grown tired of waiting for me to talk and fires another question.

'Do you know of anybody, other than Mr Adewumi, who would have had access to Xavier's computer password?'

I laugh. The grey airlessness of the room absorbs the sound, making it muffled, somehow. 'Surely someone must have told you this already. Anyone could figure out Xav's passwords; they were always a variation on "Xav is the king". He was brilliant with computers – every time I thought my laptop was dead, he'd manage to fix it somehow. But he was crap at security.'

My grilling goes on for about an hour in much the same way – me prattling, DC Riley sighing quietly to himself and taking notes. It's only after he's switched the tape off and ended the official part of the interview that a new thought springs into my mind: I can ask *him* questions too. And so I do.

'Was there something on Xav's computer, then?'

He had stood up, ready to leave, but now he sinks back down into his chair with a weary sigh. He suddenly looks incredibly sad, tired and stressed, but he answers me.

'All the files were wiped from Xavier's gaming PC, his laptop and all his tablets were smashed. His phone has not yet been located.'

'You can do some CSI-type stuff on the computer though, right?'

DC Riley rolls his eyes. 'Yes, we can do some "CSI-type

stuff". It just takes time. Just like wading through CCTV footage of the area takes time, watching numerous "play me" videos takes time. Forensics take time. Especially when Mr Bailey entertained a number of guests at his apartment on a day-to-day basis and never cleaned. Do you know that CSI found traces of more than twenty individuals in his apartment, along with traces of slime, foam, bubble mixture, dog hair, raccoon hair and novelty wig hair? This isn't a TV show, Miss Fernando, we can't get the answers in forty minutes flat, with ad breaks.' He sighs, shakes his head. 'This case.'

I'm frozen with shock at DC Riley's sudden change. I'm used to people blabbing to me; it happens a lot. But not normally with detective constables.

'You're not exactly a PlayMeep fan, are you, officer?' I ask.

He stiffens and peers at me over the top of his glasses. 'It is not for me to say, madam. But in my day, our entertainers had to have a discernible talent to succeed.'

There's this thing I heard about once, called the Spirit of the Stairs or something, which says that you always think of the best comeback when you're on the way down the stairs and out of the building. And it's not until I'm outside the police station and about to get into the car that I shout: 'OK, Boomer, let's see you produce seven high-quality original videos a week and rake in millions of views.'

Carl doesn't even flinch. He's used to PlayMeep weirdness. He just says, 'Please tell me you didn't say that to his face,' and guides me into the waiting car.

He's paler than usual today, his beard not quite as beautifully sculpted, suit and shirt not perfectly matched. The cynical part of me, the part that's survived in this business for three years, wonders what will happen to him now his highest-earning client has gone, and whether I am worth more to him now.

He presses his lips together and, in a determined voice says: 'Glad that's over. Now, Maxine_F, my leopard lovely, are you ready to sell some stationery?'

I am really not ready to sell stationery. But this photo-shoot for the Paperfly ad campaign has been booked in for weeks and they have no plans to postpone it because of Xav's death. There's no escape: I am scheduled to look orgasmic while holding an overpriced rollerball pen for the next two hours.

I've been on a few photo-shoots since I started doing this and the people who run them usually work hard to make it feel like a party, or a pampering session. There's wine, there are nibbles (posh, smoked salmon-type ones, if you're lucky), there's upbeat music playing and weird crazy props, and everyone tells you how gorgeous you are. I normally look forward to them. But after an hour of remembering Xav and feeling patronised by DC Riley, I'm going to find this really hard.

Then, when I see that horrible stationery laid out on a white table like an array of tacky surgical instruments, my enthusiasm level drops even lower.

'Is there definitely no way we can make this stuff a bit nicer?' I ask Carl.

'They'll make it look good in the photos,' he assures me.

'That's not what I mean. I mean people will go out and buy this crap, and they'll be disappointed.'

Carl gives me a wide, patronising smile and signals for me to sit down.

'In marketing, there's a sweet spot that sits between cost and perception of value,' he says. 'If we added an extra thickness of fabric on this pencil case, it would double the manufacture and shipping costs and the price, without delivering any perceived increase in value. Then your fans would be howling with outrage at how expensive it all is. This –' he brandishes the dead-rat pencil case again '– is as good as you'll get for the money we're planning to charge.'

I'm not convinced, and it shows.

'It's complicated, Maxine.' Carl's tone is snappy. 'You don't have to understand it – that's my job. You just have to look good for this photo-shoot.'

I sit. I smile. I keep my left hand angled in a very particular way because, as the stylist says, the picked skin on my little finger 'looks a bit icky'.

After ten minutes or so, there's an issue with the way the lighting bounces off my face or something, and I'm sent off to amuse myself while they solve the problem. I find a quiet corner with a sofa, slip in my earbuds and open my WhatsApp chat with Xav.

I've been afraid to look at it up until now, scared that it contained some clue about what was going to happen, something I missed, that could have saved his life.

When Xav had started sending me these links, I'd felt honoured that he'd singled out me, of all his friends, to trust with his deepest feelings. And then over time I'd come to realise that I wasn't so special – in fact, he'd picked me because, out of all his friends, I had the least power over him. He'd record a message dumping whatever heavy thoughts he had on to little old me, send it and instantly feel better. Video messages take time to watch, and after a while, when things got busier with the channel, I'd taken to skimming some of the longer ones, my heart sinking when a thirty-minute rant popped up in my alerts.

Ugh. I'm such an arsehole.

I tap on a random link from two months ago and Xav's face fills my screen. Again, I feel that twist of loss. His voice is tinny and echoey because he's recorded this one in the bathroom. I can hear his little gang, laughing and joking, in another room nearby. They were always there in the last few months, in the background, egging him on to do ever-more outrageous stuff.

I find myself wondering – could it have been one of them? Thank God it's not my job to figure that out.

Hey Padlet, he says. *Edzilla called me a psychopath today – do you think I'm a psychopath? I looked it up on Wikipedia and there's this whole checklist to identify them. Grandiose sense of self-worth, it said, which ... yeah, that's me.* He laughs and shrugs, smiling his dazzling smile. *Glibness? Yup. Superficial charm? I like to think my charm runs deeper than that, thank you very much. But, yeah, maybe I've got a few things in common with serial killers. But what if I have? I'm not the only one in this game who fits the description. We're supposed to be living in the age of neurodiversity here, so why are we poor psychos getting such a rough ride? We were born this way too. And I've never actually killed anyone. I just made a few dodgy videos and possibly stomped on a good guy's heart just a tiny bit.*

If I am, though, it's even more reason for Ed to stay away from me. My dad was right – I'm poison, I corrupt everything around me. Oh Xav. I feel a flare of pain and guilt – he looks so vulnerable, so different from the swaggering dude throwing lazy insults in the green room. *I miss the old days. I miss nobody knowing who I am. Walking down the street or into a club without being filmed or posing for selfies. I miss the Fellowship of the Yellow Pants. And Alex Malex – don't you miss Alex, too?*

A tide of nostalgia hits me, when we were just making videos for clicks and giggles. I push it back, tap on the next link, and Angry Xav greets me. He's hiding under his covers in the middle of the night, his face lit blue by his screen. Unguarded, full of regret, no sign of the flashy dimpled grin we're used to seeing on his channel.

This world we're in, it's supposed to be real. That's the whole point, right? But I feel like everyone in it is faking something. Ed's faking love, Leni's faking good hair, you're faking intelligence . . . or maybe stupidity? I don't know. Everyone's faking enthusiasm, normality, pretending to be a good person when they're not, taking money to promote things they don't like, filming stuff from a million different angles then pretending they've thrown a video together. People are secretly racist, secretly homophobic, transphobic, slagging off their fans, badmouthing the people who give them freebies, then accepting them anyway. There's one gaytuber I know who's secretly fucking straight. Seriously, what gives with that? Says he just likes the aesthetic, whatever that means. Ed says I should just keep quiet, don't make trouble, but it boils my piss, Lily Pad. I want to destroy it all.

Back home after the shoot, I have nothing to do. No, that's not true – I have lots to do, I just don't want to do any of it. If the world was still normal, I'd be doing a spring haul video right now, but how can I film myself rushing around a high-street shop grabbing clothes off railings? There's tons of products waiting to be unboxed – including a limited-edition sample of Leni's next make-up palette. It's like gold dust, everyone wants one, but it's just sitting there in the cupboards with everything else. I can't face touching it. Then there's the sunrise aerial yoga explainer – the yogi woman has emailed a few times asking about that and I've been ignoring her. I've shared a video every day for the last two and a half years, and now . . . I just can't.

Mum spent this morning compulsively checking the stats on my PlayMii account, stressing helplessly over the tail-off in views and new subscribers.

'In this business you're only as good as the last film you made,' she said. 'And if you stop making videos, you die.'

The shock of the word hit like a punch in my face. 'Mum, don't say that.'

She had the good grace to blush. 'I didn't mean it like that,' she stammered, her hands fluttering around her face batting the bad thought away – she gets extra Italian when she's flustered. 'But you need to keep creating, Maxine. If you stop, your fans will go elsewhere.'

Shortly after that she went out for a run – her go-to way of burning off anxiety – and now I am alone. I don't want to bother Frida in case I scare off my new friend, and as for Leni, she'll be busy with Andy, or making videos, or attending a beauty-industry freebie-fest. So now I am rattling around in this sterile, white luxury apartment. I have nothing else to do, so I do what millions of people around the world are doing right now.

I open my laptop and follow the hashtag.

#TheFace

#WhoIsTheFace

#TheFaceWhosNext

Fear seeps a little deeper into my bones as I read that one. Could my life be at risk?

There are already millions of search results. There are the satirical accounts, already cutting and pasting the mask on to celebrities, cartoon characters and, once, on to me.

Guys, stop, this is too much, one girl writes. They pile on her for using the word 'guys', then carry on.

Worst of all are the revolting ones praising what the killer has done.

@AllHailTheFace One less PlayMii imbecile in the world. Good work my psychopathic friend!

@facethereaper replying to @AllHailTheFace One down, hundreds to go

@Smite_The_Sinners236 He is surely doing God's work, the sinners shall be cast down! Hallelujah!

I feel anger boiling inside me, pushing up like steam.

We say we get used to this stuff – the daily threats, abuse, people calling me dumb, using sick, forbidden words like *retarded*, and worse. I've had detailed messages about why and how I should be raped. What weapons will be used on me and how long I should be tortured for. The normal procedure is to shrug it off, to train ourselves to close a message down at first glimpse of the word *bitch*. We stand back, we don't feed the trolls, but each word still bites, and they know it. And now the threats have come true. Someone really has come for one of us with a knife.

I shudder and move on, pushing deeper into the dozens of online groups which have been set up trying to solve the mystery.

I choose one of the medium-sized ones, Facehunters, and use one of my sock puppet fake-name accounts so I can join without anyone knowing it's me.

Inside, they've moved past the horror and denial and *what kind of animal does this* outrage. They're down to nuts-and-bolts investigation now. Tracking him down, bringing him to justice. That horrendous video is taken apart frame by frame. They zoom in on the knife and speculate where it's from. (I recognise it straight away – it's from Xav and Ed's kitchen. No mystery there.)

Some of them have moved on to conspiracy theories already.

Mandalor_Ian: That bobble-head shoved front and centre is from a game called Time To Kill – was Xav trying to tell us something with that? Was it a call for help?

Fenti: There's something next to it. A slip of paper that wasn't in his previous video. Hang on and I'll see if I can enlarge it.

It's a slip of white paper; I can just about make out some markings on it.

Fenti: just enlarged. Look.

Fenti (who I think is a she, but their profile picture is just a big pair of red lips) has posted a grainy image, a simple but neatly sketched cartoon of some yellow and brown underpants.

Ola: RANDOM! What does it mean?!?

James: It's probably a note from that weird fanboy Ethan.

FlaminFlaps: I rekon he did it (posts gif of Ethan looking slightly intense)

James: Nah. It's gotta be the betrayed ex (cue #TeamEd pile-on).

I scroll down to another post by Dave_361, who has set up a poll to decide what the motive was and who the killer might strike next.

Theory One: the killer is choosing mega-successful, problematic male vloggers (114 votes)

Theory Two: the killer is a homophobe wreaking vengeance on successful gay stars (74 votes)

Theory Three: the killer has something against the Dreams Inc crew. Which means either LeniLoves, Maxine_F or Ed is next (207 votes)

By now my flesh is crawling. None of these people really care. I can't imagine anyone from my online fam being on here. I'm about to throw my phone across the sofa when a new comment appears, from an account with The Face as a profile photo.

AlexM: Actually it was me. I did it and I enjoyed it. And I decide who's next.

My blood chills. Already the responses are starting to ping in from other group members.

Ola: YOU SICK FUCK!!!

FlaminFlaps: WTF are you for real?!?!?

James: If this is real WE WILL FIND YOU AND END YOU

Mandalor_Ian: Obviously a troll. Do not engage.

Ian is right, I tell myself. But my heart is hammering. It can't be a coincidence . . . can it?

I haven't heard that name in years and now it just keeps cropping up, and now I can't stop thinking about the Alex we knew, that we created. Disruptive Alex. Fearless Alex. Another menace in a mask.

Chapter 8

Sam

The first I knew about it was Xav raising the signal flag over our hideout. I was sketching at the time, looking out over the narrow strip of our back gardens and the scrubby railway siding beyond, focusing on the colours in the sky rather than the general crappiness down below. Then I noticed the sickly mustard-yellow underpants sticking up on the old beanpole next to the hut. We'd found them a few years ago in a bag of Dad's crap, brought home in a sack from a jumble sale. Polyester Y-fronts with brown edging. They were so completely revolting that we'd added them to the décor of the hut, and back before we'd had phones, they had become our universal signal for an emergency. Even now, we raised the Yellow Pants when we had news which needed immediate attention.

If Xav was calling Yellow Pants, this was big. *Oh shit, is it his dad again? Please don't let there be blood, I couldn't bear it, seeing Xav's beautiful skin cut open.*

But when I made it through the garden and down to the hut, Xav was grinning. My worry swept away, replaced by that clench of longing in my belly I always got at the sight of Xav's smile – his flashy white teeth, the sparkle in his blue eyes, that dimple . . .

'Dude,' Xav said by way of hello. Xav is the only person in the world who would ever call me anything as cool as dude. It gave me a jolt of pleasure.

'Dude,' I said back, trying to seem offhand.

It had been a couple of weeks since my big idea in the school hall, and since then things had gone quiet. But I was patient, and I was sure things had shifted a little. Eleanore – or Leni, as she was now calling herself, thanks to Xav – smiled at me a few times when we passed in the corridor. Andy often recognised my existence with a little nod these days. That's how I knew they hadn't forgotten me, I just had to be patient. There was no rushing these things.

Maybe that's what Xav wanted to talk about now. He did seem excited about something, fidgeting around on the cushions and blankets.

'I need you to make me one of your mask things,' Xav said.

Last year, I'd made a series of papier-mâché heads for an art project on fame. They looked kind of like bobble-heads – I'd done each one in the image of a celeb so that anyone could be Taylor Swift or Justin Bieber or Kanye for a day, and the teacher had gone on and on about how great they were. But why was Xav after one now?

'I'm starting a PlayMii channel,' he said excitedly. 'But it's a bit different – there's a group of us doing it and we all want to play the same character. That way it's kind of anonymous and we can mess around as much as we like. Genius idea, huh?'

'What?' My heart dropped, a dead weight.

Xav looked genuinely confused about why I wasn't jumping up and down with excitement for him, so he kept talking
about his plans for the channel, how they'd all met up one
lunchtime to talk it through and how the other kids were
basically going to do everything he wanted.

'So there's Andy, who you know – he's pretty solid. Then
there's this girl Maxine who's new, bit thick if you ask me, but
she knows what to do with a camera. There's Ed, the eye
candy. He can collab on my channel any time. Leni seems
nice but incredibly drippy, easy to boss around, I hope! She
keeps doing this thing with her eyes.'

He gave me a melting cute-kitten-stare. I was still too
weak to speak and Xav ploughed on, oblivious.

'There are five of us, so we've made up this character out of
all our initials. Alex Malex – Maxine, Andy, Leni, Ed, Xav.
Anyway, so we're going to take it in turns wearing the mask
and doing crazy stunts to post on PlayMii. Hey, you like
watching stunts, don't you?'

Seriously. Had he forgotten *everything* about that day? A
mix of anger and loss was surging up inside me and I knew
that any minute, I might – *oh shit. If I don't say something fast,
I'm going to cry. I am NOT crying over this.*

'Do you think . . .' I gulped, fighting to hide the crack in my
voice as I spoke. 'Do you think I could join in the channel,
somehow? Maybe there's a role for me, seeing as I was there,
and I basically had the idea and everything?'

Xav looked at me as if this was news.

'You know,' I added. 'In the school hall, that time all the teachers were sick.'

Slowly, a look of realisation crept across Xav's face. 'Oh yeah, you *were* there, weren't you?'

I nodded, pressing my lips together, not trusting myself to speak again. Xav's brows knitted together in thought.

'Umm . . . well I need to ask the others. Alex Smalex doesn't sound quite so good, does it, Samby? But I'll try to explain to them.'

I nodded, swallowing my hurt and shame.

'Could you make that mask, though? God, you're so brilliant at those masks, I could never make anything like it.'

I was used to being forgotten. It had happened so many times in my life, I couldn't keep count. Playing hide-and-seek in the school field, I would work my way to the back of the scratchiest hedge and wait breathlessly for It to come and get me. The bell would ring to call us in, and I would still be there, while the others had shifted to tag or football and played on without me, without even noticing I was still hiding.

We grew out of things like that, but the problem stuck. I wasn't just picked last for PE, I was often not picked at all and would end up simply standing in the field while the two teams ran off to play. I got used to finding out about parties the day after, when people came in full of gossip, scandal and, after a certain point, hangovers. So yes, I was used to being forgotten, but this time I'd been forgotten by Xav, and that cut deeper.

Still, I'd told him now, and he was on my side. He would make it right.

I mean, these people were all right to muck around with, but they weren't *real*. They were what me and Xav would call dough. All soft and squidgy from their nice easy lives – not baked hard by experience like we were. They weren't a threat to our friendship.

I worked late into the night on that mask, first creating a round cage shape with chicken wire from the garden, then mixing up the papier mâché, layering it on and waiting for it to dry. The next night, I painted, giving it huge cartoony eyes, a bit like Leni's, but more unisex. I gave it blond hair like Xav; an earring like Andy's; a leopard-print star in its hair to reflect Maxine, and Ed's dimple. When it came to adding my own distinguishing feature, I hesitated. Did I even have any? My hair was unruly but that was about it. I added a little more papier mâché to give the head a little spiky quiff – the way I'd like mine to look if it would only co-operate.

I smiled. The best of us all, combined. A splash of colour in my dull, trash-filled world. When the paint was fully dry on the quiff, I hoisted the yellow pants and presented it to Xav, glowing when I saw his reaction.

'You're a stone-cold genius, Samwise! They're going to love this. Can you bring it to the park after school tomorrow?'

It was a dingy, cloudy sky in the park that day, not really right for filming, but I caught sight of them all immediately over by the Megaslide. The Megaslide was a huge heap of concrete, about 20 feet high, which had once had a metal slide running down it. As little kids, it had been a badge of honour to ride the Megaslide, and if you went on it when it was wet, you'd shoot off the end and go crashing into the grass verge opposite. It was brilliant, but obviously too dangerous for the local council, and they'd taken the metal slide out a few years ago. The concrete mountain was still there – ugly and pointless, but too big and expensive to knock down. Xav and the others had cleared away the barriers the council had put up and Andy was standing at the top of it, holding a skateboard and wearing so much padding that he looked like a sumo wrestler.

This, obviously, was going to be stunt number one.

Aw, *man*. I wanted to be up there.

'You made it.' Xav bounded towards me. 'Guys, come and look at Alex's face!'

And they came, rushing towards me smiling and laughing. I felt a surge of hope and also panic – I rarely had this many people looking at me at the same time. I found myself clinging a little tighter to the mask, hugging it close like a teddy bear. I now understood why they needed it. Going on camera with it would be like being in a protective bubble, making you free to be someone else.

When I took off the plastic carrier bag, I could see from everyone's faces that they were impressed.

'Told you we had a genius among us,' Xav said, giving me a playful punch on my shoulder. The contact sent a flow of heat out through my traitorous body.

'It's perfect.' Eleanore smiled.

'Thanks, Eleanore,' I managed to say.

'It's Leni now,' she said lightly, but with a hint of hard, flat stone in her voice. I noticed her fingertips looked like they'd been dipped in blue and silver – an eye-catching new manicure, which didn't seem to match with the macho stunts Andy and Xav had planned.

Andy stepped forward and took the mask from me now, his fingers brushing all the extra details I'd included – the earring, the eyes and finally the leopard star. A slow grin of pleasure spread over his face. 'Oh we can cause so much mayhem with this.'

'It's brilliant,' Maxine said. Then she bit her lip. 'I'm sorry, I don't think I know your name – I'm still new here and I'm a bit crap with names and faces.'

'Sam,' I said.

She smiled at me again and whirled off, tossing a thank you over her shoulder as she raced across the playground. Andy put on the mask and followed, chasing Eleanore/Leni with a faux roar.

I think they all expected me to go, but I lingered, watching them film.

The stunt itself was pretty tame – it was no *Man Cements Head* – but as I watched, I realised there really was something special going on. The way they worked together, deftly passing the Alex head around so they could play different roles. The way Andy held up a little comedy banner saying *Help, I'm being forced to do this* before taking off. The way they dealt with the photobombing five-year-old who wanted to get in on the playground action. They all seemed natural and relaxed on camera, like they'd known each other for ever. Like they'd known each other for as long as I'd known Xav.

I felt a sudden pulse of pain and loss.

Then Xav ran up, and my stupid heart pounded with hope.

'Can you hold my coat?' he asked, shoving his jacket into my arms.

I grabbed his shirt, catching him before he ran off again. 'Did you talk to them? You know, about me?'

Xav's face looked blank for a few seconds, and then he seemed to remember what I was talking about. He rested his hand on my arm and led me over to the broken see-saw we often used as a bench.

'I've brought it up. And I think Andy's so pleased with your brilliant mask, he'd definitely be OK with it, but Lenster and Maxi aren't so sure. Some rubbish about not upsetting the dynamic or something. Don't worry, mate, I'm working on them, give me time.'

He patted my shoulder and gave me a sincere Xav smile, and then he was off again. I sat there for a few moments more, squeezing his puffy jacket harder and harder with my hands, until my knuckles turned white.

The video went live the next day, and I watched it under the blankets in my room. It was called *Around The World In Eight PlayMii Clichés*. Andy careers down the slope wearing my mask, wiping out at the bottom, ducking down below the camera, only to emerge as Maxine, who was Twabbing (remember, that summer everyone was doing that ridiculous half-dab, half-twerk dance). It then then became an unboxing video with Leni, then a reaction video with Ed . . .

Forget what I said before. Their video was shit. Their stunts were shit. They were talentless fakes. When it came, the rage was powerful, swamping everything. I wanted to roar and shout, but instead I imagined them crashing off the end of the slide – broken limbs, cracked skulls, blood everywhere, They deserved it. They deserved it all.

Chapter 9

Maxine

My bed is a heap of black fabric; my room looks like an emo jumble sale. I had no idea I even had this many black clothes – but then black does go so well with leopard that I probably wear it a lot without noticing. But there's nothing here that says funeral. Frayed black denim miniskirt? No. Flippy skater dress that'll fly up at the first breath of wind? Nope. This polka-dot blouse might work ... oh no, those are actually tiny skulls. Definitely not.

'It's no good,' I wail.

'Does it have to be black?' Frida asks from the corner of the room. She's looking at this pile of darkness with all the disgust of someone who is wearing a jumpsuit with parrots on it.

But it does. It's not just about showing respect – I know Xav would have wanted black. He'd want me and Leni in veils, a horse-drawn hearse with half the male population of London following behind, weeping and rending their clothes with grief. To be honest, he probably would have liked the skulls, but I have to think about his mum's feelings, too.

'Are you sure you can't come ...' My voice trails off awkwardly. I know it's not appropriate to drag a newish friend to the funeral of someone she's never even met, but I know I'll feel better if she's there.

'No!' A look of horror crosses her face, and then she shrugs. 'I don't do funerals, even for you. But I can help you pick something. What about this pinafore dress?'

Just then, Mum calls us through to the lounge, where she's standing in front of our unnecessarily huge television. It looks like we've slipped into a weird alternate reality.

Breakfast TV is showing queues lined up in the street outside Xav's parents' local church. Crash barriers. Traffic beeping and weaving around people who have spilled into the road. Fans huddled in pop-up tents or sitting on folding chairs, swaddled in sleeping bags. They're sipping hot drinks, waving rainbow flags and holding signs.

We love u Xav

#TeamXav

Xav: always in our ♥

ITS_XAVVVVV 4 EVAAAAA!

There are cardboard cut-outs of Xav with angel wings, Xav's face on little sticks, funereal black Xav T-shirts and hoodies and flowers – so many flowers already stacked up on the pavement outside.

'You may not have heard of Xavier Bailey until last week,' the news presenter says patronisingly. 'But since details of the controversial vlogger's funeral were leaked online, the hashtag "Xav funeral meetup" has been trending on social media, and despite the family's pleas for a quiet ceremony, people have turned out in their hundreds to say goodbye to their beloved content creator. Police have called for this to be a calm, respectful day for the sake of Xavier's family. So far, there have been no arrests following the star's brutal murder, which was posted on PlayMii by the killer. However, senior officers confirmed that they are pursuing several strong leads.'

Are they, though? It's been weeks since Xav died, and still nothing. The news report cuts to a picture of police officers at a press conference and I see DC Riley in the background, that cynical twist to his mouth still very much in place. I used to believe the police could crack any case, but now I'm not so sure.

I unlock my phone and go to the Facehunters group.

This is unreal, I type. *I wonder if he's watching this . . . I wonder if he's enjoying this?*

The group instantly knows who 'he' is.

Ola: Yes. Sicko.

Mandalor_Ian: If we're dealing with an actual psychopath here, which I think we are, this kind of attention will be likely crack to him.

FlaminFlaps: Holy shit hes prob there!!!!

Mandalor_Ian: Undoubtedly. I am in London and planning to go along today to see what I can see.

And I'll be there too. Right at the centre of it all. A wave of dread washes over me as I put my phone down. 'I can't face it.'

'You can,' says Frida, and at the same time Mum says, 'You *must.*'

But then Mum sits on the bed, puts her arm around me and, for a second, I think she's going to tell me it's OK, that I can stay home and eat ice cream out of the carton, mourn Xav in my own way. But instead she says: 'You know we're going to see Carl there today. And you know what he's going to ask.'

I look down at my lap, pretending to be deaf.

'He's going to ask when you're going to start making videos again, Maxine. The funeral's a good cut-off point, I think. You need to get back on the horse.'

'Jesus, Mum, I can't just . . .'

'I know. I'm not saying you need to do any haul videos or musical skits, but you need to say something quiet and respectful about it, and then move on. Like Leni has.'

Wait . . . Leni's talked about Xav? Trust Mum to be across it. That's what she says all the time, 'I'm across that,' like she's got everything covered. It's helpful but sometimes I wish she'd slip up.

I look down at my phone again and find Leni's latest share. Today her hair is pale lilac, her make-up subdued but shimmering grey.

'I want to get something off my chest today, as we say goodbye to Xav,' she says. 'I know a lot of you are saying that my tears for him are fake because we fell out, but I wanted to tell you a bit about our friendship. Xav and I argued from the first video we made together. He wanted to do it one way, I wanted to do it another. But every time we fought, we'd find a third way and the end result was always better than both our ideas put together. We're both stubborn people who want to do our best in everything we do, so yeah, we disagreed but we always thought we'd be able to make up . . .' Her voice breaks here and suddenly she's crying. Not fake pretty tears but proper ones, streaming down her face, slicing streaks out of her contouring. I realise my own eyes are blurring too, like she's given me – all of us – permission to weep. She smiles, and there's a kind of sad laughter in her voice now. 'Last time I saw him, I called him a fool. I was rude and petty but the more I think about it, the more I realise being a fool is no bad thing. Fools mess around and reflect your own foolishness back at you. They make you think. They make you wiser. He's *our* fool, yours and mine. Xav was ours and I'll always love him.'

Leni said it all, exactly what I'd been struggling to say for days.

Next to me, Frida sniffs. I glance up and see her wiping her eyes. I do the same.

'Look at the views,' Mum says quietly. I look, and they're astronomical. That's not why Leni's done it, though – she's found a way to be honest with her fam, and Mum's right. I need to be honest with mine.

'Tomorrow,' I said, 'Frida's taking me vintage shopping. I'll do a chat to camera about Xav before, then shoot some video there. I'll start again tomorrow.'

'OK, *cara*, let's go.' Mum's voice is reassuring. She reaches out to the table by the door and grabs a swathe of dark leopard-print fabric, draping it around my neck, adjusting it like a stylist on a photo-shoot, fastening it into place with discreet little clippy things until it looks just right.

'There you go.' She smiles. 'Perfect. Phew, I was worried I wouldn't be able to find something leopard *and* funereal.'

I stare at her, suddenly feeling hot and itchy, the fabric closing around my throat. Instinctively, my hand starts clawing it away from my neck.

'What's wrong, *stellina*?' she asks, draping it back absent-mindedly as she speaks. 'You saw all those people out there – you need to look like *you*. It's your brand, they'll expect it.'

I nod dumbly. I know she's right, and it's a lovely scarf, but putting it on for that reason alone makes it feel off, fake, somehow. As we crowd through the door, I glance at Frida. She says nothing but I know exactly what she'd advise me. *Does it look good? Does it feel right? Do you actually need a scarf today?*

When we pull up outside the church, I leave it on the back seat of the Uber.

There are shrieks as I emerge. I look round to see rows and rows of phones pointing at me, just like at a meet and greet. Crowds are pinned back from the road by crash barriers, hastily put there by the police.

'Maxine! It's Maxine!' someone shouts, a voice full of joy and excitement. Instinctively, I start to turn and smile, but Mum slips her arm around my shoulders, squeezing gently, reminding me where I am. I picture the comments in the Facehunters group: *Maxine_F grinning at Xav's funeral, kind of weird, don't you think?*

'Stay focused,' Mum says. 'Look down at the ground.'

Her guiding hand propels me forward, my feet taking one step after the other on autopilot.

Without looking up, all I can see are rows and rows of feet. I wonder if one pair belongs to Mandalor_Ian or, worse, to The Face. Despite the shouts when I got out of the car, the mood is sombre and quiet. There's a hum of conversation and I can hear weeping. *They love you, Xav.*

The church forms a hushed protective shell around the official mourners. It is cool and quiet. I shiver without my scarf.

And there it is, a coffin on a plinth in the middle of the aisle. A wooden box with brass handles, covered in a diamond-shaped arrangement of lilies – the same as every coffin I have ever seen on TV. So ordinary, so disgustingly wrong.

Xav's parents stand beside it, his mum with her face pale, one hand covering her mouth. Xav's father has an arm around her, folding her into the side of his body. It looks protective, but I know exactly what he is, and I can see that his fingers are gripping her so tightly they're red at the tips. And when he guides her into the front pew it's like he's steering her.

'Sit here,' Mum murmurs. 'Not too near the front but not at the back.' Even now she's positioning me, thinking about sending the right message. I obey, zombie-like.

I don't realise who I'm sitting next to at first, uncomfortable in his plain suit, his hair black, without the blond tips he'd taken to wearing during his time with Xav. He's bolt upright, staring rigidly ahead. His breathing is rapid and ragged, as if he's fighting the urge to cry, to scream. He looks utterly broken.

'Ed,' I whisper. He stares at me and, for a second, there's a glint of anger. I try not to flinch away. I totally deserve it; I've been a crap friend to him. But his expression softens a bit, and I reach out my hand to grip his, and suddenly we're clinging to each other, weeping as the funeral service goes on around us. This doesn't mean we're good, not by a long shot, but it's a start.

Funerals are awful, but wakes are even worse. A chilly church hall, a table of plain sandwiches which nobody feels they can eat. I'm sure Carl pushed for something fancier, but Xav's parents are set in their ways. Half the crowd here are Xav's family – the ones dressed in suits and dark dresses. And then there are Xav's friends, the real ones and the fake ones – splashes of bright hair, tattoos. Most I barely recognise as my memory for faces is really poor. There's a boy whose name I can't place, in a white shirt with braces and a black armband. He's clinging to a girl in a tulle cocktail dress, who is sobbing dramatically. She's wearing a vintage pillbox hat, with a little black netting veil. A sodding *veil*. Fuck's sake, she hardly knew him.

Across the hall, I catch a glimpse of Ed, but I can't get to him because, as usual, someone is telling me their secrets. This time it's a gamer – Jace something, I think.

'. . . I don't know how he even knew about it, it never even went online, but Xav got hold of it somehow and it's in his burn files now . . .' he says. 'I'm not a homophobe, I swear I'm not. I love Xav, I'm a proper fan. I even watched those old videos of when you all first started out. But it still looks bad, doesn't it? Do you know where those files are, Maxine? Have the police got them? Or The Face?'

I shrug and squirm away, somehow, finding a quiet corner next to the buffet. But there's a hollow-looking elderly man sitting there, his breath heavy with booze, trapping me with the sharp pain in his eyes. He has a story to share, too.

'My baby boy had five people at his funeral. The coffin was so tiny, I could carry it by myself.'

I panic. I don't know what to say – I don't have comforting words for something like that. His red-rimmed eyes fix on me; he looks devastated.

Suddenly a hand links into mine, pulling me gently out of my seat. A soft hand with a pale lilac and grey ombre manicure.

'Sorry to interrupt, Maxine, could you come over here for a minute?'

I feel awful for the poor man, but I'm off-the-planet grateful to see Leni. She whirls me away through a wood-panelled door, into a room which connects the hall to the main church. There are pegs with clerical robes hanging off them and a little hard bench. Huddled on there, knees jutting awkwardly out, are Ed and Andy.

'Max.' Andy smiles, and as we hug, I can feel him trembling slightly. It must be weird for him – he and Xav were such mates at school, then when Xav and Leni became frenemies it was obvious which side Andy would have to pick.

He pushes back his floppy blond hair with one tanned hand and produces a small, slim bottle of vodka, sloshing it into four plastic cups. For a split second, it feels like our drinking-in-the-park days.

'To Xav,' Andy says, and we toast. Then, 'To Alex.'

The liquid is hot in my throat, but I feel that sense of being crowded and poked and on display smoothing away and I'm flooded with love for Alex Malex, and everything we did. We talk about Xav, about the craziness of the lives we lead now.

'I don't know how you all do it. Leni works so, so hard.' Andy puts his arm around her and gives her a squeeze. She looks all safe and comfortable in his embrace. Andy's not my type – he's tall and fit, but also kind of soppy – but seeing them I feel a pang of longing for something. I'm not sure what.

'Well, I *don't* do it, not any more,' Ed says, a tremble in his voice. He's just staring ahead, eyes glassy. 'Everything was Xav's: the channel, the flat we shared. I was so swept up in everything, I never thought about what might happen if we split up.'

I can't imagine how that would feel – to be part of the hottest online couple in the country, recognised and loved by millions, then being alone, no channel, no fans, no future. Ed had started his own PlayMii channel shortly after splitting with Xav, but it was mainly full of rants. There was no joy in it, and it had never really taken off.

Leni's now holding Ed's hand, saying all the right things at the right time, just like I should have done.

'And did you see that *guy* is here?' Ed says, his voice a snarl. 'That *Ethan*. I can't believe he'd dare.'

Leni shudders. 'I'm amazed the police haven't charged him already,' she says, and her boyfriend nods in agreement. 'You know he was outside Xav's flat the night it happened, and he's always creeped me out.'

'Xav probably dumped him and he lashed out,' Andy adds.

Finally, my brain catches up.

'Xav and *Ethan*?' I wrinkle my nose. Of course, I've heard the rumours but I'd never thought they were true. It amazes me that Xav would be so stupid. You don't cross the line with fans. It always ends badly. 'It doesn't make sense.'

Ed shrugs. 'Xav was different towards the end. Not just in the way he treated me. He . . . I dunno, he's always been a bit insecure, a bit sensitive on the inside, but it kind of went off the scale. He kept working on those files. I guess whoever killed Xav has them now.'

'Do you know what was on them?'

Ed shrugs. Leni and I look at each other, equally clueless and once again I feel that panic in the back of my mind. *What did I do? What did we all do?*

'I thought you might know, Maxine,' Ed says. 'I know he told you stuff. Stuff he didn't feel he could tell me. Did he ever say anything that could help?'

Leni's violet gaze locks on to me too, startled. I've never told her about Xav's messages – not while she and Xav were openly attacking each other online. I feel a stab of guilt for keeping it secret from her.

'Me?' I shrug helplessly. 'I'm famous for knowing absolutely nothing.'

When the four of us emerge, the atmosphere in the church hall has shifted. The vigil outside makes us all feel trapped, scared to go out even for a few moments' fresh air and face the wailing crowd. One of Xav's crew comes forward and hugs Leni, thanking her for telling everyone's truth. Ed and Andy melt discreetly into the background. It looks like Accidental Homophobe is heading my way again and I try to lose myself in the throng of black-clad mourners, hoping to avoid him and Carl, while looking for Mum at the same time. Instead, I nearly run smack into DC Riley, who is loitering at the edge of the room, talking to a uniformed officer. Just in time I veer off, but still hear a snatch of conversation, the sheer exasperation in his voice.

'This is bloody impossible. We've been inundated, swamped with calls, texts, social media updates. And this isn't flushing anything out, it's making things worse. It's like trying to find the looniest loon in the lunatic asylum.'

I cringe. Those words confirm it for me: Detective Riley really doesn't get it. Then there's a shout from the other side of the room, a kind of strangled cry.

The officers snap into motion, moving as one towards the sound of trouble. I follow in their wake and suddenly I see Ed pinning Ethan up against the wall. Ethan's head is slammed up against the church noticeboard, crushed against updates on bake sales and Brownie meetings. Ethan struggles meekly but he's a streak of nothing, whereas Ed is well over six feet tall, strong and springy from daily workouts. Ethan twists his body limply, his feet barely touching the ground. His eyes are streaming with tears.

'I'm sorry, man,' he's shrieking, his voice high and unnatural. 'It wasn't me! I swear, I'd never! I'd never!'

My heart aches for both of them. The poor, obsessed boy and the kind, caring ex-partner who has been twisted and broken by Xav. His face is ragged with grief and rage. The officers are barking at him, ordering him to stand down, not to start any trouble, and the tone of voice they're using chills me.

Ed glances up at them and the expression on his face changes to one of fear as he sees them staring at him, a Black kid pushing a white kid up against a wall in front of four police officers. Ethan's sensed the shift. He's not struggling any more, but Ed seems frozen. The police are waiting, watching.

I want to rewind time, to make it so that this never happened, but I can't. Instead, I position myself between the boys and the police, in some stupid attempt to protect Ed. As if I have that power. I'm close enough now to put my hand gently on Ed's arm. I say his name, softly.

'Come on,' I say. 'Come home and stay the night at mine. Watch crap movies, eat junk, talk rubbish. Please. Just come.'

Slowly, the tension begins to leave Ed's arms. Ethan slithers down to ground level, crumpled with shock, parish leaflets scattered on the floor around him.

Ethan's next words come out like a sob. 'It wasn't me. I swear.'

He's not looking at Ed any more, though. He's looking at someone behind me – at DC Riley.

The officers back off, exchanging hushed whispers among themselves, probably analysing Ed and Ethan's behaviour, trying to decide which one of them is a killer. I gather up my things and get ready to leave, keeping one eye on Ed and Ethan as I do it and whispering my plan to Mum. A shadow crosses her face when I tell her – she's thinking about me leaving the church hall with a murder suspect and wondering how it'll play. But she nods and brings the Uber app up on her phone.

'Make sure you speak to Xav's parents before you go,' she adds. I'm horrified at the idea, but Mum virtually pushes me to where they're standing, next to a huge bank of flowers from well-wishers. As I approach them the sweet smell of too many lilies hits me in the face like a sickly wave.

I murmur something about being sorry, something lame and pointless, and flee as quickly as I can, pretending to inspect the nearby flowers.

There are black-swathed wreaths, bouquets, a floral rainbow flag with his name on. A kid in a vintage jacket and black trilby hat is taking close-ups of it on his phone, trying different artistic angles. And then at the end of the display, an arrangement of the most beautiful, crazy-looking flowers I've ever seen, with a card tucked into the stems.

Eternal Love from Alex M.

It's probably nothing.

How many Alexes subscribe to Xav's channel? Probably hundreds.

How many Alexes had Xav dated since breaking up with Ed? Also, possibly hundreds.

This isn't evidence; this is nothing.

But when I join Ed at the door, I still have the card in my hand.

Chapter 10

Sam

'What are you afraid of?' Alex Malex asks the camera, bobble head tipped to one side in a questioning pose. 'Spiders? Public speaking? Your PE teacher? Those aren't real fears. What are you *really* afraid of?'

Xav told me there was much discussion about keeping Alex's voice gender neutral. Eventually they had downloaded a voice changer app which disguised their gender brilliantly but also made them sound a bit sinister. It worked well, adding a thrill of menace to an otherwise feelgood video.

The next few shots change in rapid fire as each Alex member, wearing the mask, confesses their deepest, darkest fear.

'I'm afraid of people not liking me,' Leni says, hands held up to the Alex mask as if she's shy – a glittery manicure ruining the gender-neutral thing.

'I'm afraid of rejection,' says Andy.

'I'm afraid ... I'm afraid I'm not as smart as everyone around me,' says Maxine.

'I'm afraid of jumping off this,' says Ed, pointing at a zipwire.

And finally, Xav – what could he possibly be afraid of? He's lolling back against a wall, looking relaxed and wearing a seriously fitted T-shirt which does things to the bits of my body that I try not to think about.

'I'm afraid my sick sense of humour will get me into trouble one day,' he says, shrugging.

This was Alex video number four and something had shifted. It's not just the sudden upping of their editing skills, either. The first few posts had just been silly stunts and cartoon capers, but this one feels different. In this one, each Alex member tries to face their fears in different ways. Ed throws himself down the zipwire (he actually cries at the end. Pathetic.) Andy pretends to ask Leni out on a date, and she says yes. Maxine sits in a leather *Mastermind*-style chair (from Andy's dad's study) and answers a bunch of trivia questions: apparently Tipperary is in Australia (because it's a long way away), and in 1066 England was invaded by William the Conker. Xav's right, she's not the sharpest tool. The final shot is Xav, making a string of the most offensive but also howlingly funny jokes you could possibly imagine.

It's every bit as stupid as their previous videos but the difference is that it has a heart. The mask has a kind of meaning now. Like you or me, or anyone watching could be wearing it to face their fears. *Je suis Alex Malex. We are all Alex Malex.*

As if any of them – apart from Xav – had any real problems.

Xav sent me the link on the night they uploaded it. He seemed to have forgotten his promise to talk the others into including me. *Maxine wouldn't budge,* he said when I nudged him. Then: *Soooo . . . what do you think?*

I felt a boiling rage deep in my belly that spread, like molten steel, throughout my body. *I hate them, I hate them, I hate them.*

Wow, that's great, I typed.

Afterwards I set up about a dozen different aliases and posted as many negative comments on the channel as I could.

Priviliged wankers.

These people r full of shit

The one with the sparkly nails is literally the most annoying girl on the planet.

Not funny. Not clever. Just stop.

The next day, as I made my way to my meeting with the school pastoral officer, I could feel the ripple effect the video was having on the school. I heard reactions and chatter: *Yeah, they're in year ten, I think . . . I know, it's gone viral . . . That guy's abs, though . . . Xav Bailey? You know Xav, everyone knows Xav . . .*

The sick rage was still boiling inside, and it made me want to do something big and loud, to throw a chair out of the window, grab a passing year seven by the throat and rip his stupid phone out of his stupid hand. Of course, I didn't. I sat meekly in an empty classroom opposite Call-Me-Bronwyn and discussed How I'm Getting On.

She talked about anger-management techniques and mindfulness, and I told her yes, actually, I have a few friends now. We're going to make a PlayMii channel together – something I couldn't quite believe she swallowed, even though it was so very nearly true. And then the question came:

'Any improvement at home at all?'

I'd come prepared for this question, steeled against it. Because this was the question that kept social services out of our home, which kept me and Dad together, the long thin thread of sanity stretched tight between us. If it broke, we'd both be lost.

'Oh yes,' I lied, plastering on a smile. 'Dad and I have reached an agreement – he's going to meetings about the drinking and we're tackling the house one room at a time.'

On the way to the canteen, I saw Xav coming towards me in the corridor and, for a moment, I didn't know how to react. Were we still secret friends or, since I'd created the mask for the channel, would he admit to knowing me now? I started to raise my hand in greeting but at the last moment I bottled it and buried both hands in my trouser pockets, fixing my eyes on the floor as he walked past.

Back home, my lie to Call-Me-Bronwyn came back into my head. Maybe that really was how to handle it with Dad. We were sitting side by side, picking at our Iceland chicken jalfrezi in front of *Midsomer Murders*, and it felt like one of Dad's good days. He ruffled my hair and called me 'a good lad' with a wry chuckle, leaving me feeling a little bit angry, a little bit proud. I still never knew how to feel when he said that.

SAY SOMETHING NOW. Alex's creepy voice urged me in my head: *Face your fears.* I cleared my throat.

'Dad.' My voice came out as a whisper. 'All this stuff . . . could we maybe just tackle one room at a time?'

Dad looked at me, his grey face blank with shock. I'd done it, I'd mentioned the enormous, junk-encrusted elephant in the room. The thing that had driven Gran away, that meant my aunt no longer spoke to us, the thing I'd tried to talk about time after time, but never quite had the courage to say out loud. *Idiot. I should have stayed quiet. We were OK, weren't we? I was coping . . .*

But my stupid voice kept going.

'Maybe . . . it would be nice to be able to get in the bath again,' I said quietly.

My heart hammered. I looked up at him, suddenly rigid with fear. What would it be this time? Crying? Rage? Silence?

He leaped up so quickly, I didn't have time to react. Pilau rice scattered over me, the sofa, the floor.

Without speaking, he swept out of the room. I heard his footsteps on the stairs, passing into the bathroom. With dread rising in me, I rose and walked out into the hallway.

'Dad?'

CRASH. A full plastic storage crate came sliding down the stairs, slamming into the stack of boxes behind the door. The boxes wobbled dangerously but held.

Dad stood at the top of the stairs and dropped another armful of papers and old photographs over the side of the banisters. Memories fluttered down into the hallway like snow. I caught a glimpse of Mum in a blue polka-dot dress, laughing and spreading her fingers over her pregnant belly.

'Bath's empty,' Dad said. I heard his footsteps across the landing, his bedroom door slam. I knew I wouldn't see him again that day.

That's the problem with mental health issues. All this well-meaning advice might sound like a good idea. It might make sense when you read it in a lame self-help guide, or if someone says it to you in a counselling session, or at a my-parents-are-pointless-losers support group, but that doesn't mean it's going to work. Dad drank and hoarded things because those were his hang-ups, and the only person who could stop it was Dad. That was his responsibility. It was up to me to cling on, to keep the rest of our lives together and stop anyone finding out and taking me into care.

So, Alex Malex, what was *I* afraid of? Oh, nothing major – just being hated and excluded by everyone I knew and my dad drinking himself into a coma because I pushed him to the edge with some stupid comment about the bath. *Oh, Alex, you're so right, I should face my fears.*

The next day at school they were all there, sitting on the low wall beneath the statue of the school's founder, Thomas Greech, aka Old Grouchy. A pretty pretentious thing for a bog-standard Lewisham comprehensive to have, but less impressive when you got closer and saw his feet were covered in chewing-gum blobs, scratched initials and pigeon crap. No wonder he had a face like someone had slapped him. Still, the spot under Grouchy was generally reserved for the highest-ranking kids, the ones who'd Arrived. Alex had rocketed them up the status league tables.

I sidled closer, standing behind them, hesitating. They were chatting away, planning their next puerile, pointless video that they probably thought was 'totally going to change the world'.

'God, Xav,' I heard Leni saying, exasperation in her voice. 'It's a great idea, but where the hell would we get our hands on that much slime?'

'Details, details, Leniloo.' Xav waved his hands airily as if sourcing slime was someone else's problem. Maxine hovered nervously between them, unsure of which side to pick, but it was Ed who drew my gaze. Ed, who was leaning on the wall next to Xav, whose hand was so close to his that it was almost touching him. And then I saw it, a tiny movement, Ed's little finger reach out and stroke Xav's.

No. No. *No.*

Swallowing a yelp of dismay, I took a step forward. My foot brushed Andy's sports bag. The zip was half-open and I could see he'd lovingly packed the Alex mask in there, with padding around the edges to prevent any damage. I looked down at it, feeling the urge to smash it to pieces. But it was still my work, and one of the nicest things I'd ever made.

Peeking inside, I could see the wire mesh that supported the head had become slightly banged up. I crouched down, straightened it out. Then, carefully, and making sure nobody could see me, I got my pliers out of my art supplies bag and snipped at several wires, bending them carefully so that they poked inwards, and would stab and scratch and cut whoever put the mask on next.

It felt good, but I wanted to hurt them even more, to reach into their lives and teach them never to ignore me again. They'd come to regret revealing all their greatest fears. All I had to do was think of how to use them to my advantage.

Chapter 11

Maxine

A weird buzzing feeling wakes me up, my eyes crack open and I realise I slept on the sofa last night. Ed is still slumped on the other one, head buried in the expensive, nondescript grey cushions. I become aware of a hot, sore sensation on my cheek. I've fallen asleep with my face on my phone. Blimey, I must have been exhausted. It buzzes again.

Half awake, I thumb into it and see texts from Frida planning to meet up today, and dozens of notifications from the Facehunters group. Yes, I'm that sad now. I get alerts. Mandalor_Ian has published a full report on the funeral, complete with photos through the crowd of us all going in, like a line-up of suspects.

Maxine looks devastated, i didnt think she cared abt Xav that much, one person has written.

I stare at the photo he'd taken of me and see a scared kid, staring out at the crowd like I'm expecting them to bite me.

RU saying its her?!? Fenti posted.

Jamie: Nah. Can you imagine Maxine outwitting the police? 😂

Thanks, Jamie. Now I'm too stupid to be a crazed killer. Not sure whether to be thrilled or insulted about that one.

She still hasn't put up a video since it happened, Fenti responded. *Just that one post on Insta. Cd she be hiding something?*

Then there's a later picture, a blurry one, of me getting into a car with Mum and Ed.

What are those 2 doing together?

Trying to mend our friendship, that's what.

As soon as I got home last night, I covered our stupid leather designer sofa in blankets and made a huge bowl of popcorn. Then Ed and I lolled around, watching ancient episodes of *Glee* and searching online for our all-time favourite Coach Sue Sylvester quotes. When we got to the episode where everyone breaks up with each other and sings about it, my eyes started to get all hot and itchy and wet. Crying at old episodes of *Glee* – at a *Coldplay song*. Cringe.

Embarrassed, I tried to hide, dabbing my tears with a fleecy blanket. Stupid show, manipulating me. I couldn't even tell why I was crying – I haven't had a break-up in for ever. I don't have time for dating and suitable blokes have been thin on the ground.

Come to think of it, maybe that's *why* I was crying.

Then I heard a sniffle from Ed. I glanced up at him; he met my eyes and burst out laughing. Then that laugh became a cry, then a hug and things suddenly felt a tiny bit better.

'I think this is the first time I've laughed properly since it happened,' Ed said. 'It's been horrible, Max. Xav . . . he was absolutely shitty to me and now he's gone and I'm sad, and

I'm angry, I still love him, and I still hate him, all I want to do is shout at everybody. You, Leni, the feds. Especially them. You know the knife had my fingerprints on it and I'm like: "Of course it does. Until a month ago, it was my fucking knife." And I can't tell them what I was doing the night it happened, which makes it even worse.'

Oh God, Ed really is under suspicion.

'Ed. You must tell him. Whatever it is, it can't be that bad.'

Ed's stare had such anger, such contempt in it. 'You're telling me I should trust the police? Even though I get stopped and searched all the time, but when I get gay-bashed in the park they suddenly don't have time to investigate? I'm not like you and Xav, Maxine, am I? Xav always used to tell me to forget it, that together we'd use our mega-influencer power to make the world colour-blind, but that's a crock of shit. I'm an angry Black man, it's all they can see. I can't tell them where I was.'

My mouth was dry from all the popcorn, my head fuzzy with shame at not seeing the reality of Ed's situation before, at being so cushioned from it all in my comfy, leopard-print world.

And worst of all, I remembered the thought that flitted through my head when I talked about it with Leni, about how Ed had seemed so *angry*.

Shit. I had to work on myself, work on this. This wasn't acceptable.

But how could I help him now? I guess just be there for him, be his friend, listen.

When I spoke, my voice came out in a croak. 'You can't tell the police, but you could tell me if you like.'

Ed's face hardened, like a shutter had gone down. 'You shouldn't need me to.'

Now I glance over at him, stirring and waking under his blanket. He's still in his boring white shirt and suit trousers from yesterday, the tie long gone. He still looks uncomfortable in it – I'm used to seeing him in the totally-on-point hip T-shirts and tight jeans he and Xav always used to wear. Sometimes, when they were still loved-up, they even used to match their clothes.

'Jesus, this settee's uncomfortable,' he says.

'This isn't a real flat for real people,' I apologise. 'At least Mum put blankets on us after we dropped off, so we didn't freeze. Coffee?'

'Oh God, yes.'

I go through to the kitchen and fire up the bean machine. Even though I didn't drink last night, I feel hungover.

'Dehydration,' Ed says, hunching over his coffee cup. 'Combination of crying and not drinking any fluids. I feel like I've shrunk.'

This simple exchange, so boring and normal, sparks a tiny flare of positivity inside me. *I haven't lost him.*

I want to tell him I'm sorry I let him down, that of course he's bloody angry, it's only natural. I want to say I know he didn't do it, that dressing up in a mask and uploading a murder video is about the most un-Ed-like thing on the planet. But I don't want to destroy the fragile peace we've made, the little bubble of contentment that has formed around us and our coffee mugs. So instead, I hold out a tin and say, 'Biscuits?'

It'll have to do for now.

Just then, the entryphone goes and I buzz Frida up. She sails into the kitchen, all jangling bangles and palm-tree print, her unruly black curls pulled into a topknot and held with a silk flowered band.

'I hope you're prepared to shop, because I'm . . . oh.'

'This is Ed,' I say, and stop myself from adding 'Xav's ex' just in time. Imagine that, imagine being introduced as some person's ex for the rest of your life.

Ed and Frida are staring at each other warily.

'Don't worry, Ed, you can relax. Frida's not #TeamAnything, she's just my mate.'

Mum serves us all badly made scrambled eggs for brunch and we make stilted conversation. You know that weird thing when friends from two different worlds meet up and you don't know which version of yourself to be? That's what it's like. Frida is quiet and awkward and nothing like as fabulous as she usually is; Ed clams up. By the time he heads home, I'm relieved.

I apologise to Frida for Ed's spikiness and then ask her a favour. 'I know you've got all this shopping planned, but I need to go back to south London today – there's something I want to check out. Will you come with me?'

In my bedroom, I pull on leggings and a top without paying much attention for a change. I fix my make-up again and fumble through my pinafore dress pocket, until I find the Alex flower card. On the front, next to the handwritten message, was a sorrowful-looking angel, the kind Xav would have despised as cheesy crap. On the back is the name of the florist that organised the delivery.

I unlock my phone to call a car but Frida puts a bejewelled hand out and stops me. 'Come on,' she says. 'Let's go to the station. Slum it with the civilians for a change!'

Rays of sunlight hit us as we step outside. Squinting across the street, I can see a small knot of people and, as I look, one of them raises their phone.

'Bloody hell, did you see that?' Frida is outraged.

'It's normal. I don't get it as much as Leni and Xav . . . as Xav used to.'

'But I don't want to be photographed by randoms in the street!'

'You get used to it.' My main problem is that I can never remember who everyone is – I once mortally offended the owner of quite a popular fan account by swanning past without saying hello. So now I make a mental note. *Blonde with leopard jacket . . . girl with high ponytail . . . and . . . is that Ethan?*

I feel a jolt of unease. Why would Xav's fan-and-possibly-boyfriend have switched his attentions on to me?

'Come on.' I link my arm with Frida's. 'Let's get moving.'

The trip to Lewisham is hot and crowded. We find sticky seats in the corner of the carriage and I tell Frida about Alex Malex, about the excitement of creating the channel, the way it swept around the school like wildfire, changing me from no-mark to mini-celebrity in the space of a term, and then how it all came to an end.

'I wish I could go back and change things. I was so caught up in my own problems with Dad, and missing Mum, that I didn't see that someone else was struggling and, even if I had, I didn't feel like I had any power to make a difference. It's funny, isn't it? How school makes you feel so small and helpless, and trapped in the role everyone else has given you.'

Frida is quiet, and I realise that I'm doing to her what everyone normally does to me – dumping a whole load of heavy emotions on her that she's just not equipped to deal with. Just like me, she probably doesn't have a clue what to say.

After a few moments, she smiles and squeezes my arm. 'You're a good person, Maxine.'

She means it – her voice has this deep, sincere note in it that reassures me. I worry sometimes that I've latched on to Frida too fast. I mean, we only met five weeks ago, and she knows more about my life than Leni and Ed do. And I know she's got things about herself she's not ready to share yet. My eyes flicker down to the white lines on her arms as I think this. But it's good to hear her say she cares, and I believe it.

Still, I don't want to be let off the hook, not for this, so I shrug it off and change the subject. 'I know it's mad, coming halfway across town, and I'm sorry about missing out on the shopping, but I can't help feeling that this Alex card has something to do with what happened. Maybe if I get more proof, I could go to the police with it.' I picture myself trying to explain all this to Detective Riley and fail. But still, I have to try.

Arm in arm, we walk out of the station on to the high street. It's so weird, being back here again. At the funeral yesterday, I rushed out of the car into the church. This is different, a total immersion in my memories of the two school terms I'd spent at Dad's.

There's the corner shop where we used to fill up on sweets after school. There's the park, still scrubby and wind-blown with old takeaway wrappers and empty cans of Nurishment. I lost three door keys in a row and for a while Dad stopped 'trusting' me with them, so I'd often come here to hang out until someone else got home. The huge slide Andy skated down for our first stunt looks so small now. Hal's Kebab has been replaced by something called Ocean Fry and I feel a burst of sadness that I'll never taste Hal's chips again. I hesitate at the end of the road where Xav's funeral took place yesterday, but the street is empty now – a few tattered rainbow banners tied to the railings are the only sign that anything different happened there the day before.

Frida shivers out of sympathy as we turn left into a narrow street of Victorian houses, grubby front gardens and tatty, greying walls. Suddenly neither of us wants to chat. We keep our heads bowed. Then I realise where we are and stop short, shocked.

'Xav's old house,' I say, pointing up. We both shudder.

I only went there a couple of times, and even then, I never made it over the threshold. But I know what went on in there, the violence, the bullying that had twisted something in Xav.

No wonder he had moved out as soon as he could.

The house is tatty but not as run down as some of the others in the street. The net curtains at the window are fresh and white, and there's a fat tabby cat looking smugly out from the windowsill. It doesn't look like an evil place, but not all evil is as visible as The Face.

'Let's get out of here,' Frida says.

I couldn't agree more.

The Flower Agency is just a few streets away, a shop painted in stylish slate grey, with big, bright statement blooms dotted around. One wall is covered with a display of glass vases of all different shapes and sizes. The girl at the counter looks up from her phone as we come in.

And in two seconds, her face transforms into a wondrous smile.

'Oh my *days*,' she says.

I smile back. Thank the vlog gods – the assistant at the Flower Agency is part of my fam. Her name's Keisha and she's lovely. We pose for selfies (I agonise privately over whether I'm supposed to smile or not), then she tells me about her mum's arthritis and her boyfriend's failed attempts to find a job, and how at sixteen she's supporting them both and trying to get her Instagram following off the ground.

113

'I'm sorry I'm going on, but I feel like I know you,' she says. 'I guess you've just got . . .'

'. . . one of those faces,' I finish, and we both laugh. I wish I could help her somehow. She'd be a great influencer, so natural and fun to listen to. But it's harder to break through these days, with so many trying. I grab her IG name and promise to give her a boost.

She looks awkward for a moment, and then blurts out a question. 'Why haven't you said anything yet? You've gone so quiet. People are worrying.'

'I know,' I say. 'I'll put something up soon. I'm working on it.'

Keisha looks relieved, and then suddenly remembers where she is. 'Oh, I forgot,' she says. 'Do you want to buy some flowers?'

I shake my head. 'Actually, I want to find out about a bouquet that was sent to the funeral yesterday. It's a bit of a weird one. I just want to satisfy my curiosity about something.'

I show her the card and a photo I took of the flowers: 'Do you know who ordered these?'

'Wow, protea at this time of year? That would cost big bucks – the season's nearly over,' she says. 'It's my boss's handwriting on the card which means it was probably an online order. Hang on, I'll try to look it up.'

She clacks away on the computer with long, perfect nails. 'OK, here it is . . . yes, someone ordered it online. Umm . . . obviously I can't give you the PayPal details but there's an email address. Does the name ring a bell?'

I crane over her shoulder, then feel a surge of fear, an adrenaline release so strong I want to run out of the shop, screaming until I have no breath left in me.

Calm, keep calm. Breathe in. Breathe out.

'I'll write it down for you,' Keisha says as I fight for control. 'alex.malex321BANG@gmail.com. Funny email address, isn't it?'

Chapter 12

Maxine

The pages Mum has written lie on the hall table with a Post-it note on top. *Gone to meeting. Here's a few thoughts. Just to get you started.*

Mum has written a fake vlog script for me, talking about Xav's death. I flick through and phrases jump out at me, sensitive, thoughtful things I would never say. *At this sad time . . . I just want to express my sympathy . . . My heart goes out to Xav's family and fans . . .*

I can't do it. I can't upload this pile of old tripe, and I can't think of what I want to say instead.

So what if people are expecting something? So what if I lose hundreds of followers overnight and bring my whole career crashing down around me? I'd rather do that than say something well meaning but hollow and fake. I screw the paper up and shove it in the recycling.

I go to my room and shut the door firmly before throwing myself down on my bed and staring at the gmail address, scrawled on the florist's notepaper.

I have the email address of a killer. Possibly. Maybe. Now what? Do I just drop my old non-existent pal Alex a line and say, 'Would you mind handing yourself in to the police?'

Do I tell Detective Riley? I'm not filled with confidence that he'd take me seriously.

I need more than this to convince him.

Opening my laptop, I type the address into a blank email. My fingers feel like rubber and every single part of me is screaming not to do this.

I type a message, then erase it. Then another one, over and over.

Are you The Face? No.

Did you kill my friend? No.

I hate you, murdering scum. True, but no.

There is no right wording for this email. There is no way it's going to end well for me but I've got to send it. I've got to do *something,* for Ed. In the end I type: *Who are you?* Then press send.

I stare at the screen, refreshing, refreshing. But nothing happens.

I spend the rest of the morning dicking around on the Facehunters page. News of Xav's burn files has leaked out, thanks to a panicky-sounding video by Jace D the Accidental Homophobe. He blurted out the news on a video this morning, while wearing a T-shirt with *Pride Ally* on it in rainbow letters. The speculation is that The Face is going to hold us all hostage, blackmail us with our little secrets, but that doesn't make any sense.

Isn't it obvious? I write. *The Face was IN those files, whoever he really is. That's why Xav's computer was wiped and his phone went missing.*

117

Fenti: Wait WHAT? His computer was wiped & phone taken? When did this come out?!?!

Oops. Great work, Maxine.

I backtrack, saying it's a rumour I'd heard online, I couldn't remember where. But the team takes it and runs with it, making a (very long) list of influencers and other celebs Xav might have dirt on, and cross-checking who was doing what that night looking for alibis. I am assigned two creators to check up on – Jace D, and a gamer girl I vaguely know. Fenti gets me. Just my luck – Fenti and Mandalor_Ian are the only ones who seem to know what they're doing.

Things are becoming too uncomfortable now. I log out and go back to thinking about what info Xav might possibly have on me. It could be anything – a wrong word, a slightly off-colour tweet, but I genuinely think there's nothing there. I try so hard not to offend anyone that I occasionally veer over into boring.

But then something does occur to me.

No, it couldn't be that.

But what if it was?

Ohhhh shit.

I've gone all hot now, that breathless plummeting feeling you get in your guts when you know you've done something wrong and are about to be found out.

Because I suddenly realise that Xav didn't just have access to the stuff I put online; he used to fix my computer for me, which means that he'd had plenty of time to poke around in my history, my files . . .

Flicking the lid open again, I search for a folder called *Old*.

There it is. Click.

There's tons of stuff in here – half-made videos that never worked out, ancient schoolwork, tons of Alex photos, and . . . it's not there.

I scan through it again, making my search alphabetical. Still nothing.

I feel a flood of panic in me. It's not earth-shattering, not the dirtiest dirt in the world, but about six months ago I got pissed off about Leni ignoring me and jealous of her being so successful, and I made a diss video. I appeared with my face caked in terrible make-up and a clown wig, and ranted about how I was so graceful and ethereal that I didn't need my old loser friends. It was completely petty, very satisfying to make at the time and never meant for public viewing. If it got out the whole world would hate me and – even worse – Leni would never speak to me again.

And it's gone.

I search *Leni_diss* just to be on the safe side. *No results.*

Xav could have just copied the file, but oh no. He must have moved it deliberately, knowing it would freak me out when he was ready to release the files. I feel sick.

Bing.

The email alert makes me jump up. I refresh my screen and there it is.

A message from the Alex Malex account.

Thank you for your email. Your message is important to us and we will get back to you shortly.

I don't know what I was expecting, but it's not this.

Bing. Another message, again just one line.

Just kidding. You know who this is. And I have a job for you.

There's this rush, a wave of fear and horror as the words sink into my brain – the feeling that I've just broken something that can never be repaired.

The logical part of my brain is still fighting this new reality, telling me this can't be real. It's a hoax, it's a random fan pranking me. Why would the killer send flowers to the funeral? Why would he use that name? This can't be *him*.

But the words sit there on my screen, blinking black and white. And the terrified-small-animal part of my brain knows it's true. This is a monster who dressed up to kill, posted a video of a murder – he loves the drama, the fear. And now, I've given him a window into my life, a new audience.

A new victim.

I realise I've backed away from the laptop. I'm pressed into the corner of my bed, up against the plush headboard, as if putting distance between me and the keyboard could somehow take back what I've done.

Stupid, fucking *stupid* me.

Bing.

Have you calmed down yet? Here is what I want you to do. I want you to find those files, and if you do not, there will be consequences for you and your friends.

I snap the laptop shut and stand there for a while, just staring at its dumb, sticker-covered lid. I think about throwing it across the room, hearing the screen crack, keys scattered all over the floor. I think about stamping on it hard, crunching my heel down and buckling the metal. But that won't change the message on there. Won't undo my idiotic email.

I take a step back towards the bed. Then another. I open the laptop with the tip of my fingernail, like it's going to scorch me. I stare at the text, and stare and stare. And then I click reply.

What do you mean? I type.

Just find the files. Xav was your friend – nobody will suspect you if you go looking. Find them, or there will be consequences.

My heart is thumping so hard, it feels like my chest is going to burst but the outside of me feels numb, like I'm made of rubber. I can't move, I can't breathe. I have to show this to the police. Detective Riley will have to believe me now. I'm still staring at the screen when the next message comes in.

Do not go to the police. They won't find me from this email, and I enjoy arranging consequences. Do you know that Leni_loves takes a run alone in the park every morning at 7.15 exactly? I do. Just find the files.

I slam the laptop shut. This is too much. My brain can't cope with something this strange, this wrong. I don't care what this Alex person is saying, I'm calling the police now.

Detective Riley's mobile number goes to answerphone after two rings. I leave a message telling him I need to speak to him right away, that I have important information about who the killer might be. I start trying to explain about flowers and emails, but my voice comes out all garbled and squeaky. I trip over my words and I'm worried about messing it up: coming over all 'maccabree' will stop him taking me seriously.

'Please just call me back,' I say.

When I hang up, the apartment seems cold, quiet. *Think, Maxine, you dummy. THINK. There has to be a way out of this.*

I type a message to Leni: *Stupid request, but could you not go running for a few days? I've seen a few weird posts on a fan page, stay safe xxxx*

Leni must be drowning in threats and 'weird posts'. I only hope she takes me seriously.

As I press send, I look out of my window to the street below. The girls from this morning aren't there any more, but there's a skinny black-clad figure leaning against the wall opposite, playing with his phone. Ethan's still there. Suddenly he looks up, straight up, at my bedroom window. His gaze locks on mine. I freeze with panic.

Could he be something to do with The Face's threat?

I try to get my head around the idea of quiet, shy Ethan being The Face.

I guess it's possible. He's obsessed with Xav, thinks it's fine to root through people's bins, and Leni's radar is usually pretty good but ... I close my eyes and picture him in the green room, half-laughing, half-choking, mouth full of M&Ms, and I just can't ...

Yeah. But look where my brilliant judgement has got me so far.

OK, so he might be The Face. Small chance. Small-ish.

But he also might have the files.

I have to do something. One more hour in my room with that laptop, one more moment of sitting around doing nothing, and I'll explode. I come to a decision.

I leave by the back door. The cool evening air calms me, helps some of my panic ebb away as I slip around the corner, press my body close to the building. I wait there, breathing slow and steady, until the obsessive fan, the one that my friend Ed plus half the internet thinks is a murderer, starts walking home for tea.

And, at a distance in the half-light of dusk, I follow him.

Chapter 13

Maxine

I've been followed a fair bit in my time. I don't mean stalkers – usually, I'm just trailed around shopping malls by small groups of kids who are too scared to come up and say hi, so they lurk behind clothes racks pointing their phones at me until I spot them and wave them over. The difference between what they did then and what I'm doing now is that they *wanted* to be seen. I don't – and I have no idea what I'm doing.

From the moment that email appeared in my inbox, my body's been full of this weird adrenaline energy, pushing me to move, to act, to do *something*. And, right now, that strange impulse is shoving aside normal Maxine, the girl who would much rather be binge-watching cheesy shows while eating ice cream. Normal me is still there at the back of my brain screaming, *WHAT THE HELL ARE YOU DOING, YOU IDIOT?* But I block the words out and keep walking.

As I tread carefully down the street behind him, with Mum's black running hoodie pulled up over my stupid, conspicuously curly hair, the pounding of my heart is almost unbearable. How does Jason Bourne cope with this stuff?

My phone's in my hand, and every time it looks like he's going to turn around, I kind of lift it up and look intently into it, like I'm watching a PlayMii video and definitely not following the skinny kid with the ITS_XAVVVV limited-edition messenger bag. My hands are clumsy, fumbling as I unlock the screen. I'm terrified that at any moment I'm going to give myself away by tripping over my own feet, or sneezing.

OK, break it down, Max. What are you afraid of?

I still can't get my head round the idea of Ethan being The Face – especially since the emails, which sounded too cold, too calculating to be him. I remember when he started popping up in Xav's videos as a glorified prop – as target practice in *Truth Or Dare Water Balloon*, then wrapped in cellophane and hopping around after Xav and Ed in *We Made A Living Plastic Mummy*. A needy, geeky outsider. Sometimes fan, sometimes friend, maybe something more in the aftermath of Xav's break-up with Ed. I still don't feel I know him at all. I still don't feel safe with him.

He's at the bus stop now. A few metres back, I spot a garden with a pine tree growing by the gates and step back behind it, bend over my phone, only letting my eyes flicker up every now and then. Thank the vlog gods, Ethan is genuinely glued to his own screen. His earbuds are in and he's gazing at a video, but it's too far away for me to see if it's one of Xav's.

By the time the bus pulls up, there's a bit of a queue. Ethan gets on and I see him go straight upstairs. I join the back of the queue, sit on the bottom deck a few seats back, next to an old lady in a red coat with a neat vintage clutch bag on her lap. After a couple of moments, I sense her shifting her body language and turning to me.

Oh please no, not now.

'Ooh, you don't half look like my daughter,' she says. 'She moved to Australia last year, hasn't even called.'

I say 'mmm' as quietly as I can, just in case Ethan can hear my voice from upstairs. But she keeps talking: there was an argument about a will, apparently. As the lady continues to offload, I grab an abandoned *Metro* paper and hold it up in front of me, while nodding in all the right places. With Ethan safely upstairs, my heart rate begins to slow. Common sense starts to seep in.

What the hell am I doing here? What do I think I'm going to learn? Should I just give up and go home?

I'm about to press the bell for the next stop, but the thought of going back to the flat, to my room, and sitting there waiting for The Face to make his next move is just . . . I can't do it. I refresh my phone. There's a short message from Leni: *You're freaking me out.* I reply lightly, saying she should just take care, nothing specific to worry about. The lie makes me feel achingly alone.

The bus eventually stops on a quiet suburban road. It's a bit run down but in a nice, homey sort of way. I hear feet on the stairs and hold the paper up even more, pretending to study the entertainment section. *All I need is a pair of eye holes cut in it to look like a complete comedy cliché.* Now would be a really stupid time to start laughing at how ridiculous it all is but I can feel it bubble up inside. I bite my lip.

Ethan gets off and I murmur a hasty goodbye to the old lady then jump out of my seat, through the doors before they close, and follow.

A few streets later, we come to a row of terraced 1970s houses. Ethan walks down the path of one of them, rummaging for keys. He turns slightly and I spin around, my head down, grab the latch on next door's gate, and go through it like I was headed there all along.

What happens next happens fast – barking, growling, a blur of mouth and tongue and teeth. The dog is all muscle; it cannonballs into me, knocking me to the ground, pushing all the air out of my lungs. I curl up into a ball, tucking my head under, but I feel the dog's jaws connect with my shoulder, tearing into the fabric of my hoodie.

'Buddy, NO!' Ethan's voice. The dog's weight is wrenched off my back, there's the sound of rustling packets, a hand on my shoulder.

'Are you OK? . . . *Maxine*??'

It takes twenty minutes of sitting at his mum's kitchen table before I'm calm enough to speak. I sometimes say that my job is like a constant adrenaline rush, but I know now that nothing compares to being threatened by a murderer, followed by stalking a stalker and then being attacked by a crazed spaniel. My shoulder still throbs slightly but Ethan has looked at it and assured me the skin isn't broken.

'Sorry.' He shoves a flowered mug of weak tea into my hands and I take it. 'Buddy's off his meds at the moment and my neighbour keeps shutting him outside, poor thing. Lucky I had that bag of crisps on me. He loves crisps.'

I nod and stare down into the tea. It has floaty bits in it. I drink it anyway and it's very, very sweet.

'Mum says sweet tea is good for shock,' he says.

And so here we are. The stalky, murder-suspect superfan and me, the failed detective, drinking tea together, making conversation. How terribly, terribly British. I take another sip and the sweetness does sort of calm me. Ethan's mum is on to something.

I look straight at him for the first time – he's pale, even paler than usual. In sorrow, his face is kind of beautiful, in a sharp-cheekbone, emo-boy way, and while he's still hurting, he looks strangely more like a grown man than he did when he was hanging around Xav.

'Maxine,' he says, 'why were you in my next-door neighbour's garden?'

And there it is, the million-dollar question I don't have a decent answer to. His hazel eyes study me closely and I remember what he was like before – a bit intense, maybe. A bit disrespectful of personal space, but not . . .

I glance up and something odd catches my eye. It's in the laundry basket by the washing machine – a snaggly scrap of black hair, a glimpse of white rubber, red lips . . . It's that *thing*. That mask. The Face.

I'm frozen. My guts twist in horror and my legs are almost kicking against the laminate floor, but fear won't let me stand. I fight to stay calm, not to let on what I've seen.

But Ethan's noticed. He walks over to the laundry basket and grabs it, like it's just a normal, everyday item.

'It's not the one from the video Maxine, really it's not,' he says.

Now I look more closely, I can see that it's different. The hair is lighter and it has more of a killer-clown vibe about it.

'It's just a joke mask Xav gave me. He was experimenting with different masks, trying to find the scariest-looking one. He wanted me to kill him. If I'd done it . . . oh I wish I'd done it, then he'd be alive.'

He chokes back a sob, gripping that horrendous thing in one hand so that the rubbery face twists and distorts. Another tide of irrational fear washes over me. My body is pressed so hard against the kitchen cupboards that my back hurts, but Ethan's words are starting to sink in. They match up with Xav's behaviour in that final video. It's starting to make sense.

'It was supposed to be a prank, wasn't it?'

Ethan nods, then explains how they'd planned it together. Ethan would wear the mask to 'murder' Xav, then Xav would go into hiding for a couple of days, release the files and watch the mayhem from afar. Had they really expected that to work? I couldn't imagine Detective Riley being amused when the supposed 'murder victim' came out of hiding. But then, Xav was never one to think that sort of thing through.

'I was all set to do it, but a couple of days before he changed his plans. He said he'd thought of a better killer. Someone funnier.' Ethan's fighting to keep the hurt out of his voice, even now.

Silence hangs between us for a moment and I realise something about Ethan. He doesn't waste his words, doesn't speak unless spoken to.

'Did he tell you who it was?'

'No.'

'Did you have any suspicions?'

'I thought it might be Jace D. They were spending a lot of time together.'

Accidental Homophobe? That's a shocker.

'That night I waited outside Xav's flat to see. I didn't see anyone go in at all. But later, I thought if Xav was planning to make his fake death realistic, he might have got the person – whoever it was – to climb in through the utility-room window. I did that once when I was hiding from Ed, and there's no security cameras there.'

'What happened next?' I realise I'm interrogating Ethan just like DC Riley would, but he doesn't seem to mind.

'The police came and I ran off. Stupid, but I thought Xav had got pissed off and called the cops on me. They arrested me, and that's how I found out Xav had died. I didn't even get a second to think about that. They're all, like, did I have sexual relations with the victim? Where's his phone? Did I love him or hate him? And all the time I'm thinking, *he's gone, he's gone.*'

His voice fractures again. He sits down on the metal chair next to me, elbows on the table; the tips of his long fingers are drumming against his temples, harder and harder. 'I don't know what to do now, who I am. I went to Xav's every day. Now I can't. I can't go on the fan sites because everyone hates me. I can't go to Leni's because she calls security. So, I go to yours. I hope you don't mind.'

Do I mind? Well, yes, but that seems so unimportant, so irrelevant right now. And I suddenly know with absolute certainty that, whatever he is, and however different his view of the world, Ethan is not The Face.

'But the police know you didn't do it, right?'

Ethan shrugs. 'I'm still under caution. And I don't know what to do with this.' He lifts up the mask and I feel another knee-jerk surge of dread. 'I shoved it in Mum's linen basket upstairs, but she must have brought it down by accident. I can't keep it and I can't throw it away. What if someone goes through my bins and finds it?' He looks slightly sheepish when he says this.

'Listen, Ethan, why I followed you . . . what I wanted to ask is . . . do you know who has those files?'

'I wish I did,' Ethan said finally. 'It might make the police – and the fans – leave me alone.'

As I walk away from Ethan's house, I feel strangely stronger. The crazy afternoon of emails and threats seems absurd to me now. It can't be real. Why would The Face pick me to find the files, anyway? I hadn't seen Xav for months before it happened and hardly anyone knew about the messages he sent me. Maybe I've overreacted; maybe it was just some sicko playing a prank and I've stupidly fallen for it.

I get on the bus feeling stronger. More realistic.

By the time I'm at home, I've talked myself out of most of my fears. The email has to be an empty threat, some weirdo having a joke. I'll ignore it, hand it over to DC Riley when he calls back, then start making videos, get back to my life. It's time to be me again.

Chapter 14

Sam

That morning Old Grouchy was wearing a thong on his head. There was a logo on the front, which sat just under his craggy Roman nose. It said *Party Animal*.

I looked him up on Wikipedia once and the result was depressing and predictable. Up-himself Victorian who made a fortune 'in cotton' (translation: slaves and kids working in cramped factories) before scattering some money out into the community to make himself look good.

I was late for school, so there were no cool people lolling against his plinth now. I sidled up and gave it a little kick, which hurt me more than it did him.

Still, the sun was out and I lolled back against him and let its warmth soak into my chilly body. The boiler had broken at home again and I'd woken up freezing. I looked out over the school driveway, the blue metal gates flung wide open, and tried to imagine myself hanging out here, waving to friends and acolytes as they came in. Then I looked down, caught a glimpse of my drab, stained school trousers and scuffed black trainers, and reality snapped right back into place, hard and ugly. That's when my foot nudged on something plastic on the flowerbed below. Looking down, I noticed a phone had fallen out of someone's bag and on to the ground, where it was partly covered by the soil. A mid-range model with a leopard-print case.

Wow, Maxine really is disorganised. I smile, unable to believe my luck.

The week before, when my fingers had twisted the metal loose in that mask, I'd felt a thrill, a stab of excitement, the same way I felt whenever I watched an especially batshit stunt online. Later on, I noticed a scratch on Ed's pretty fore-head and I was even more certain. If they wouldn't let me into their stupid little gang, I'd mess with them, disrupt their lives in any way I could.

I was still joyously posting shitty comments on each video. *That girl who's afraid people don't like her? I don't like her.*

How stupid do you have to be to not know you're stupid?

Itching to push that guy off a cliff and see if it cures his fear of heights.

Who wants to hear what this bunch of smug priviliged kids have to say?

Some of them were immediately pushed down by fanboys and girls from the school, but a couple of comments had been liked. Not everybody was a paid-up member of the Alex fan club.

And now I had Maxine's phone, I could take their suffering to a whole new level.

My heart beat hard as I palmed the phone, rushed into the toilets and shut myself in a cubicle. Registration could wait – I suddenly didn't care how many late marks I got.

Maxine had exactly the same cheap-ass phone as I did, and because she never cleaned her screen, I could see the marks her fingers had left when she drew a pattern to unlock it. I was in within five minutes and, oh, what a goldmine.

WhatsApp: Endless conversations with Leni about how obvious and full-on Andy's crush was. *He's sweet but so, so into me. Am I ready for this?* Leni wrote. Ugh. The Alex group chat was an endless blasting of ideas and video clips. It would take me hours to go through it all, and it was all so sickeningly fun, I felt more left out than ever.

Facebook: Loads of photos of a middle-aged woman with Maxine's surname (her mum, I guessed) posing in various American locations and writing *Missing U Stellina xxxxx* on Maxine's page. Lame GIFs and heart-warming memes from a nan in Italy.

Facebook Messenger: Lots of messaging with her mum. The older ones were variations on: *Miserable with Dad and Glenys. They are making me sleep in a cupboard like Harry Potter.* The newer ones were about all the fabulous new friends she'd started hanging round with (*boak*).

Instagram: A grid full of leopard-print things in shops. Selfies in various places around town, with and without Leni.

Photos: A series of really embarrassing mirror-selfies where she's trying out various duckface poses. Some girls can carry off duckface, but Maxine really can't – each is more searingly cringeworthy than the last. I chuckled for ages over those.

PlayMii: Ooh, this was interesting. Maxine had her own channel, Maxine_F. I wondered if she'd told the others about it. She hadn't shared it on any of her social accounts, never mentioned it in any of her WhatsApp chats. It was almost like she was keeping it a secret. *Hmm . . . this could be useful.*

I watched a couple of them – a clever sketch about body image, shot with bendy funfair mirrors and a video tour of her bedroom at her dad's house, which really did look like a walk-in cupboard. There was a rail of shirts hanging over her bed, which she'd tragically tried to jazz up with fairy lights.

Now I had a choice: I could be discreet and do nothing, continuing to spy on her, or I could rampage through her apps causing maximum mayhem. I wished I was one of those cunning, thoughtful types, but rampaging was more my speciality. I spent the next twenty minutes making as much random mischief as I could.

Facebook Messenger: I sent links to two of Maxine's most recent PlayMii posts to her mum. I didn't bother to check what they were – most kids don't want to share their PlayMii channels with their parents, so there was bound to be something troublemaking on there.

Instagram: I posted the most horrendous duckface selfie I could find with the words *Yaassss! Queeeeen!! #selfie #me #myself #love #cute #beautiful #model.*

WhatsApp: I typed out a message to the year ten girls' chat group. The message went something like this: *My good friend Leni, who you all know as Eleanore – because that's her actual name – is crushing on Andy. I mean she LOVES him and not just because he's completely loaded, although that helps.* 😁 *But I hear*

he can be slightly creepy and a bit of a priviliged tosser. And also,
that he has a tiny penis. Does anyone know if that's true?

I chuckled to myself. Don't you just love a bit of sophisti-
cated humour?

The pips went for the end of first period and I heard the
corridor outside flood with noisy, bratty voices. Time was up.
I had to act fast – get Maxine's phone back to her without her
seeing me do it.

I ventured out of the toilets and headed for the science
block, where I caught sight of Maxine's dark hair outside Lab
Four. She was frisking herself, rummaging through her pockets looking panicked.

Smiling, I polished the cracked screen with my sleeve,
handed the phone to a passing year seven kid.

'That girl over there just dropped her phone,' I said. 'I'm
late for class. Could you give it back for me?'

The year seven gave me a withering look – bloody hell,
even they caught the scent of loser off me – but she did what
I asked.

Later that day, I went to geography. As usual I was hunched
over my phone, when suddenly I felt a whisper of movement
as someone slid into the seat next to me. I looked up to see
Eleanore and she smiled.

Maxine still sat at the front of the classroom, abandoned by
her friend. Her head was down on the desk, her dark curls
pooled around her. I wasn't sure if she was crying, but I liked
to think she was. I knew what Eleanore was like – she could

be weirdly sensitive sometimes and not afraid to dish out the silent treatment.

Whatever. I fired up the video I'd been watching, *Crazy Girl Superglues Stuff To Face*, and the two of us watched Crazy Girl adding a selection of tiny plastic dinosaurs, Hello Kitties and unicorns to her forehead. It was just like old times.

Leni smelt different – she wasn't drenched in perfume like a lot of the year ten girls, but there was a cloud of subtle scent around her that I couldn't put my finger on. She'd also stopped wearing her hair in a shy flick over her face to hide her braces. I didn't notice make-up much on the whole, but I couldn't miss the shimmer of mauves and greys that made her eyes seem bigger and brighter than before.

But the biggest change was the way she carried herself. Even now, when the whole year group were laughing about 'Maxine's' messages, she had a serene smile, a grace about her, like someone was filming her 24–7. I don't know why none of us had seen this specialness before. It made me almost afraid to speak to her.

But if I wanted to mess with the Alex team, Eleanore was the perfect place to start, mainly because she was aware of my existence.

'About Andy . . .' I began.

'There's nothing going on,' she snapped.

'Oh, of course! No! Good!' I said. And I left it there. One thing about staying silent at school for years and years is that you know when to shut up.

Leni waited a few moments, then turned her iridescent eyes on me. 'What about him?' she asked, arching a perfect brow.

Gotcha.

'You know what happened with his last girlfriend, don't you? He got a bit . . . intense . . . when she tried to cool things off with him.'

Leni reacted immediately – her posture went rigid and tense.

'What do you mean?' she asked.

'Um . . .' I looked down, as if I suddenly felt really awkward (and realised that, for the first time in years I didn't feel awkward at all! Who knew torturing people was the cure for my terminal shyness?) 'He used to send her things in the post. Dead things. And, well, you know I saw him following you home last week and I was worried.'

'He *what*?' There was a toxic mix of emotions in her voice: disbelief, anger, a dash of fear. And then she remembered to put her mask back on and said, 'Oh, I'm sure you must be mistaken.'

I told her I hoped I hadn't spoken out of turn, that I thought she'd known already. I told her to forget I'd ever spoken and cued up another silly video to watch.

It wasn't altogether a lie. Xav once told me Andy's ex-girlfriend really had found him too full-on. He was all about big, overly romantic gestures: champagne and expensive chocolates, and whisking her off to stadium gigs and posh dinners – the kind of thing that works in films but is a bit much in real life. And once, after a row, he'd sent her a dried-out rose – which was technically a dead thing, wasn't it?

I was doing her a favour really. And if it created tension in the happy land of Team Alex, then ah well, so be it.

By the end of the day I felt flushed, drunk with pleasure. I couldn't believe how smoothly it had all gone. All my shyness, my bad nerves, had evaporated because I was playing a role and I realised maybe that was the key. One day, when Xav and I were out of here, I'd start again, reinvent myself from scratch.

'Where shall we go, when we escape?' I asked Xav in the hut that evening. We were lolling back on the bean bags, drinking cider that Xav had brought with him. Something about watching my dad's decline made drinking feel like poison to me but I didn't want to reject a gift from Xav, so I took tiny pretend sips.

'Oh, I dunno,' he said. 'Ed wants to go to university in Edinburgh, for some reason. Scotland sounds nice.'

'Nicer than Indonesia? What the hell is *in* this cider?'

Xav laughed and squeezed my hand. 'Sorry, I'm not in the mood for games tonight.' He waved his phone at me lazily. 'Do you think I should ask Ed out by text or to his face? This is ridiculous, I don't usually stress about this stuff, but Ed's different. Ed's ... he's hot but he's also funny, and he's got this cute computer-geek side – you know I'm a sucker for a nerd – and, well ... he's *Ed*.'

I reacted without thinking. My hand shot out in front of me, grabbing his phone and flinging it across the hut, where it clattered to the floor next to some old bottles.

'Shit, man, what was that about?' His blue eyes stared at me with shock. I wanted to stroke the side of his face – in fact the effort of keeping my hands by my side was so exhausting, I was almost shaking.

'Sorry,' I said. 'There was actually a spider? Dangling from a web? Just above your screen?'

Could that possibly have sounded any more pathetic? *Actually* a spider? Xav nodded slowly in a way which told me he wasn't fooled. And suddenly I got this flash of insight: Xav knew. He knew exactly how I felt about him, and he'd always known.

I'd always assumed he had no idea – the way he treated me so offhandedly, picking me up one moment, dropping me the next. He'd never do that if he knew, surely?

Despite all my insecurities and fears, I had never once, until that moment, imagined that Xav didn't care about me.

I forced that thought down, but it added itself to the whirling mix of anger and hate and resentment deep inside. I was losing everything. I had to find a way to fight back.

Chapter 15

Maxine

Ola: Still nothing from Maxine. Not one video since the night before TF struck.

Fenti: She's not TF though, you know that, right?

Ola: Yeah but her fans are raging. She needs to do something soon.

LilyPad (i.e. my sock puppet account): Maybe she's just worrying about what to post, maybe she's struggling to say the right thing.

Fenti: She needs to do something even if she just supports Leni's no-hate campaign.

Mandalor_Ian: LilyPad is right. I'm a bit older than you lot. OK a lot older. These people are just teenagers. They make good videos that people want to watch but they still have loads of growing up to do. That's why I joined this group. They don't deserve to be victimised, so can we just focus on the detective work?

Ola: OK boomer. You don't get it. She owes it to her fam.

My fam are, as Ola says, going apeshit right now; it started out with concern for my mental health but now it's turned into full-blown anger. The nicest ones are saying: how can we support you when you're not talking to us? The not-so-nice ones are accusing me of hiding something, of being a cold-blooded killer.

I only went into the group chat because I saw my name – my real name – being mentioned. I've been trying to avoid it since my emails from Alex Malex and my pathetic attempt at sleuthing. Three days on, it all seems a bit sad now, people playing detective. How did I ever think we could make a difference? Shorn of new information, Facehunters is reduced to analysing creators' videos from that night, nit-picking discussions about whether Jace would have had time to get to Xav's house from the game launch he'd attended that night, the significance of an umbrella in the background of Leni and Andy's live stream from that night (*Fenti: Is this really a live video? Why did she have an umbrella WHEN IT WASN'T RAINING THAT DAY?!?!*)

Ola, who I think has her own start-up PlayMii channel and is obsessed with online etiquette, stamps on this one really quickly: *You can't fake a live stream on PlayMii. It's just not possible.*

And then, of course, there's Maxine_F's outrageous media blackout – why didn't I upload anything after the meet and greet?

Fenti: she's hiding something.

LilyPad: Maybe she was just knackered and went to bed early?

As the days have passed with no word from the Alex email, I've wondered more and more whether the person mailing me is just a fantasist. Someone online pretending to be someone else, just like me. I'm not saying I've forgotten about it – I still jump every time my phone makes a noise. It's just the idea of a fake-Face trying to scare me for shits and giggles makes more sense than the real Face risking capture to recruit little old me as a detective.

'Maxine.' Mum's voice drags me away from my screen. 'Are you going to film something today?' She's fixing me with her stern, brown-eyed gaze as she cradles her morning coffee.

I look up from my phone and my Wheaties and promise I will, but there's still too much going around and around in my head. I tell her I'll try and get something up by the end of the day.

She puts her hand on my shoulder. 'I know it's hard, I know it's been a shock for you, but . . .'

I shrug her hand off, feeling a twist of anger. All she's worried about is the precious channel. When did this happen? When did we stop dancing around the kitchen to the radio or scoffing popcorn in front of Friday night films and become a business partnership?

I text Frida. *I need to get out of here.*

Come to mine, the message comes back. *I'm on study leave and I don't want to study.*

I feel a flush of pleasure – in the eight weeks or so we've known each other, Frida's never invited me to her place before. I get the feeling she's not particularly proud of it and I'm super excited that she's finally letting me in a bit. I message back straight away in a flurry of enthusiastic emojis: *Yes please!!!*

It's quite a long Uber ride between my place and Frida's, and on the way I think about telling her everything – my stupid move with the email, the horrible blood-chilling reply and my feeble efforts to tail Ethan. I'm not a secrets person. They itch at the back of my mind all day, cast surreal shadows in my dreams at night. I'm a sharer, it's what I do. But would Frida laugh? Or would it scare the living hell out of her? I can't decide which result would be worse.

Maybe I'll wait until after Detective Riley has returned my call. If he thinks it's nothing, it'll become nothing more than a silly joke, something to laugh about. *Do you remember that time we trailed all the way across Lewisham looking for that florist?*

Frida lives in zone six. Her flat's in a tatty block of 1970s town houses, too far out of town even to be hipster territory. I asked her once why she doesn't live with her parents. She'd shrugged and said, in a fake-cheery voice: 'They're dead. Carked it. Shuffled off their mortal thingamabob. Deader than a dodo sitting on a doornail. New topic, please!'

She's an orphan – is that what makes her so brave, so determined to live on her own terms?

Frida's kitchen is gloomy and crowded with dirty coffee cups, bits of cereal stuck to the worktops and a grill that looks like it hasn't been cleaned since the millennium.

'My flatmates,' Frida says, a long-suffering note in her voice. 'They're both guys, both work shifts and never spend any time here. I've given up nagging them to clean and I refuse to do it for them. So I tend to just keep all my cups and stuff in my room.'

While she gets them, I wander through to where I think the sitting room might be, open the door and freeze in horror. It's not a sitting room – there's a bloody great bed in the middle of it, and a hairy bloke in boxers spread-eagled there, snoring.

I yelp and shut the door, my face burning.

'Jimmy's on nights,' Frida says, laughing. 'Come on, follow me.'

She leads me up a cramped staircase, the cream carpet worn in the middle and grey with dust at the edges, and pushes open the first door on the left.

Wow, what a difference. Like the rest of the flat, Frida's room is cramped and painted in a kind of murky beige, but that's where the resemblance ends. Every inch of the walls is studded with tiny plastic stick-on hooks, each one hung with a different, colourful accessory. Resin bangles, silk roses, the multicoloured scarves I've seen her wear in her hair. Spangled earrings are pinned to a bright ribbon, a cactus brooch stitched out of felt. Postcards are dotted between and fairy lights trail over, under and through, lighting the whole thing up. From floor to ceiling it's nothing but gloriously messy light and colour.

'Do you like my filing system?' she says. 'It might look a bit untidy but it's actually super organised! I know where everything is.'

'You've seen my room,' I say. 'This is about a million times nicer. There's no need to apologise – you've made this room into something special.'

She looks down, embarrassed but glowing from the praise. Her hands are nervously pushing her sleeves up and down and I glimpse the scars on her arms again.

I know her well enough now to know she won't say anything until she's ready, so I swallow back a question and make myself comfortable on the chair, which is covered by an African wax print throw.

'What used to be there?' I point up at a set of shelves, the only empty space in the entire room.

'Umm . . . hats.' She cringes. 'The one accessory that really never worked out for me. Now – tea, coffee or do we steal Jimmy's novelty gourmet gin?'

'Do you even have to ask?'

The afternoon kind of pans out from there. We spend the next few hours drinking terrible flavoured gin (although I notice Frida's not drinking nearly as much as I am), chatting and half-watching a horror movie Frida describes as 'seminal'. I must admit that when it comes to films, my taste is closer to Ed's.

I just wish I could find a way to fix my friendship with him.

'He's still so broken,' I tell Frida. 'I want to help him but it's way above my skill level. I'm no expert. In fact, I'm no expert at anything.'

Frida gapes at me. 'What are you talking about? You're a flipping PlayMii sensation! You have millions hanging on your every word!'

'Yeah, OK, I can hashtag and I'm all right with a thumbnail. But I don't feel like I *know* anything. I mean, Xav knew his games. Leni knows make-up and beauty, and now she's guiding everyone through this horrible mess. You should see her videos – they're so wise and insightful. She's got this whole stop-the-hate campaign going. Even the trolls can't think of anything mean to say about her. Meanwhile I'm . . . struggling to figure out what to say.'

A shadow of a frown crosses her face and she lets out an irritated sigh.

'I love you, Maxine,' she says. 'But you need to break out of your nice comfy PlayMii bubble and grow a pair. Walk away if you want – you don't have to do this for ever. Or use your voice to say something you mean. Post or don't post, but for fuck's sake, own it. This is why I hate PlayMii so much – it's so *self-centred*.'

I reel back, the sting of her words making my cheeks hot like I've been slapped. I feel a flush of rage. How can she judge me? She has no idea. She'll be calling me 'lucky' next.

But then she doesn't know about the emails, doesn't know what's really bothering me.

I feel a heavy thud of dread in my chest. I'm hurt and angry, but I don't want to fall out with the only real friend I have.

For a few moments there's silence between us, just the screams of the victims on-screen. Finally, when Frida speaks, it's quiet.

'I have my own mad stuff going on,' she says. 'Nothing like as big as yours, nothing I can't deal with but . . . it made me cranky. Sorry.'

I wonder if she's ready to open up now. I struggle to think of the right thing to say but her harsh words are still simmering away in my mind, and there's a flicker of anger still there. After years of watching everything I say and do, of not stepping out of line, I'm afraid to speak honestly.

And then she waves her hands dismissively in a blur of rings. 'First-world problems. I'll deal with it eventually, in my own way.'

Classic Frida understatement. I know not to push any further.

'Back to the end of the world then,' I say, turning back to the tablet. 'Come the apocalypse I'll have no useful skills to offer a plucky band of survivors. They'll probably throw me to the zombies so they can get away.'

Frida fixes me with a thoughtful gaze. 'Well, you'd better brush up on your running skills, then. Your only hope is to be faster than the other survivors. More nachos?' she asks, grabbing the empty bowl and heading for the kitchen.

'Of course. When is the answer to that question ever no?'

We put the film on pause so as not to miss any gore, and Frida disappears. I lie on my back and stare at the amazing walls for a few moments, when her tablet makes a plinking noise.

I don't mean to look at it – I mean, why would I? It's probably just a message from a college friend or incoming junk mail. But above the frozen onscreen zombies, I see the PlayMii logo flash up. I hold my finger on it and the first line of a notification pops up in that annoying twee language the app likes to use.

Hey Frida! Feast your eyeballs on 4 new uploads from KTX201, StanForXav and CarmenGeddit1.

Frida, who only minutes ago was slagging off the whole PlayMii world, and who carries around the sort of phone that belongs in a museum, has the PlayMii app on her tablet.

Frida's bedroom door begins to open and I jump halfway across the room, pretending I haven't seen the updates. My heart is pounding. I'm ashamed of snooping, angry at Frida, and underneath it all there's a growing sense of unease. *Why would she lie?*

'I've got to go.' I just about manage to squeak the words as I grab my bag.

By the time I get home I'm a raging mess of doubts, confusion and fear, but also anger. At Mum, at Frida, at myself for not being grateful enough, even at my fam for demanding everything and not letting me keep one shred of my feelings private.

I sweep past Mum, who's at her desk staring at PlayMii analytics. She glances up and says: 'Are you wearing jeans? I thought we'd agreed jeans don't work on you,' then looks back down again.

Once I'm in my room, I shut the door and go to one of my favourite filming spots, in front of my shelves. My hands are trembling as I set up the camera and adjust the Gorillapod, my brain pulsing with anger and fear and rage. I turn it on and talk.

'I don't know what I'm supposed to say. I really don't. I have no words of wisdom to share about what happened to

Xav, no comfort. The whole world thinks I'm some stupid airhead, so I can't understand why you're expecting any kind of sense from me! If you want someone to be the queen of your heart, check Leni's channel, she's nailing it right now.

'Everything I have to say can be summed up pretty quickly. For those of you who say he deserved it: fuck you. He's a nineteen-year-old millionaire – that sort of thing can make a guy say stupid things, so cut him some slack. For those of you saying Ed did it, or Ethan did it, or even *I* did it, fuck you too. My friends are not killers. I am not a killer. We're fucking influencers, not knife-wielding assassins.

'And for that one person out there who did do it, fuck you a million times over, you demented bloodthirsty prick.

'There, that's my reaction video. I'll be back soon with hot new hauls, fun explainers and exciting merch news, just as soon as I can get through the day without crying. Maxine out.'

I don't edit, I don't think. I just push the tears from my cheeks with my sleeve and upload the video. Once I'm sure it's gone live without a hitch, I change the password to my channel, turn everything off and bury myself under the duvet cover.

After fifteen minutes, Mum taps on the door and suggests I might want to take the video down. I ignore her.

She tries the door handle, but it's locked. Turns out this soulless apartment has excellent strong, lockable doors.

After five more minutes, the gentle knock has turned to banging, and she's asking for the new password so she can do it. She says it could start a horrible backlash, that I should think of the Paperfly people, and the other deals she has in the pipeline. She doesn't say, 'Are you OK, love?'

'Actually, fuck you too,' I murmur from under my duvet.

And then my email alert bings and my heart drops in horror.

It's him.

That was a very stupid mistake. Now someone is going to get hurt.

Chapter 16

Maxine

It's morning and I'm lying in a shaft of light, thumbing through the reactions to my video. Over the past forty-eight hours The FU, as people have been calling it, has been shared more times than almost any video I've ever made, even the Disney Princess Explainer which has been live for over a year now. Eventually Mum gave in and stopped begging me to take it down.

'You've hit on something here,' she said, as if my outpouring of rage and hurt had been a clever ploy to gain more followers. Leni's cornered the market for people's hearts; I'm the new queen of anger.

Out there in the world, there are people reacting to what I said. People worrying about my mental health, people complaining about my 'potty mouth', others accusing me of fakery and cashing in (thank God I remembered to turn off ads before posting it) and my fam cheering me on.

But it's that one reaction, the one that came to me in an email, that shakes me.

I had almost convinced myself that Alex wasn't really The Face, that he was just a cranky weirdo with a twisted sense of humour.

But maybe I was wrong.

I know I should tell the police, but DC Riley is still going to voicemail, and besides, what if The Face gets to my friends before the police find him? I feel completely paralysed, unable to make a decision. I'm just thumbing blindly through people's comments on my pointless, destructive FU.

Then – a series of alerts, one after the other, from Facehunters.

Holy shit!!!

NOOOOO!

😮 😮 😮 😮 😮 😮 😮

This is it. He's struck again.

It's linked to a live newsfeed. The headline: POPULAR PLAYMII STAR HOSPITALISED AFTER BRUTAL ATTACK. ATTACKER POSTS VIDEO ON STREAMING SITE. I see a glimpse of a face I know, a face I last saw sipping coffee in my kitchen, and I start to shake uncontrollably, my skin cold.

Ed. It's Ed.

I don't have a number for Ed's parents; I just know the hospital from the news reports. I am going to show up there like any random fan. I just have to get to him.

I message Frida, forgetting my strop, shrugging off the fact that I've ignored her worried-sounding texts. I'm being an arse, but I don't care.

Please help me.

Her reply: *Always.*

On the Tube to the hospital, we stare at our phones and try to piece together what happened from the shreds of information which have leaked out. The video has already been taken down – much faster than last time – but stills from it are still circulating. There's a shot of Ed, lying unconscious on his bed at home. I recognise his ancient, faded emoji duvet, crumpled and twisted around his legs. A close-up of Ed's face, a bright splash of blood on his temple. And then The Face, grinning wickedly in the semi-darkness.

A newspaper headline: MASKED ASSAILANT ATTACKS SECOND STAR . . . ATTACKER WORE SAME MASK AS XAV SLAYING. FLEES THE SCENE AFTER POSTING ATTACK ONLINE.

A TV channel: showing the outside of Ed's parents' tiny semi, swarming with scenes of crime officers.

A tech site: *Has the cult of the influencer had its day?*

Twitter: *Trending In UK: #Thefacestrikesagain*

Someone on Reddit: *This is probably the most traffic Ed's boring solo channel has had so far.*

'Why do this?' Frida says. 'What kind of sicko shares a video like that? I don't get it.'

But I do. The Face posted that video for me. I did this. I ignored the Alex Malex emails. I didn't believe the threats. I dropped the FU.

I'm still trembling out of control, my whole body freezing in the stuffy Tube carriage as I hunch over, my head in my hands, and sob. Frida strokes my back, but I shrug it off. I don't deserve comfort. I might as well have painted a target on Ed's back.

Outside the hospital, I hesitate. A small group of people has already gathered by the doors. Someone is holding a candle; others are holding banners with *The Face Will Not Break Us* and #OurFool on them.

I can't go past them; I can't fix my face in neutral right now.

'Stay here a second, then follow my cue,' Frida says. I wait behind a bin as she rushes towards the crowd of people, all colour and clashing bangles. She says something to them and after a moment of staring, they all charge around the corner as one, rummaging in their bags for their phones. Frida beckons me forward.

'I told them Leni_loves just went in the side entrance,' Frida says. 'That *was* the right username, wasn't it?' She looks genuinely unsure and I don't have the mental energy to wonder whether she's bullshitting me.

Inside, I haven't a clue which way to go, but Frida leads me from department to department through a rabbit warren of corridors, stopping here and there, charming scraps of information out of hurried staff.

'He's not in ICU, that's a good sign. First floor.'

I follow the bright flutter of Frida's palm-tree-print headscarf through a pair of swinging double doors. There's a couple of police officers by the reception desk but one's talking into her radio and the other one is talking to a nurse and making notes. Frida strides confidently past them, linking her arm in mine so we're walking in step.

And there he is. Alone, his beautiful face swollen, his eyes half closed. Frida melts discreetly into the background.

Now we're this close, my voice has failed. There is no way I can explain that this was my fault, absolutely nothing I can do to make this right. The word *sorry* tastes bitter in my mouth.

'Mate,' Ed croaks. 'You look worse than me.'

'Ed, I'm so sorry . . .'

'Not dead.' His voice sounds exhausted. 'It's a plus. Been beaten up before, will be again.'

A tide of guilt crashes through me. I lean against the side of the bed, my hand finding his. It's the only part of him that doesn't look bruised.

'I'm sorry I let you down, Ed – so many times.' My voice cracks here under the full weight of my shame, the knowledge that he's here because of me. I can't tell him, I'm too afraid of what The Face will do, but part of me knows it's cowardice, too. *Would he ever forgive me?*

Ed's eyes are troubled. He's not thinking about my silly guilt complex – his mind is on something else, and eventually he speaks.

'I just . . . every time it happens, every time someone hits me I think I'll be faster next time, I'll be stronger, that I'll stop it, but some people just have this mean violence in them, it makes them quick. He just hit me so fast I went straight down, and though I tried to push him off he kept hitting and hitting. He waited until my parents were out, must have come in the window . . . tore the place apart looking for those files –as if *I'd* have them.

'And there was something else which threw me off balance, too. Just stopped me in my tracks. It wasn't until they were putting me into the ambulance that I put my hand up to my face to check my split lip and I noticed the smell on my knuckles where I'd tried to fight him off. He smelled of Problematic. He was wearing Xav's signature scent.'

Frida makes a little sound from the corner, a gasp of shock, and Ed's gaze fixes on her for the first time. He tenses; his eyes widen. His hand pulls me closer until my ear meets his mouth. I can feel his breath as his dry lips form another, whispered sentence.

'Watch out for her.'

Just then there's an angry tap on the glass pane in the door – a nurse looking irate, motioning us to get out.

'Ed, what are you talking about?' I ask. But the room is suddenly full of medical staff. Moments later, we're out in the corridor being told off in the most patronising way possible. I stare over into Ed's window, but he looks pretty out of it now. The nurse is fussing at his side.

Frida is all innocence, talking us out of our situation while I stand beside her gaping, wondering.

Watch out for her.

How well do I really know my new best friend?

Later that night the phone rings.

'This is DC Riley. Apologies for the delay getting back to you but as you can imagine things have been busy lately.' His voice sounds officious, and tired, but not quite as offensive as usual. Maybe they're getting desperate. Desperate enough to listen to someone like me. 'I understand that you have some information you'd like to share about an email?'

I swallow. Clear my throat. Hesitate for a long time before finally answering.

'I'm sorry, officer, false alarm. I was just overreacting, getting silly ideas. You know we all get a lot of weird messages.'

He tries to push me, to get more information out of me and I want to tell him, I really do. But then I remember Ed's bruised face, that grinning maw on the video. Leni could be next. I could be next. The only way to get out of this is by keeping quiet, doing what The Face says.

I have to find those files myself.

Chapter 17

Sam

Leni and Xav were having an argument when I got to the park. I saw it as I crossed the grass towards them, picking my way around the litter and enjoying the spring sunshine. It was the first properly sunny day of the year, just right for filming an Alex flashmob in the park. Some twenty-five kids from our year had shown up, wearing masks as instructed, to be a part of it. It was just a shame Xav and Leni couldn't agree on how to do it.

I already knew what the dispute was about as I'd listened to Xav rant about it endlessly the night before. All it boiled down to was that Leni wanted one thing and Xav wanted another, and she wasn't giving in. Usually, the only person who said no to Xav was his dad, and all the hatred and resentment he had against him was being directed straight at the sylph-like girl in jeans and a floaty satin hummingbird blouse.

I kept a little distance from the action, found myself a comfortable patch of grass to loll back on and watch the show. Xav was all drama, waving his arms and tearing at his perfect hair in frustration. Leni was standing stock-still, facing him down. She had just coloured her hair for the first time

– pale, silvery blonde with a modest streak of violet at the front, which she'd plaited. It had got her a reprimand from school but no serious punishment, and other girls were already starting to copy it.

From a distance she looked calm, but she was clutching the Alex mask tightly. I could see her long graceful fingers were white at the tips, her eyes hard as they looked across into his. She was the immovable object, Xav the irresistible force. I felt a click of understanding in my brain: *there's no way these two could work together for long. One channel can't have two stars.*

As I watched, Maxine, barefoot and wearing a leopard shirtdress, tried to pull Leni away from the confrontation, pointing at the trees, the light, the assembled kids, anything to distract her. But it had gone too far for that now. People were starting to drift away, and I wondered if the video would even get made.

And then I saw a figure creep up behind Xav wearing a rubber Miss Piggy mask. He waited a couple of moments, a strange presence lurking behind Xav's back, and then tapped him on the shoulder. Xav jumped about three feet into the air.

Then, just like that, Xav and Leni were laughing. Xav started chasing the pig across the field, tackling him to the ground, rolling . . .

Ugh. Fucking Ed. He really does get Xav.

The kids started to come back, Maxine fiddled with the music, Andy seized the Alex mask from Leni, and I saw his fingers brush hers, accidentally on purpose. As he did so, he murmured something in her ear. Leni bit her lip and smiled.

I slipped on the ghost mask I'd found in one of Dad's boxes and joined in with everyone else. The video was taken down later after the Unfortunate Incident, but I still have screen grabs somewhere and can see myself, dancing one beat behind everyone else, dropping the ball when it was passed to me. Not that anyone noticed.

Sometimes it was an advantage being invisible. You could watch things, tweak things, a powerless microbe playing God. After the filming stopped, when everyone else had settled down to toast their success, I amused myself by finding Maxine's discarded shoes, scooping up some dog poo with an old crisp packet and popping it inside them. Pleased with this childish gag, I went to get some more, planning to slip it into Ed's messenger bag. But a voice called me back.

'Sam?'

'Oh Elean . . . Leni, hi . . . I was just leaving.'

'I thought that was you under that ghost.' She smiled, and the world went into soft focus. 'You know how I could tell? You're the only person still in school uniform.'

I shrugged. 'Couldn't be bothered to change.'

Leni sat down on the grass, slim legs crossed, and patted the patch next to her. I obeyed, wondering why on earth she was talking to me now, how she had noticed me when nobody else had. I hoped she hadn't seen what I'd done to Maxine's shoes.

162

'That's not it though, is it? I've never seen you out of uniform,' she said, her voice still light and airy. 'You can be honest with me.'

At that moment, I forgot my hatred of her, my anti-Alex campaign. She was the first person to actually ask me about myself, to question why I looked the way I did.

But where the hell could I start?

I could feel the burden of it then, the weight of losing Mum and baby Daniel, of lonely Dad clinging to his trash and his booze, and his dreams of a perfect son. No wonder I'd pushed my real self so far down inside me that I didn't even know who I wanted to be any more.

She moved closer to me. Her hair smelt like sweets. Her gaze fixed on my face, steady and serious. I felt like the centre of the world – almost like the way I felt when Xav looked at me.

'You can trust me,' she said.

At that moment, flushed with courage by her sudden attention, I managed to blurt out the question: 'Why didn't you and Maxine want me to be part of the Alex channel?'

Leni looked at me, an expression of shock on her face. 'What are you talking about?'

'Because it was all my idea, you see, the channel. And then everyone forgot it was my idea, and then Xav said he'd ask you guys if I could be a part of it, and you said . . .' I didn't need to finish that sentence. A sudden realisation, a rush of insight, made me feel sick.

Leni said nothing, waited for me to fully understand what had happened.

'Xav never asked, did he?' I said.

Leni's eyes were sorrowful as she shook her head. 'Xav can sometimes be . . .'

I nodded. I knew.

My head spun. Why would he exclude me like that, cut me out of my own channel? And then to lie.

I wanted Leni to go now, to leave me to my anger and tears, but instead she stayed, resting her hand on mine, squeezing with a gentle pressure.

'What were you doing with Maxine's shoes earlier?' she asked. Then, seeing my face, she added, 'Don't worry, nobody else saw you.'

'I . . . erm . . . there's dogshit in them.'

Leni looked appalled. 'Oh! Sam, that's terrible!' And then she was laughing, free, uncontrollable peals of laughter. I expected her to get up, to warn Maxine, but instead she turned to me. 'I could do with unwinding a bit. Don't suppose you've got any booze, have you? Proper booze?'

I started to shake my head. Like I said, it wasn't my thing. But then I remembered that Xav kept a stash of cheap whisky in the shack. We'd never brought an outsider in there before; it was our sacred space. But right now, nothing between Xav and me felt sacred. I'd had enough of his hypocrisy.

'Come with me,' I said.

*   *   *

I was expecting Leni to be disgusted by the shack, but she didn't complain as I opened a flap of fence by the railway, then led her down a brambled path to our hideout. And when I pulled aside our tattered curtain and apologised for the state of the cushions, she just said, 'Wow, this is cosy.'

The bottle was tucked into the cushion of the knackered car seat we sometimes sat on. I handed it to Leni then, after a moment's hesitation, took a slug myself, and then another. Not being a drinker, it started to affect me almost straight away. I felt warm, and my shoulders relaxed for what felt like the first time in weeks.

'So, this is your place and Xav's?'

'Built it a couple of years ago out of my dad's junk. It's more or less watertight and, so far, nobody else has found it. It's an escape for both of us.' I stopped myself after that. I might be raging with Xav but he hated people knowing about his dad, and that didn't seem like the right way to hurt him.

Leni and I sat opposite each other in the fading light, her eyes focused on me, alert, thoughtful and intense. I felt a wave of gratitude that she'd even noticed me. But why had she? Why did Leni see me when I was cellophane to everyone else? And what did she want from me? I fidgeted uneasily, broke off eye contact.

'So come on, tell me,' she said, finally. 'Should I . . . I guess I should ask what your pronouns are?'

I exhaled slowly, suddenly so tired of it all. It was a good question, a sensitive question, but Leni was barking up the wrong tree, in the wrong forest, on the wrong planet.

'I'm cisgender, so I'm she/her, just like you,' I said. 'The reason I blur the line a bit with how I present myself has nothing to do with gender dysphoria. It's . . .'

I ran out of words. I'd never really tried to explain it before – the bizarre, complicated, Dad-exposing truth. I took a breath. Where could I even start?

'Dad always wanted a son,' I began. 'When Mum got pregnant with Daniel, he couldn't hide it, didn't stop going on about how he was going to take him camping and fishing, raise him as an Arsenal fan. He'd never done any of that stuff with me and as I listened to him, it kind of felt like I was fading. And then Mum went into labour too early, there were complications . . .'

I remembered the day Dad picked me up from my aunt's, the day he came back from the maternity hospital without a baby, and without Mum. My face had been raw from crying, but Dad's was blank. He could barely look at me.

There were weeks of silent breakfasts, of dinner in my bedroom, of talking to Dad only to have him turn away. Out of grief and sleeplessness, a desperate need grew. *Look at me, Dad, just look at me.* One night in my room, raw with desperation, I cut my hair brutally short.

As I watched it all fall away, I felt lighter, cleaner, like what I was doing to myself was right. I was sure this would shock Dad into a reaction.

I trod carefully downstairs – the junk was already beginning to build up around us – and slid on to the sofa next to where Dad sat slumped, the blue light of the TV flickering on his face. It took him a while to turn, to face me, and when he did, he looked at me properly for the first time since it had happened. The corners of his mouth pulled into a little twist of a smile and he ruffled my hair in a way he'd never done with me before, in a way he probably longed to do with the son he'd never have. 'You're a good kid,' he'd said.

Slowly, all my feminine clothes went into bin bags and piled up in the spare room with Daniel's things. They were probably still there now, buried for ever under boxes and black plastic sacks. Now all I wore were trainers, hoodies, tracksuits. Inside the house I was Dad's good kid; outside I was a faded ghost. I told myself this was what I wanted, but it was for him. For us, to keep the family together.

'So, you did it for your dad,' Leni said. And then she smiled. 'And it didn't make a difference, not even a tiny one, when you realised Xav was a bit more into boys than girls?'

'Of course not,' I snapped. 'Xav's bisexual, he likes girls too – sometimes. Not so often maybe but . . .' My shoulders sagged as I realised she was right. 'God, how pathetic. I'm so pathetic.'

At that point I was grateful for the whisky, because instead of crying I started to giggle. 'How could I possibly think that Xav would notice *me*?'

Leni leaned forward until our foreheads were so close, they almost touched. Her liquid gaze held mine and with one perfectly manicured hand she stroked my hair soothingly. Her voice, when she spoke, was soft and kind, her words full of comfort.

'Oh Sam, of course he will. But Xav doesn't like timid mice. You have to stop hiding away, you have to *make* him see you.'

I knew she was right. I didn't have a plan, not then, but I had a need. I would make him – and everyone else in the school – notice me once and for all.

Chapter 18

Maxine

We planned to make a video at a fairground once, long ago, back in the Alex days. Andy was desperate to go to the shooting range, to see how many cuddly toys he could win for Leni. Xav wanted to get Ed on to the ghost train for obvious, make-outy reasons. I was just hoping to film myself on the bendy mirrors and incorporate it into a silly video I was planning on body image. Problem was, we got the date wrong and the morning we turned up, the field was deserted. Colourful litter blew across the bare grass – discarded puffs of candy floss, sparkly streamers. A pile of broken glow-sticks had just been dumped under a tree. Tangled in the branches above, a warped, deflated Goofy balloon twisted in the wind.

That's what Xav's flat looks like now. A scene of mayhem, fun, carnage and destruction, abandoned and forgotten.

Over there on the balcony there's a palm tree swaying in a pot and a few buckets of sand from the homemade beach Xav created in the middle of last winter.

Above my head is the zipline which runs from the top of the stairs to the lounge area, where the ball-pit used to be. There's still a tangled orange wig hanging from the wire, which the police obviously didn't see fit to bring down.

Of course, there are no files left here, and no X Marks the Spot treasure map. The police have been over and over this place before they declared it safe to go back into, and if the burn files were here they would have found them, and they would have come talking to me and Leni, and everyone else on there.

But I have to start somewhere. And besides, Ed's asked me to pick up some of his old designer stuff so he can sell it on eBay, which is how I managed to get my hands on the key.

The floors have been swept clean, but there's still junk everywhere, a lot of it smudged grey with fingerprint dust. I remember DC Riley's comment and feel a pang of sympathy for the scene of crime officers who have to make sense of all this. How do you know what's relevant? Could there be a clue on that half-empty bottle of Problematic eau de toilette? What about the shiny freebies, stacked up in their boxes? The Hawaiian leis? The assortment of rubber dog toys?

I could be here all day. And that's even before I go into That Room. The one with tattered remnants of crime scene tape sticking to the door frame. The place where Xav was killed.

I'll do my nice easy job for Ed first. Xav and Ed shared a bedroom upstairs, first door along. My sneakers squeak on the polished floors, echoing off the bare walls, and I admit for the first time that I feel uneasy being here alone.

And that I feel like I'm being watched.

It's ridiculous. There's nobody here, but the atmosphere in the flat is off-key, wrong somehow. A draught sweeps through the hallway, brushing my cheek and sending chills through my body. It should be stuffy in here, after being closed up for so long. But it's not.

The bedroom's pretty normal by Xav's standards, although the bed has been stripped. Just behind the door, there are two built-in wardrobes, and as I reach to open them, I find myself hesitating, my hand shaking just a little bit. *Don't be daft, Maxine, there's no one in there waiting to jump out at you.*

But as I slide the door aside, something is moving, rushing towards me.

I scream, flinging my arms up to defend myself.

It takes less than a second to realise that I've just been attacked by about ten thousand pounds' worth of designer T-shirts, jeans, shorts and hoodies, tumbling out of the over-filled shelves on to my head, but my heart is hammering, the illogical scared-animal part of my brain screaming *run*. I'm not sure whether the police took it all out and put it back in badly, or whether Xav was just that messy, but when I open the next cupboard – very carefully – I find neat piles of folded clothes in colour-coded order. These must be Ed's. I grab my rucksack and start stuffing them in.

My phone beeps as I work, but I ignore it. The Facehunters group has taken an awkward turn. A while back, Fenti reported that my social media had gone dark just hours before Xav's death, the day I publicly called him out for the first time. My whereabouts that night were completely unaccounted for – at least as far as they were concerned.

And now, Ola, who I used to quite like, won't let it go. A debate is raging between Team Maxine (*Do you really think*

MAXINE is capable of evading the police for weeks?) and another group I'll call Team Hater, who just love the idea of me being a secret psychopath. They're a small group but they're loud.

We think we know these people, Ola writes. *But we don't. Not really.*

And I wonder if she's right. I like to think I'm honest with my fam, but I've always kept a bit back. Made myself seem nicer than I am in real life. Layered myself in make-up to hide the bags under my eyes and that weird freckle thing on my cheek. Lied through my teeth whenever anyone asked me if I was OK, banged on at every opportunity about how lucky I was, when I wasn't feeling lucky at all. Was I wrong to do that?

Then there are the messages from Frida. I haven't seen her since we visited Ed and I still don't know what to think about it, so I'm burying my head in the sand. On the one hand, what Ed said chilled me to the bone, but on the other I really miss my funny, wise and impossibly colourful friend. I know she's holding something back, but her secrets can't be that bad, can they?

As I'm shoving the last of Ed's bland but expensive T-shirts into the bag, I hear a noise. A creak, a crack, a something. The kind of noise that old houses make even when they're empty. But this isn't an old house – it's a brand new, technologically advanced smart apartment.

It must be the air conditioning kicking in because I opened the door.

That must be it.

Creak.

I clench my fists, set my jaw and tell myself to stop being a total idiot. Nobody is here. The place has been locked up since the police finished here. And Ed is the only one who has the key.

Except The Face. The Face could have Xav's key.

Shut up, Maxine.

I suppress a shudder, go down to the kitchen and look in the fridge. I once read that you could learn a lot about a person from what's in their fridge. This one, though, is completely empty and cleaned out apart from a bottle of hot sauce in the door.

I shut it again, and see the front is studded with fridge magnets, holding down endless pictures of Xav, Ed and the rest of his crew of hangers-on. I look at them all and wonder vaguely if I should speak to them. They were with Xav every day – he could have passed the files to any one of them.

But then I remember those mocking shouts in the background of some of his messages to me. The contempt in his voice when he spoke about them. 'They don't care about me . . . well, apart from Ethan, maybe. If I deleted my PlayMii account tomorrow they'd drop me like a stone.'

I pocket the picture, but also take a photo of Xav and Ed together on a night out, trying to share a bar stool, teetering, laughing. Maybe Ed will want this one thing, this little slice of a happy memory, along with all the T-shirts.

Next, I open the kitchen junk drawers and rifle through. I suppose, despite all common sense, I'm half-hoping to find a stray SD card, or a USB drive with BURN FILES written on it, but of course there's nothing like that. Just loads of spare batteries, string, a user manual for the toaster. There are also a few scraps of paper crumpled at the back. On a sticky note, Xav has scrawled a selection of letters and numbers with my name next to it.

Cheers, Xav. It's my computer password left over from the last time he fixed my laptop. Way to go, Mr Security.

Then I see a piece of paper I haven't seen in years. It's ripped out of a school exercise book, folded multiple times and faded yellow.

At the top, scrawled in elaborate red and black biro is the title: *DTM List*. It's Xav's legendary list of all the people who were dead to him. I run my eyes down the list of names. The first one, *Dad*, gives me a twinge of sadness as I remember the sour, domineering man at the funeral. It feels wrong to take the list, so I photograph it to look at later.

As the camera clicks, I hear another sound – the softest of steps in the hallway outside. I freeze. I'm not imagining this. My heart is hammering so hard that I can feel the blood pumping against my eardrums. *Thud, thud*, drowning out all thought, all reason. I can't think straight, can't breathe.

And then I see it. A figure flitting past the kitchen door, treading softly as a dancer. Medium height, all in black, hood up.

Panic tightens my throat. Part of me wants to scream, get the waiting over with. Shaking, I creep forward, watching the figure turn and pad over to Xav's junk shelves. It picks something up in its gloved hand, something small that gleams red. It looks like a mobile phone in a shiny metallic case, but I can't see it well enough to tell, and I'm too terrified to move forward for a closer look. I just want to go. Get out. I don't care about finding the files. The figure is heading for the stairs now and I see the hood slip slightly and catch a glimpse of pallid skin and mouse-brown, close-cropped hair before the figure pulls the hood back up and continues into the bedroom.

This is it. This is my chance. I have to get out the door.

Come on, legs. Move. I take a step, another, and then adrenaline surges through me and I'm running towards the front door. My sneakers slip, and pain stabs my ankle as it twists, but I keep moving through the agony, through the fear until I'm out of the door, down the stairs and safely in the newsagent at the end of the street.

Still panting for breath, I buy the biggest bar of chocolate I can find and cram it into my mouth. It stops the worst of the shaking but my heart is still throbbing, a heavy bass in my ears. Astoundingly, I'm still clutching the rucksack with Ed's stuff – which is a good thing as no way would I have gone back in there to get it. I call an Uber and stay in the shop until it arrives.

It's only once I'm in the car that my heartbeat slows and I start to think straight. That couldn't have been The Face. Ed had said the attacker was as tall as him. The person I'd just seen was shorter. *Could there be more than one person looking for the files?*

I ask the driver to let me out at the park near Leni's. I've arranged to meet Ed at her place, but I don't want to get there too early and mess up Leni's schedule. Besides, I need to calm myself down first. So I walk. I do circuits of the park over and over until the backpack feels damp and unwieldy under the hot afternoon sun. It hasn't rained for weeks, and the stubbly grass is covered in students and office workers stretched out, their clothes rolled up, exposing their midriffs to the sun. *Normal life.*

I think about sitting on that back step outside the meet and greet, chatting to Frida before all this started. I think about how nice it would be for the two of us to go out for a drink, to talk nonsense and laugh until our stomachs hurt. And then maybe to tell her everything, ask her advice and hope that she'll open up in turn.

I unlock my phone and type: *Sorry I've been a crap friend. There's been stuff going on with me that you don't know about.*

I erase that last sentence. I don't want to make this all about me. When I meet her, I'll tell her everything. It's what I should have done right at the start. I finish the text: *Let me make it up to you – got tickets to a thing on Tuesday. Free drinks!!! Please come!!!!*

I add a sprinkle of pleading emojis then press send. It seems strange to look at that message. A friend. A party. A little island of normality in the surreal nightmare of my life.

Flopping down on a park bench, I flick through my photo reels, looking at the selfies we've taken together.

Then I get to the image of Xav's list. There's a name on it which snagged in my mind earlier. I stare down at it, a strange feeling filling up my chest. I remember the things Xav said, about missing his old buddy who would do anything for him, something about yellow pants. I think of that broken figure in the background of the first Alex video. And I think, *Who would have done anything for Xav in school? Who would hide the files and keep quiet for him? Who had reason to hate the whole lot of us and would be happy to see us brought down?*

Suddenly I'm bolt upright as the name snaps into my head. Sam.

Chapter 19

Maxine

'Aw man, that's the maddest thing I've ever heard!'

Wow. I had expected some doubts about my Sam-has-the-files theory from Ed, but this is pretty extreme.

'Um . . . why?'

'You know Xav. Once you're on his list, that's it. There's no way he was secretly talking to Sam.'

I want to say: *But I just saw the list, and Xav wrote your name on then crossed it off.* But that would be cruel. The bruises around Ed's eyes have faded slightly, the stitches on his forehead have come out, and he looks different – like he's becoming something new. The touches of bleach in his hair that made it a darker echo of Xav's are long gone. It's close-cropped now, with simple tracks at the sides, and he's wearing the kind of relaxed, loose-fitting clothes Xav used to hate. He looks so bloody brave and optimistic and I feel another twist of guilt.

Looking around the room at Ed, Leni and Andy, I suddenly feel so tired of lying to my friends. A few months ago, I would have been beyond excited at the idea of spending an evening sharing a takeaway with these three, but now I feel worn out and heavy with secrets. I try and argue the point, convince him that Sam could be sitting on the files, but he seems strangely stubborn about it, so I give up and hand him the rucksack of clothes.

'You could have asked me to help,' Leni tells him, looking a little hurt. 'You know, I'd have happily done it.'

Ed shrugs. 'I just thought you'd be busy being . . . you know, *you*.'

Leni lets out a little sigh and I notice for the first time that she's looking tired. It's hardly surprising; she's posted long-form videos on PlayMii every day since the funeral, combined with shorter films, photos and posts across all her platforms. Her channel has become the place for Xav's grieving fans to come and share their heartache and she's launching a campaign for a more forgiving world. She's even handled the commercial side gracefully, too. When she previewed her upcoming make-up palette, it somehow didn't jar at all. It's a huge task for anyone and, even though she's always been unstoppable, shiny and strong, she's starting to look a bit ragged around the edges.

Today, Leni's hair is candyfloss pink, with green at the ends, and she's wearing a typical Leni-relaxing-at-home outfit – printed silk pyjamas and cashmere socks scrunched around her ankles. But it's weird – her pyjama top is buttoned up wrong and she's fidgeting constantly with one of the tassels which hang from her sleeve. I glance down self-consciously at my red-raw picked finger. I know a nervous habit when I see one.

She untangles herself from Andy, holding up a camera in her bejewelled-manicured fingers and taking a breath.

'Say hi, everyone.' She pans the camera round, and Ed just about has time to turn sideways on so his bruises don't show. I raise my hand and waggle my fingers. Almost without thinking, I make sure my T-shirt is in shot. It's part of a sponsorship deal and the clients will love the fact that it's making an appearance on Leni's channel.

We talk on camera for a while, about how lovely it is to be together. Leni hits exactly the right note, even when talking to Ed. I expect him to look awkward and sad but he doesn't. I think he's grateful to be able to talk about it publicly, to admit he's grieving as well as hurt and angry. Andy shows off the new #OurFool tattoo on his tanned wrist and grips Leni's hand as he shares stories of their friendship. 'I always felt like I could tell him anything – he would never judge, probably because he'd done far worse things himself!'

We all laugh, even Ed. And then Leni the Perfectionist makes us do the whole chat again so she can cut the best bits together. Just as everyone's getting sick of filming, the food arrives.

'I guess I'm on that DTM list, too,' Leni says sadly, as she unpacks the boxes and chopsticks on to her glass coffee table.

'No, you're not, but . . .' I clamp my mouth shut, but it's too late – everyone wants to know what I was about to say.

'Andy's on it,' I admit. 'I guess because he took your side when you fell out.'

Andy's eyes flicker down to the tattoo with a slightly rueful expression.

'I don't suppose *you* have those files?' I ask.

Leni laughs. 'I wish I did! I'd have given them to the police ages ago – although obviously I'd look at my own file first!'

I wonder what's in her file. Leni's dirt can't be that bad, but then we all have things we don't want our fam to know. My face is hot as I remember that horrible diss video. Another bloody secret.

'I'm fairly sure I know what he had on me,' Leni says, her fingers twiddling with the tassel on her sleeve. 'I lost it with a fan one time, at an event, and Xav filmed it. It was that week we all did the Speak Up Against Prejudice campaign, remember? At the launch, there was this girl who just came for me, shouting, pushing, until I was stuck in a corner with her shrieking into my face about how I had no right to talk about hate, how I'd never experienced it, how sheltered and privileged I was.' Leni's sparkling finger twists faster and faster around the tassel. 'I hadn't slept much at all that week – you know how it is sometimes – and I felt ashamed because I knew she was right. I'm a lucky, privileged person – what did I know? But then she got closer and closer, and the shame kind of came out as anger, so . . . I shoved her. I screamed at her to get the fuck away from me. It was unforgivable.'

The tassel snaps off. Leni looks at it blankly and I reach across to hold her hand, but Andy's already there.

Yet another lesson to me: just because Leni makes it look easy, it doesn't mean she's not working like crazy in the background like the rest of us.

'Xav caught the whole thing on camera. And if you edit out the bit with her yelling at me and edit out the bit where I said sorry afterwards, all you see is Leni_Loves going apeshit at a fan. I mean, it's probably not enough to get me cancelled, but it's bad.'

'He was such a bastard,' Ed murmured.

'Hashtag Our Bastard,' I say. We all laugh faintly, and for a moment there's silence but for the slurping of noodles.

'Well, that's our dirt,' Andy says, looking at me. 'How about you?'

I shrug, aware that I'm looking twitchy and uncomfortable. 'No idea. Really, not a clue. All my stupid mistakes take place in public.' Excellent. Another lie.

'There is another theory knocking around.' Andy leans forward, showing a newspaper report on his phone. It says: PLAYMII MAKES MILLIONS FROM XAV MURDER. A brief ad ran before Xav's murder video, and a journalist has calculated how much money PlayMii made from it before it was taken down, then added in the money they've made from increased traffic to Xav's channel, and all of our channels since. *Bailey's murder has led to a renewed interest in longer-form video and the platform's established online personalities.*

'What, so people are saying PlayMii did it?' I'm stunned. I can't get my head around this idea. I've met the PlayMii execs and, while I'm sure they'd sell their own granny for an increased share price, could they really do something like this?

Andy shrugs. 'There's a lot of anger online about it.'

'But it can't be,' I say. *Not if the killer's after the files.* I think of those emails, those threats. They didn't come from a corporate assassin.

I need air. Leni and Andy are trying to photograph each other's chopsticks as I go, and Ed is tucking into the sesame prawn toast, so nobody really notices. There's no window in the bathroom, so I go into the bedroom and open the window, look out into the dusk and breathe.

Outside, leaning against the iron railings of the square opposite and sheltering under the branches of a tree, is a dark figure in black jeans and trainers. Standing. Waiting. Is it just a fan? The same figure that I saw in Xav's apartment?

A surge of fear. I slam the sash window shut, heart hammering. *I can't live like this. I can't.*

Looking around for the first time, I realise Leni and Andy's room is really untidy. Usually it's a place of white light and serene beauty, with pale walls covered in Japanese art, vintage mirrors, Andy's Kendo gear on display and a four-poster bed I've coveted for ever. But today, it's a mess. There's a trail of yesterday's clothes leading from the door to the bed, her expensive jacket crushed and trampled like she doesn't care. The famous umbrella that got the Facehunters in such a flap is discarded in the middle of the floor; an upturned make-up palette beside it has scattered iridescent colours all over the wooden floor.

This is wrong. She and Andy are usually such neat freaks. She must be in a worse state than I thought.

I have to find those files for her too.

Suddenly feeling uncomfortable, like I'm spying, I rush back to the food but my appetite has gone now. Half-heartedly I crack a fortune cookie: *You Will Be Meeting A Dark Stranger.* Great.

Ed and I leave together, his arm threaded through mine. I glance over at the tree where I saw the dark figure and realise that it's actually Ethan standing there, dressed in head-to-toe black like always. I give him a little wave, and hurry Ed away before he sees him. And then I ask the question that's been bugging me.

'Ed, when I came to see you on the ward, you said something to me, something about my friend.'

Ed's arm tenses up just a little, but his tone is light. 'Oh God, what did I say?' He cringes. 'I was hallucinating all over the place that day. I don't know what painkillers they had me on, but at one point I thought a nurse had babies growing on her head instead of hair.'

'So it really was nothing?' It seemed like something at the time, but Ed looks at me and smiles.

'Really nothing. Your friend looks really fun. Maybe we can hang out sometime.'

I fall silent. I don't want to push him, don't want to find out that he's lying. I want to trust Frida and need both of them so badly right now.

Later that night, I start looking for Sam. I have no idea what her surname is, so I search various Class Of school groups looking for likely members. I end up digging through old schoolmates' Instagram accounts until I discover that a few of them were followed by someone called Sam Gam. The profile photo is a hobbit from the *Lord of the Rings* films. Not helpful, but it does match up with the shy, geeky figure I remember.

I click on the account. Not much stuff there, just enough photos for me to guess Sam's preferred fandoms – *Game of Thrones*, the Grishaverse, nothing earth-shattering. Her follow-list of favourite PlayMeeps, TikTokkers and YouTubers is much longer and more impressive, a finely curated list of the craziest, most off-the-wall stunt and prank channels. Then there's a heartbreaking list of fifteen friends.

Updates stop completely in mid-July three years ago, just after we'd both left the school for good. She posted one farewell picture and left.

It was a photo of a gravestone.

It's ancient, ivy-covered and cross shaped, and carved with a scroll that reads, THY WILL BE DONE. I know it's too old to be Sam's, but it makes me shiver.

Now I have a name to go on, I begin to search for Sam Gam elsewhere. Facebook, Tumblr – she was on all of them. Each one has the hobbit photo and the tiny number of friends or followers, and each one is frozen in time.

I feel a low pulse of dread in my stomach.

Sam had been lonely, vulnerable, full of rage and sadness. Where is she now?

An idea comes to me – the kind of idea that makes me slightly uneasy, but it's all I can think of doing at the moment. Opening up a new window in my browser, I go into the Facehunters group, pick a few of the more sensible group members, the ones I trust to be discreet, and invite them to join a small, private breakaway group.

Sorry about the random information, but I'm trying to find someone who might be able to help with the burn file situation. I've been poking around in Xav's past and a name keeps coming up, an old friend of his. I was wondering if any of you might be able to turn up more information than me?

As I share the details I know so far about Sam, fears of a witch-hunt flash through my head and I add at the bottom of the post: *This is not, repeat NOT a suspect. Please don't share with the rest of the group.*

After ten minutes or so there's a tap on the door. Mum's voice, full of excitement.

'Maxine, quick, the stationery samples have arrived! Paperfly says they want to be ready to launch at VC!'

My heart sinks as I switch back to reality. VC, officially known as VlogCon, was usually the highlight of our year. But how can I face three days of meeting and greeting my fam at a huge conference centre and acting as if everything is normal, pretending to like my amazing new stationery range? I have no choice, though, do I?

But as I head out to perform in the world's least sincere unboxing video, my phone vibrates and beeps.

'Come *on*, Maxine,' Mum shouts impatiently.

I can't resist. I click on the first update from Facehunters. Someone's found a video hidden away in a dusty corner of PlayMii, posted by sam_gam_03. It's called *Liar Liar (Yellow) Pants On Fire*.

The camera is moving through a dark, wooded area. There's no music. A train shrieks past; twigs crackle under the camera operator's feet. Slowly you become aware of another crackling sound, see a glint of light in the dark. And then you see it. A fire. Roaring, raging, sparks pushing up to the sky. It's huge, terrifying. Out of control.

Chapter 20

Sam

Of course, I was the last to find out. I came into school and there was a buzz, a hum of anticipation. Girls were comparing make-up choices in the back of registration. The boys smelled like they'd taken a bath in pure undiluted Lynx and taken ages styling their hair to make it look like they hadn't bothered styling their hair.

This was the thing with not being on the school WhatsApp group, or any of the other private chats that were going on. I never found out about anything until the day it happened. But there was clearly a party tonight.

As I sloped down the corridors in my usual holey black school trousers and supermarket trainers with the front of the toes flapping off, I only had to eavesdrop on a few conversations to find out what was going on.

Andy's house. After school till late. Today.

That explained the universal excitement. Andy's parents went away a couple of times a year, leaving him with his elderly hippie grandmother who let him throw the most outrageous parties. Everyone was invited.

Well, almost everyone.

I felt a surge of bitterness crashing into my head like a wave until I could feel nothing but anger, pain and rage.

Since Leni had told me about Xav's lies, I had spent hours just lying on my bed at home, stunt videos playing over and over on my phone – a mind-crushing reel of screams, crunches, manly whoops and rock music. But I wasn't watching the screen. I was telling myself my own story, over and over. Sometimes as the tragic main character, sometimes as the loyal, stupid flunky. The parrot in *Aladdin*, *Polly wanna cracker*. I never really expected Xav to be my boyfriend, but I always thought he was my friend. I could feel my grip on reality slipping. I didn't care.

And now, lining up to get into class, I kept my head down, staring at the scuffed floor, too ashamed to look anyone in the eye – until I caught a waft of Leni's scent and looked up to find those eyes fixed on me.

'Hey,' she said gently. 'You coming tonight?'

'I have no idea what you're talking about, seeing as nobody here ever tells me what's going on,' I snapped.

'I'm telling you now, Sam. Come on, I'll meet you there.'

I couldn't speak, I was so amazed and flattered and taken aback. I was happy that Leni had started noticing me, but I always thought she'd go for the Secret Friends option like Xav. I never thought she'd want to be seen with me. I felt a flicker of excitement in my chest. *This could change everything.*

But I'd felt that once before, hadn't I? And look how that turned out.

By the time I got to the party it had been going on for a couple of hours and it was already coming apart at the edges. The thud-thud of the music could be heard right down the street and when the door opened, it hit my eardrums as if it was a solid thing. I was used to squeezing through front doors but this time it was a press of people, rather than boxes of used yoghurt pots, in my way.

The hallway was full of people looking up at Andy, who was straddled over the banisters wearing the Alex mask. His admirers below were holding their phones aloft, chanting, 'Slide, Alex, slide!'

The push of the crowd swept me further inside. There were kids everywhere. Kids in the narrow Victorian hallway, kids on the stairs, kids sitting on the kitchen counters looking out over the garden, where Andy's grandma walked barefoot in the evening light, wearing a floaty dress and spinning around with her arms outstretched, like an inspiring Instagram meme.

Xav was holding court to a group of adoring fans, sitting on a high stool at the kitchen island, talking and waving his hands wildly. As the first properly Out boy in the year, he had seen a lot of abuse and ignorance but by sheer force of his personality, he'd managed to spin it into superstar status. It meant kids who were nervous and scared about expressing their sexuality flocked to him. The wise old bi man of year ten. I could see him now, talking to a starstruck-looking year nine boy, who seemed like he was growing taller with every word Xav said.

There was no chance I'd get near him. But at least there was no sign of Ed yet. There'd be no Maxine, either

– according to Leni she'd been grounded for losing her key again. And possibly for getting dogshit in her new shoes. I didn't feel so good about that now I knew about Xav's lies. I could see Leni, though, leaning against the wall in the sitting room, away from the crowd, sipping clear liquid from a crystal glass through a paper straw. As I got closer, she smiled and slipped her hand into her bag, pulling out a slim bottle of vodka and splashing some into another of Andy's parents' expensive highball glasses.

'That's a lot,' I said, then felt a flush of embarrassment as nobody complained about getting too much booze. I didn't want to mess this up – Leni was about the only person I didn't hate right now.

'It's a party,' she said, shrugging.

I pretended to drink it.

After that, time passed in blur and confusion – the crowds, the noise and the attention made me dizzy and drunk without drinking. I smiled. I danced. I whirled around Leni as she encouraged me to dance faster and faster. We did silly selfies. I had never been in a party selfie before; people didn't really want to pose with me. My heart beat faster and I laughed just for the feeling of it, the bubbles of joy coming out of me. Suddenly I wanted to see Xav, to show him that, yes, I *could* do parties and fun.

I noticed we'd danced our way over to the kitchen door and I saw Leni's gaze flicker in that direction, her mouth forming a little 'o' of surprise. I whirled round to see what she was seeing and . . .

I froze.

Xav and Ed kissing. So softly, so gently. Ed's hand stroking the side of Xav's face. Xav was cradling Ed like he was a precious thing. Neither of them seemed aware of the outside world, the gawping, gossiping kids around them, and I knew then it wasn't just attraction or lust. This was serious.

Out of the corner of my eye, I saw a glint of blue and purple – Leni standing just behind me.

'Oh God, Sam,' she said. 'I'm so, so sorry.'

At her words a tear, a *fucking* tear, forced its way out of my eye, trickling down my cheek. I pushed it off my face, rounded on her. *Did she know? Is that why she wanted to dance with me for so long? Was she protecting him?*

I didn't wait for her to answer me, just surged on through the partygoers. All the fury I'd kept boiling away was flowing through my body, filling me with strength, courage and the desire never to be fucked over again. I didn't think about what I did next, just grabbed Xav by the elbow, dragging him back, away from Ed.

I heard Ed's yelp of shock, and other kids' gasps. I was vaguely conscious that the music had stopped but inside I was nothing but rage, and my rage was focused on Xav. My secret friend, my betrayer, who was staring at me in horror and disbelief, as if a poodle had suddenly turned on him and bitten his leg off. Triumph flushed through me. This felt *good*.

'What's up, SFF?' I sneered. 'Everyone!' I announced to the room. 'I'd like to call your attention to the fact that Xav

Bailey and I have been friends for years. Yes, a loser like me. Every time you tell him a secret, he comes back and tells it to me. Every time he has a problem, I'm the one he comes to. And yet the second I ask him to do something that makes my life just one tiny bit less miserable, what does he do? Fuck all.'

I shoved Xav back, catching him off-guard, and he fell ungracefully.

'Good luck with him, Ed-wood, Ed the dead, Ed-ing-for-disaster. You can both go fuck yourselves.'

I spun round and the crowd parted for me, like that story from the Bible, as I stormed to the glass doors at the back.

Outside it was cold and dark. The grandma had wandered off but Andy and a bunch of his mates were practising skate-board stunts on the patio. He was still wearing that stupid mask, as if it made him invincible. My heart was pounding and my skin was like fire. Tears of humiliation streaked down my face as I bit back angry sobs.

Oh God, what have I done?

But I couldn't regret it. I couldn't be ignored by my best friend a second longer.

Behind me, I heard the doors open. A slice of party noise slid out and then the door closed again. I knew it was Xav even before I turned around. His scent carried on the air to me, producing the same melting-inside reaction it always did. *He has come to me. He's walked away from a room full of friends and supporters to get to my side. He finally understands.*

Oh God, Xav, I still love you, and if you apologise now, I will love you for ever more . . .

'What the fuck was that, Sam?' Not Samwise, not Samster, not Samalamadingdong. I felt like I'd been punched.

I turned slowly, my arms crossed as if that offered some kind of protection for my heart. The words stuck in my throat. I wanted to tell Xav how I felt, how I loved him from afar, and then I wanted him to gather me in his arms and comfort me. But I knew now that that was never going to happen. Xav didn't care about me, or Leni, or Maxine, or even Ed. Xav just cared about Xav.

'You never asked them,' I croaked. 'You said you'd ask them if I could join, but you didn't. You lied to me instead.'

It took a couple of seconds for Xav to adjust from outraged lover to confused SFF. I could see the thoughts flying through his head like shadows. How to play this – how to play *me*. How to make it all work out perfectly for Xav.

Behind him, Ed was standing in the window, one hand up against the glass, his face sorrowful, although he had no concept of what was going on here. Xav glanced back at him with such longing on his face that I wanted to puke.

'Go on,' I spat. 'Say it. You can say it, Xav.'

'All right, I will,' he flashed back. 'You're not PlayMii material – you're too strange and too shy, you wear the same clothes all the time, and you do that cringing thing with your shoulders. People forget about you. You're one of life's forgettable people, blending into the background. You lack the necessary charisma.'

Suddenly he was smiling, and a high, breathless little laugh came out of him, as if he was suddenly free to be the real Xav, to tell me what he'd really thought about me for all those years.

Silence. I hugged my arms in closer around myself, cushioning myself against the wave of devastation I knew I'd feel.

But it didn't come. Instead, something else – a sick, venomous tide of loathing. Too much anger for me to even speak.

'Xav, *mate* . . .' A voice behind me. I whirled round to see Andy staring at us. I saw the mask in his hands and I knocked it on to the ground, stamped on it. Harder and harder, until my beloved work was just crushed wire and rainbow flakes of paper. Andy stared at me, his face frozen in horror. Then he let out a pained cry of loss, almost like a sob. Xav roared with rage. And I ran.

I fled home through the dark, not caring about the drunken yells from outside the pub, the hidden dangers in the park. I was aflame, a ball of energy pushing the world away from me.

I went straight to the back of the house, tore the roof off our hideout, sending the corrugated metal crashing down towards the railway track, ripping the ragged curtains aside and grinding the yellow pants into the mud with my trainer.

Petrol. There is petrol somewhere.

Rummaging in Dad's shed, I found it, an ancient stinking metal can, which I emptied all over the rotten wooden walls, the cushions and moth-eaten rugs. One flick with a match and that was it.

Whoomp.

As the flames began to climb, I went back to my bag for my phone. Even through the trees, the heat of the flames warmed me as I started filming.

Chapter 21

Maxine

This year, every party worth anything is taking place in the top room at Soho's Panopticon bar, and the annual Dreams Inc Pre-VC bash is no exception.

There's a small red carpet leading across the grimy, chewing-gum-spattered pavement to the entrance and it has photographers and fans on either side of it. As we pull up in the cab, the tension is coming off Frida in waves.

'I didn't realise it would be this sort of party,' she says faintly.

I tell her not to worry, to get out of the other side of the cab and not walk in with me. Sure enough, nobody lifts their camera as she dashes in, even though she's wearing a faux fur coat that's way too warm for the summer heat, a purple satin playsuit with a Bettie Page motif and clashing red suede platform shoes. Some people might say she dresses like that to get attention, but I know better. She's just being Frida.

I stay outside for a few moments doing selfies and notice that among the photographers and PlayMii fans, there are a few people holding banners. One says PLAYMII MURDERERS. Another says PLAYMII = THE FACE. Another one says JUSTICE FOR XAV.

'Maxine!' a voice shouts, and I look up, getting ready to smile and pose. But I look into an angry face – a girl with purple hair, a green beanie rammed down on top of it. 'How can you make money for these people after what they did to your friend?'

I'm so shocked, so lost for words that I scamper inside.

The tide is turning against PlayMii. The Facehunters group has gone crazy since the reports on PlayMii's profits. Even Carl has come under suspicion by the sleuths on there as he gets a cut of all our earnings. *Follow the money*, Ola posted, along with a link to her deep-dive into the company's finances. I think she must be a trainee accountant or something. The figures blurred in front of my eyes. Her thinking makes sense . . . except that PlayMii doesn't care about those files, and I know The Face does.

Tonight was supposed to be fun, a chance to be normal again after two months living in the shadow of Xav's death. But now all I can think about is him – and that hideous face. Frida slips her hand into mine as we climb the backlit white steps inside. I'm not sure whether she's comforting me or I'm comforting her, but I grip hard.

Built on to the roof of an old Soho pub, the Panopticon is like being in a futuristic space capsule. All the walls are lit in white; cameras peer down from every angle, feeding footage of the revellers on to big screens over the bar. The more outrageous and eye-catching things you do, the more likely you are to end up on the big screen – which means a free drink. *The Times* reviewer called it a 'post-modern hellscape', which somehow made it even more popular. It also specialises in this year's must-have drink, a foul concoction called pis-en-lit.

We make our way past a stack of goodie bags at the door – nobody comes to an event without freebies – and into the main room, which echoes with the low jangle of hipster background music and the clash of influencer voices. They're all here – the great, the good and the controversh. There's a posse of girl game reviewers taking a group selfie; that guy who invented the Flinch dance . . . then look, there's Jace, the Accidental Homophobe, who seems to have got over his shame and is taking his turn on the ice pis-en-lit luge. I spot Leni, a flash of aquamarine in the crowd, and Ed, talking to a hot barman – *good for him*. Then there's Carl, lounging in a large booth in the corner, surveying the room like he owns it. Maybe he does.

It's a good opportunity to dredge for information on the files, but right now my priority is to nab a booth and talk to my friend. I grab Frida by the hand again and pull her towards an empty one. She slides in opposite me, her eyes wide with fright. She is definitely outside her comfort zone.

I want to tell her all about the emails, about Ed's weird reaction to her, apologise for my paranoia, but right now she's not ready for that. She needs a drink and a laugh, and so do I. I grab two glasses from a passing waiter's tray, hoping they're not pis-en-lit.

They are. We both take a sip and splutter.

'Ugh, it tastes like pee,' she shouts over the music. 'Where can I get a vodka and Coke?'

'On it.'

I jump to my feet and snake through the crowd towards the bar, running slap-bang into Jace D, who gives me a massive hug like an old friend, then pulls me aside and asks anxiously if I've heard anything about those files.

'Not a thing,' I say. 'Why do you keep asking me? It's not like Xav and I hung out all the time.'

'But I know you spoke.' He's clutching my arm now at the elbow, and his thumb is starting to hurt me. 'Xav used to send you messages, tell you stuff.'

I stare at him, seeing something else for the first time. Xav wouldn't tell just anyone about his messages, which means . . .

'You and Xav? But I thought you were . . .'

'I *am* straight,' he growls at me, his face twisted into an expression of loathing. 'It was one kiss, one fucking time, and it disgusts me. I'm not a fucking homo.'

The words hang there for a moment and I'm frozen in shock. I see that sort of stuff online all the time but never, *never* has someone dared say that word to me out loud.

'You need to go, Jace,' I say, my voice flat. Just then a flicker of motion draws my eye, and I see that our faces have been captured on the cameras and beamed on to the screens above the bar. My shock and outrage, Jace's snarl. I hear a voice nearby say, 'Ooh I wonder what *that* was about?' I look around in time to see Jace heading out of the door, greedily grabbing a goodie bag as he goes.

Luckily my face doesn't stay on the screen for long. By the time I get to the bar it's changed to the Flinch dance guy, doing the Flinch dance. Ed's still lolling against the bar, nursing a bottle of beer.

'Blimey, that looks good in this heat,' I say. 'I'll have one of those and a vodka and Coke, please.'

The hot barman smiles this warm, engaging smile and goes to get it for me. It's then I notice it, the way Ed's eyes follow him. I see the barman glance back at Ed and . . . ohhh. Second big gay secret realisation of the day.

'You've met someone new!'

Ed's answering look can only be described as impish and I throw my arms around him, beaming with happiness.

'I might as well tell you: Maxine, meet my sweet alibi.'

'You mean . . . ?'

'Yup. I was with him the night Xav died. But you mustn't tell anyone, Max. He's not supposed to be in this country. He came here on a student visa, dropped out of uni and stayed. Being gay's illegal where he's from, he can't go back and . . . I've just done it, haven't I? I've dumped all my secrets on you like everyone else, and now you're going to end up having to lie to the police, all thanks to me.'

'Shut up,' I tell him. 'You're not a random stranger on the bus, you're my friend. You're supposed to be able to tell me things. I'm just happy you've found someone in all this craziness.'

Just then I glance up and see Leni's face fill the screen in a classic Leni pose, violet eyes as large and wide as a Disney cartoon bunny, a sunburst of a smile on her lips. I realise with a jolt that she's sitting in my booth with Frida, who's looking deeply uncomfortable. I dash back their way carrying the drinks.

It takes me a couple of seconds to make the introductions, then Ed slips into the seat next to me and, to my surprise, he and Frida smile at each other. But she still looks overwhelmed, smaller than usual somehow. I want to draw her into the conversation, but Leni speaks first.

'I see they've put samples of your new stationery in the goodie bags.'

I groan. That's all I need. I wonder if there's time for me to get over to the bags, which are on a table by the door, and somehow sneak all the samples out, but just as I look over I can see someone take one and leave. There's no stopping it now. I feel stupid, failing on my first proper venture into merch. Leni would never have let this happen to her.

So instead I change the subject, talking about Jace D's outrageous comment, about PlayMeep gossip, about anything except The Face and the files.

Soon Ed's giving us the inside info on the worst of Xav's hangers-on, and Leni's chipping in. Andy is filming us toast with pis-en-lit cocktails we have no intention of drinking. Frida is still looking pale, lost and a little bit trapped in the booth. I try to steer the conversation elsewhere.

'Frida doesn't do influencers, she's at college, does something with sculpture,' I say.

But Frida's still hanging back. Then she gets up and says something about needing the Ladies. It's only after five minutes that I realise that she's taken her coat and bag with her.

She's gone.

I feel a flash of guilt. I've just done to her exactly what Leni is always doing to me. I dragged her to something filmable because it was easier for me – even though I know she hates PlayMii, even though Panopticon is clearly not her kind of place. Shit. I grab my things and rush out into the street but there's no sign of her. I have no idea how long ago she left.

A message blinks up on my phone. *Sorry I had to go, headache.* So obviously a lie.

I don't want to go back in now, so I make my way to the cafe next door and order a tea. Ignoring the clutch of JUSTICE FOR XAV protestors chatting in the corner, I find a table, flip open my phone and put my earbuds in. I want to check again what Jace D was doing on the night Xav died. I don't want to think it, but Jace seems to be the one most worried about Xav's files.

Jace said he was a fan of Xav's in the early days, so he'd know about Alex Malex.

Jace is obsessed with finding the files and knows Xav confided in me.

Jace is a homophobe who behaves aggressively when challenged.

Xav and Jace had a Thing, despite Jace's bigotry. Maybe Xav wanted to take things further . . . or maybe Jace did and hated himself for it?

Jace could have gone to the game launch, then rushed over to Xav's flat after it finished – he'd have had time.

Could it be him? Have I just have picked a fight with The Face?

But when Jace's channel finally appears on my screen, the first thing I see is my own name – in the title of his latest video – uploaded half an hour ago.

My stomach lurches in panic. There it is, splashed across the screen, the thing I've been afraid of for months now.

I GOT A SNEAK PREVIEW OF MAXINE_F'S NEW STATIONERY LINE – AND IT SUCKS.

Jace is waving the dead-rat pencil case, the inflated price flashing up on screen in neon green, with five exclamation marks after it. And he's telling it like it is.

'Maxine is ripping off her fans, making a mockery of the people who put her where she is today. I'm insulted, and frankly you should be insulted too.'

Quickly, I jump on to my other social apps to see the response. #MaxineRipoff, #MaxineIsOver and, randomly, #DuffLeopard are all trending. I've seen this stuff happen to PlayMeeps before and I know the anger will only get worse when the stuff hits the shops next month.

I feel like I'm in freefall, my insides turning over and over as I plummet downwards. Hands shaking, skin hot and cold. It's happening – everything I've worried about since I first saw those Paperfly samples. I was right; Mum and Carl were wrong. But I'm the one who's going to get cancelled.

Chapter 22

Sam

The fire burned late into the night. I hoped the smoke would make its way up and through Xav's bedroom window, filling his room with the stink of ashes and destruction. I hoped he would see the flames and understand that he'd trashed his oldest, closest friendship for good.

I walked away from the flames, wiping the petrol-stink off my hands and on to my brushed-cotton joggers. Up in my room the fire glowed so brightly that I didn't need to turn my bedroom light on. I flicked straight to PlayMii and started my own channel there and then. I decided to call it *Wile E. Coyote TV*, after the indestructible cartoon character who falls off cliffs, gets blown up by dynamite and comes back fighting every time.

My first upload was called *Liar Liar (Yellow) Pants On Fire*. I didn't expect anyone, even Xav, to see it, but it felt good to put film of the fire out there. My next post would be something far more memorable.

Looking up from my editing, I noticed that the glow from the fire was now lighting up my dull blue bedroom walls. Outside, delicate sparks were drifting up through the night air, weaving around the smoke. Beautiful destruction.

But then an uneasy feeling crept through me. That glow was too bright. Too vivid. I dropped my phone and climbed on to the bed to look out properly.

The garden was on fire.

A spark must have jumped from the wreckage of our hideout to the old car seat on our side of the fence, and now it was being eaten by flames, the plastic cover swelling and popping in the heat. The fire was spreading to the washing machine carcasses, stuffed with old clothes. I watched in horror. *This isn't possible. The garden's too damp. It won't spread any further.*

But now weak little flames were licking the edges of Mr Birch's fence, clinging on and growing, feeding, coming closer. My heart hammered in my chest.

'Dad,' I shouted, rushing through to his bedroom.

The stench of beer hit me the moment I got in. The sad huddle on the bed didn't move, despite the crash I'd made coming in, and I knew I wouldn't be able to wake him.

'Come on, come on, COME ON!' I was screaming now, pulling at his arm. He rolled over, groaning slightly and swearing, the stink of his breath hitting me full in the face. I yelled in his ear. 'DAD, DAD, *PLEASE*!'

Blue lights flashed, lighting up the walls of his room, showing the piles of paper around him, his face crumpled into the pillow. Bangs and crashes on the door outside. I scrambled to my feet, running down the stairs, kicking up plastic bags and empty containers as I ran.

Pushing the boxes of yoghurt pots over, I wrenched the door open for the firefighters outside.

Through their masks I could see the shock in their eyes as they saw our packed assault course of a hallway, the path they'd have to battle through to get to our back garden.

'I'll show you the quickest way,' I said, darting through the mounds of junk, hearing their clumping boots behind me. I shoved things aside that hadn't been moved in years. Sharp edges cut my hands, jabbed at my stumbling bare feet. It felt like I was running in slow motion, swimming through crap. A warm red glow shone through the kitchen window, casting long fuzzy shadows as the fire brigade rushed past me and out.

It took moments to put the fire out. The flames never reached the patio, although the house was filled with the stench of smoke. 'Local yobs on the railway sidings again,' one firefighter said with a shake of his head. 'You're lucky the neighbour called when he did.' Mr busybody Birch protecting his precious vegetables, I imagined. Once the life-or-death danger was over, there was the aftermath: the tea in a Styrofoam cup, the blanket on my shoulders. The questions.

'How long has it been like this?'

'Are social services aware?'

And, in a gentle voice, 'You know you're not doing him any favours protecting him like this, don't you?'

I was the one who set the hideout on fire, who destroyed half the garden, but in the end all the condemnation was for Dad, who had come downstairs, blinking blearily, moments after the fire had gone out. The incident was logged, the right people informed, and within twenty-four hours I was staying with Auntie Fiona across town for a few days, 'to give your father the breathing space to sort himself out'.

It wasn't permanent, everyone went to extraordinary lengths to tell me, especially Auntie Fiona, who had just done up her spare room in pristine shades of white, gold and purple, and probably didn't want a teenager living in it. But as I lay on the never-used duvet cover, staring at the pointless fake flower in its purple vase on my bedside, I knew things had changed for ever.

Closing my eyes, the future spun out in front of me. Without me cooking our meals, getting him up in the mornings and sharing TV marathons, Dad would get worse, lonelier, more desperate. More like me.

My phone was in my hand before I knew it, thumbs flicking, searching. A man jumps through fire. Another dude breaks into a European museum and climbs on all the dinosaur skeletons. Another guy throws himself into a shark pool at an aquarium, wearing Bermuda shorts and an inflatable rubber ring. Each clip sent a buzz of adrenaline running through me, feeding my anger and my need to make an impact, make a difference. Make people look at me differently.

You lack the necessary charisma. Xav's words cut deep because they were true. I was forgettable, part of the background in every classroom, at every party. But you don't always need charisma to get people's attention. Sometimes bravery, imagination and the urge to do something completely outrageous will do it too.

So that was what I was going to do. Something big. Something amazing. Something that would make sure Xav would never, ever forget me.

Chapter 23

Sam

I've had it with you fuckers. See you on the flipside.

I posted the message on all my accounts, telling everyone where I was going and what I was going to do before I sneaked out of my new, too-clean bedroom.

The fact that not one person reacted to my post fuelled my bitterness. There was no apology from Xav, no concern from Leni. Even Great Auntie Jean in Australia, who usually showered cheesy emojis on everything I put on Facebook, didn't drop so much as a GIF. Probably because of the swearing.

It was all such bullshit. Even the name on my profile, the one everyone used, was something Xav gave me. Nobody had called me by my real name since primary school, not since Xav and I had gone through our *Lord of the Rings* phase, questing through the playground with him as the hero of the story and me as dopey but ever-loyal Samwise Gamgee. *I'm worried about you, Mr Frodo; I love you, Mr Frodo.* Long after Xav had stopped being Frodo, I kept on being faithful adoring Sam, named by him and bound to him, until pretty much everyone had forgotten my real name. It was time to stop.

But if I wasn't Sam, who was I?

Maybe I was this. Wile E. Coyote: genius.

I locked my phone screen and melted into the darkness of the quiet street.

Our school had the best security system known to the Western world. They probably spent more on cameras than they spent on sports equipment or library books. There were signs everywhere telling us that we were being watched and that the school had a zero-tolerance policy on vandalism. There were cameras over the main gate, cameras in the hallway and a complex alarm system which tripped if you tried to get into any of the main buildings.

There was also a broken bit in the wire fence behind the science block that peeled back enough to let a medium-sized human through.

It's amazing how focused I was, given the fact I was so full of rage. The task kept me grounded and sane. Aunt Fiona was shocked that I'd even wanted to go to school the Monday after the fire, but I had a plan now. I kept my head down, ignored Xav and the others. Even when Leni tried to talk to me, I ducked away, pretended not to have seen and walked around school with my notebook instead. Because I had a mission.

So now, as I squeezed through the hole, I had a map with me, a plan of every single security camera and a route round most of them. I also had some climbing equipment, a small folding stepladder stolen from Uncle Adrian's garage and a large and very heavy axe. The handle caught on the fence, but with a few tugs I managed to break it free without causing too much noise.

I crept around the edge of the field, slipping into the shadow of the science block, hoping that my black hoodie and joggers wouldn't show any movement, that I'd be just a flicker of darkness on a CCTV screen. Pressing myself against the wall, like some kind of amateur ninja, I couldn't help laughing to myself. When I reached a safe spot, an alcove with a fire door in it, I secured a bandanna with skull patterns across my face, pulled my hood back up, attached my phone to a selfie stick and turned the camera on myself. It didn't pick up much in the darkness, but that was probably a good thing. Not, I told myself, that I particularly cared about being expelled. I had nothing to lose.

'Welcome, everyone,' I said. 'Allow me to introduce myself. I'm Wile E. Coyote: genius. For years, the children at this school have been terrorised by the craggy and judgemental face of its founder, Old Grouchy, a notorious colonialist, racist and exploiter of the poor, who thought his murky past would go away if he chucked a bit of money at his local school.' Holding the camera further away, I brandished my axe. The light from my phone made it gleam delightfully in the dark. 'Tonight, Old Grouchy gets his comeuppance.'

My hands were shaking. I couldn't quite get the shot right, so I did it a few more times, over and over. But the more I did it, the worse the shaking got. I realised that I was hiding here for another reason. I was too scared to move, to make this thing real.

Come on, you useless charisma-vacuum, I told myself. *Do it. Follow through on this one thing in your life.*

I took a huge gulp of air, shoved the axe head-first back in my rucksack, then started to move.

The side of the science block was fine, but as I came to the front of the building, I knew a worse problem was waiting for me. Twin hazards: the security cameras trained on the front gate and the floodlights which lit Old Grouchy from below. I was banking on the fact that the cameras were monitored offsite – last summer a bunch of kids had broken in and had a barbecue on the front steps, and it had taken the guards around forty minutes to get there. If I moved quickly, I could get the stunt done in a matter of seconds.

One, two three . . . GO.

Come on feet, I said GO.

I took one more breath and launched myself forward, running headlong across the forecourt, throwing an old towel over the anti-climb spikes at the top of the plinth and using my ladder to get high enough to clamber over the base to the statue itself, which started around two metres up. Then it was simple – hand over hand, feet notched in the crevices of Grouchy's pretentious cloak, fingers finding a hold until I was at the top, one foot nestled in the crook of his arm, the other resting in the book he was holding. Up close, the statue was flaky and old, and tiny chips of it sloughed off as I gripped Grouchy's shoulders tightly with my legs and wrestled the axe out of my bag.

Oh God. Clutched in my inexperienced hand, the axe weighed a ton and now that I was here, I wasn't sure how I could cling on with my legs and swing it with enough force to lop his head off.

I had to try.

Then I remembered the bloody camera. I was supposed to film this, wasn't I?

By the time I'd leveraged my phone out of my bag, attached the selfie stick and clamped it between my neck and shoulder I was beginning to realise this wouldn't work. I pressed record and hoped for the best.

'Here goes,' I told my audience.

Hot panic flooded my face; my hands were shaking uncontrollably now as I took a deep breath, shuffling my legs down, out of the way of the axe. I gripped it at the top of the handle, close to its head for extra control, and swung.

With a clang it rebounded off the stone, vibrating so much in my hand that my grip loosened. The axe slid out of my hands and my balance failed; my legs started to slide downward. I dropped the phone too as my arms flailed. I threw them around Grouchy's shoulders as my legs finally gave way. *What a fucking disaster, you fucking, fucking moron.*

I lost my grip and slithered down, feeling the spikes rip my joggers, scrape and slice into my legs as I fell into a shameful heap on the flowerbed below.

For a moment I lay there, silent sobs racking my body. What a failure. What a total and utter failure. Then I opened my eyes and saw something amazing, something miraculous.

In my struggle not to fall, I'd somehow managed to rip Grouchy's head clean off. It was lying next to me half submerged in the flowerbed.

Sitting up, cross legged, I cradled it lovingly and began to laugh.

My phone lay nearby – the screen was cracked and the selfie stick was destroyed, but it was still working. I flipped the camera back on to myself. My face looked flushed, excited and alive. My heart sang.

'Well that wasn't especially graceful,' I said. 'But look! Grouchy has fallen!'

I held the head up. His nose had been partially chipped away and the fluffy moustache was gone. A gurgle of laughter fought its way up from my belly.

'How are you feeling, Grouchy? Are you ready for Phase Two?'

Compared to the beheading, Phase Two was going to be easy. Now I needed to put the head somewhere visible, somewhere disruptive that would make everyone laugh at the old goat, and I knew just the place. At the top of our building a disused flagpole jutted out horizontally. I could hoist Grouchy out on to it in a net shopping bag, and when the kids came in the next morning, it would be dangling comically over the school forecourt.

But I had to go *now*, before security got here.

Bundling the head up into my bag, I grabbed the folding ladder and scaled my way up to the main building fire escape.

I knew this was alarmed to hell and, sure enough, screams and wails soon began to fill the air. *If I go fast enough, I can make it.*

My legs were on fire, springing up the staircase, the scratches on them forgotten as I ran, feet clanging on the metal. At the top, a high gate blocked my way on to the roof, but I scaled it easily. I barely noticed the scrape of barbed wire on the inside of my arms as I went over. I felt a wetness on my forearms – blood, maybe? I kept going.

And then I was there. A gentle breeze ruffled my hair, cooling the sweat on my skin and, in the distance, I could see a faint light on the horizon. The darkness had taken on a bluey-grey shade now. A new day was coming.

I wondered what Xav would think when he saw what I'd done.

I wondered what everyone would say when the video went live. The whole school would watch it. If I edited it right, made it funny and offbeat, other PlayMeeps would share it and promote it. It would go twice around the world in a few hours. It would go viral.

I just had to finish. Crouching down, I tipped the head into the sturdy net bag I'd bought especially for the occasion. The remains of his nose poked comically through one of the holes. *Serves you right, Grouchy.*

But there was one problem. The rope on the flagpole hadn't been used for ages – as soon as I tried to tie the bag on, it broke, the pieces crumbling away in my fingers. The only way I could do this was by hooking the bag over the end of the 2-metre-long pole.

I could do this. I had to do this.

In fact, shimmying out on to this flagpole would take this stunt to the next level.

Propping the phone up so I could film myself, I went low on my belly, hooked the bag on my arm and started to move.

I pushed myself out, felt the pole give slightly, and flakes of white paint came off in my hands, but it held. I felt it could easily take my weight. But as I got further out, the flagpole began to flex and there was a series of sharp clicking sounds, the metal under strain. My hands trembled, knees pressed together, and I became aware of a throbbing in my forearms where I'd cut myself, a pain in my lower back where I'd fallen. *A fine time for the adrenaline to wear off. I don't have time for this.*

Then the sound I was dreading – a car coming down the deserted streets towards the school. I'd taken too long. Security was here.

I couldn't go any further; I had to go back. As I moved, Grouchy slipped from my grasp and crashed to powder on the ground below. But I held on tight, inching back and back and back up the flagpole, towards the building, towards safety.

Relief. That was so close, too close.

Still astride the flagpole, I clung to it, thankful I'd survived, dreading the moment when I'd have to pivot my body round to climb on to the roof.

And then it happened: I heard a sound behind me and

twisted instinctively, tipping my balance, and suddenly I was falling. There was nothing below me, only air. Rushing, weightless seconds of freedom ...

And then a horrendous, unending wall of pain.

Chapter 24

Maxine

By the next day, it's all over the internet. The PlayMii gossip channel Piping_Hot_Tea has even done an explainer video complete with infographics all about my trashy stationery. I've watched it over and over, and so have about seventy-five thousand other people:

Things have taken a maccabree turn in the life of popular British PlayMeep Maxine_F. Since the murder of her sometime-friend Xav Bailey, our airheaded friend's content has become more and more erratic. First, she doesn't post for over a month after Xav's death, despite fans urging her to speak out. Then she blows it all out of the water with the devastating video known as The FU. After that, it's business as usual for our gal, with explainer videos on dodgeball and aerial yoga, and a dramatic unboxing of her new stationery products, set to launch in UK stores next month, but then . . . [and here there's a graphic of a cartoon bomb exploding] Bang. Turns out she's planning to rip people off with her new stationery line and the whistleblower is none other than Jace D, a close personal pal of her dear departed buddy Xav. Is Maxine as dumb and innocent as she looks, or is she every bit as money-grabbing and desperate to hog the limelight as Xav was?

Mum is behind me, pacing, talking into her phone.

No, we will not comment.

Yes, we will release a statement in time.

No, Maxine is not planning to upload a video today.

Well, you'd need to talk to the Paperfly office about that.

Her face is pinched and taut, her arms gesticulating on overdrive. Her anger fills her – it blazes in her clipped words, sits between her tight shoulder blades. I want to scream *I told you so*, but I don't. Anything I say now will make her blow.

She was like this the week after what happened with Sam. Stretched tight as a guitar string, the smallest movement making her hum with rage.

The school carried out an investigation, talked to Sam in hospital, interrogated us one by one, watched all our videos and hers, and the explanation was clear. PlayMii had made Sam do it. Envy of our channel had pushed her to try an extreme, dangerous stunt. Dad and Glenys were summoned to school for a meeting; Mum dialled in on Skype.

I can still remember that small feeling, my legs dangling from the too-high chair, a pile of rubble (which I later found out was the remains of Grouchy's head) on a tray on the headmaster's desk.

He talked a lot about tradition, respect, school values, while Dad and Glenys nodded agreement. He talked about the fact that we should be concentrating on our studies, not messing around with videos, that we had to take the Alex channel down immediately and that, henceforth, video-streaming apps were banned from school property.

'Ridiculous,' Xav had snorted later. 'As if we were to blame. Sam's crazy, obsessed. She would do literally anything to get my attention. Honestly, I'm glad she's not coming back to school, I'm a bit scared of her.'

But Leni and I talked a lot about it after that and it was obvious. She'd done it because we'd excluded her, we'd forgotten her. And maybe Xav was to blame for some of that but, still, I'd stood by and let it happen. We all had, except maybe Leni. Unlike Sam, we weren't expelled – Andy's dad was on the board of governors and argued we hadn't explicitly told Sam to do what she did – but the Alex channel was over.

At first, I'd thought Mum's fury was directed at me, but then I realised she was angrier with Dad, Glenys, the school. Thinking back now, I think she just felt guilty, being so far away. Within a month, she was back from the States, cutting her contract short and transferring me back to my old school.

It was a relief not to be 'The Other Alex Girl – you know, the daft one who's not Leni' any more.

Bing. An email brings me back to the here and now. A message from the Alex email which contains only two words.

I'm waiting.

Please, I'm trying, I reply. I cringe at the words, the idea that I'm giving this evil person exactly what they want, showing

I'm afraid, that I'm doing his dirty work like a good little amateur detective. I want to send one back saying, *Why me?* Of all the people in the world, why pick me – a person famous for not having two brain cells to rub together?

It must be because of the messages. Whoever it was must have known about Xav confiding in me. Could it be Jace?

And then I'm groaning, slapping my forehead at my own stupidity. The Face had Xav's phone – he would have seen the messages when he stole it. It could be anyone.

It also means there were no clues in them; he must have watched them all by now.

Unless . . .

No. The Face would have had time to see the messages were there, but there was no way he could watch them. I know from pretty much every TV crime drama made after 2010 that the police can track phones. He must have swiped the phone, then later realised he couldn't risk keeping it.

The Face isn't perfect. He isn't all-knowing, all-powerful. And by now, he is getting scared.

Which means I have a chance. I can think my way through this somehow.

I shut myself in my room and check the video messages Xav sent me once again. One by one, I upload them all to my slow, ancient laptop so I can see more detail, take more precise screenshots. It takes long, ugly hours to go through them all. Watching Xav's gorgeous, sad, royally manipulative face as he works out his demons. Sobbing. Ranting. Unsaveable.

This time, though, I take a step back. I look at this the way the Facehunters would – as a mystery to be solved, rather than a friend in pain and about to be murdered.

Edzilla called me a psychopath today . . . I'm not the only one in this game who fits the description.

Ever think you know someone, then realise you got it so wrong? I don't trust anyone, Maxi-Pad, not even myself.

Thanks for letting me dump all my secrets on you. I don't think you know just what a time bomb you're sitting on.

Time to burn it all down. I'll be in touch.

I jot the words down on sticky notes and stick them to my wall, printing the DTM list picture and pinning it next to them. I look at the photo of Xav's crew. His arm is around Ethan, who looks thrilled to be there. Various others are smirking for the camera. Jace D is on the edge trying to look cool.

I'm missing something, I know I am, but if I look at this stuff for long enough, I'm going to see a pattern. I'm going to work this out.

I go back to watching videos, but then then my laptop screen goes blank for no reason. This happens sometimes, but this time I'm grateful. As sensible parents who aren't my mum would say: I need a screen break.

I shut the laptop, turn off notifications on my phone, and put on some loud, loud music. Then I throw open my wardrobe doors and drag out the boxes inside – all the tat I hid away when we moved here. It's time to make this room my home.

The unicorns, llamas and sloths go into a bin bag, along with the rose-gold lamps, the framed art with inspirational quotes and the fake succulents I use for Instagram flat-lays. Out comes all my old junk. There's the string of naff fairy lights, a PlayMeep cliché, but one I love so much. Out comes the dressmaker's dummy, the art project. A bunch of books I forgot I loved. Mr Dodo, the cuddly chicken-ostrich-dinosaur thing from my childhood. My posters – oh my beloved retro band posters, how I have missed you!

By the time I've finished, my hands are grubby, I'm sneezing from all the dust but I'm in a teenager's bedroom again, surrounded by things I actually want to look at. One last thing to do.

My pinboard is massively out of date. There are photos here of the leavers' ball at my other school, friends I've lost touch with, a shot of the Alex team hanging out in the park on the day we did the flashmob, just before I found the dog-muck in my shoe. I can just about see Sam in the background – a hunched figure, half turned away from the camera.

I stare at the picture for a moment, getting the feeling again that I'm missing something. Then I replace it with one of me and Frida vintage shopping.

By the time I've finished, I feel better, and almost like making a video again. Just a quick one on finding your own (chaotic) interior design style. But when I reach for my phone, I see I have a lot of notifications from the Facehunters group. A *lot*.

My phone is showing previews of the mentions in reverse order, so I can't quite figure out what they're on about.

FlaminFlaps: Fuck, has @LilyPad disappeared? Where are you girl?

Ola: @LilyPad where RU? GET ON HERE U HAVE 2 SEE THIS.

Ola: OMG this is major!!

James: i fort there was summat about her

Mandalor_Ian: let's not rush to conclusions but I have to say this does look bad.

FlaminFlaps: So there's a link between this girl and Xav. And now there's a link between this girl and Maxine. Holy shiiiiit @ LilyPad was right!!!!!

I thumb my way into Mandalor_Ian's original post and I see he's shared a picture.

It's an image I recognise straight away, the selfie I took with Keisha at the flower shop for her Instagram. In the background, not knowing she's in the photo, and with her head turned slightly away from the camera, is Frida.

And now, just minutes after looking at my pinboard, she's so familiar. The line of her jaw, her profile – although the nose is slightly different and her overall look has completely changed. My first response is denial – this can't be her, I'd know. But I can't ignore it now. I don't even need the Facehunters to spell it out for me.

Mandalor_Ian: It took a while, but look, @LilyPad, I found Sam. And she's friends with Maxine.

Chapter 25

Sam

The first thing I saw when I opened my eyes was Happy – a warped and badly painted Disneyesque dwarf looking down from a stained, pale blue wall next to me. I stared at him, trying to square where I'd been before to where I was now, feeling starched cotton under my head instead of asphalt, hearing whooshes and beeps, and somewhere in the room out of my field of vision, a child weeping, whimpering in pain.

Where? Hospital?

I noticed a bundle of old coats piled in the chair underneath Happy, and after a couple of blinks, my vision came into focus and I realised it was Dad, his grey skin sagging and relaxed in sleep.

I couldn't feel any real pain – not yet, that would come later when the drugs wore off fully – but there were parts of me that were stiff, parts of me that were numb. I lifted my fingers, some bandaged, to my face and felt some stiff kind of dressing across my nose. I tried to move my right arm and realised it was in some kind of splint or cast.

It was then that the realisation formed in my head.

I fell off the roof. My stiff, bruised face twisted into a grin and delicious, manic laughter bubbled up inside me.

I fell off the freaking ROOF and survived. That's EPIC.

I was dizzy with happiness that I'd done something that stone-cold crazy and lived to tell the tale. It was heady, addictive. *This must be how those Russian dudes feel every day.*

Dad shifted in his chair, waking up. I shut my eyes instinctively, trying to fake sleep. I wasn't ready to talk to him yet. Moments later, I felt Dad's unnaturally soft fingers stroke my hair.

'Oh, Kerri,' he said.

I hadn't heard him say my name in a long time – using it would have punctured the warped, almost-a-boy pretence we'd created so long ago. Now, though, he was whispering it over and over, his voice so full of loss that I had to bite the inside of my lip to remind myself to keep still. Dad's tenderness felt so wrong, heavy on my head, pinning me down. I realised the painkillers had stopped working and agony started to seep from my bones into my blood. I kept my eyes shut. Reality hit me like . . . like a concrete school courtyard. This wasn't epic, it was humiliating. I was an attention-seeking failure.

I kept still, forced my body to relax, to feign sleep hoping Dad would stop stroking my head and go away.

'I'm sorry. I'll be a better dad, I'll clean up. I'll be better.'

I couldn't bring myself to believe him. But it was a very, very long time before the stroking stopped.

The children's ward was a cramped place – big on toys, cartoon murals and false optimism, low on space and proper equipment.

The kid next to me, a three-year-old on dialysis, cried through the night, wailing *don't wannit, don't wannit* while his parents said soothing, pointless things and choked back their own sobs. If I sat propped up against the pillows, which they sometimes let me do, it meant locking eyes with the seven-year-old boy opposite, who threw endless questions at me. Was I a boy or a girl? How did I break my elbow? What was wrong with my nose and were the doctors going to give me a nose job? How bad were the cuts on my arms? Was there a lot of blood?

Once a clown came in – full face paint, balloon animals and honking nose, straight out of a children's story book or a horror movie. He took one look at my face and glided smoothly past me on giant, flappy feet to the toddler next door. But I still watched him out of the corner of my eye. I heard the kid's voice change from scared to sceptical to honking laughter, watched the clown's gloved hands produce feathered flowers out of the kid's ear, twist what looked like a blown-up yellow condom into a giraffe. The clown was all movement and vivid colour. Colour was the key – it distracted and disguised. The bobbing yellow flower in his purple hat drew your eye away from the fake bouquet up his sleeve. The wide red painted-on mouth hid the clown's stubble, last night's hangover, the fact that he was an ordinary man.

Xav was all colour, a Pride rainbow on acid that had taken a shower in glitter. Leni was bathed in blue light wherever she went, like she was sitting on the bottom of a swimming pool on a sunny day. Maxine was earthy and warm. Ed was all energy, like a zigzag of bright yellow.

Me, I had always been grey marl.

The clown glanced over me and poked out his tongue. I looked away.

The nurse with too much eye make-up came over and drew the curtains around my bed.

'Children's ward is always a weird place for teenagers,' she said. 'But you don't quite belong on the adult one yet, so you're stuck here, I'm afraid.'

I looked up at her and took her in for the first time. The children's ward nurses all wore slightly different uniforms, variations on a blue top with short sleeves, trousers and hideous shoes. Most of them had tried to customise their uniforms in a sad and desperate way, with silly brooches and lanyards, but this nurse really stood out. Her braided hair was wound into a high bun, with a brightly coloured headwrap around it and she wore more crazy colourful badges and pins than anyone else.

She worked her way through my obs quickly, taking my temperature without fuss, and on the inside of her wrist, I saw a tattoo of a tropical flower, surrounded by rich green leaves.

Again, colour. I couldn't stop looking at it. She saw me gaping and smiled.

'The Trust doesn't really approve of tattoos – or headwraps – but they need the staff, so here I am.'

'It's lovely but . . . weren't you nervous when you had your tattoo done?' I said. 'Didn't you worry about what people would think, whether you'd lose your job?'

She shrugged. 'Sometimes you just have to be yourself, do what's right for you and let other people deal with it. So how are you feeling today? Not going to jump off any more buildings, I hope?'

'I didn't jump, I . . . oh, it sounds silly now I say it, but there was this boy . . .'

'You're right, that does sound silly.' She shook her head and a stray braid loosened itself from her bun. 'No boy on earth, no matter how incredible or how good at kissing, is worth that.'

'You haven't met Xav. You'll get it when you see him – he's just one of those people. You'll like him. He doesn't care what people think, either.'

But was that true? Hadn't he ignored me, turned his back on me because I was too cringe for his PlayMii channel? And where was he now? As soon as I was able to, I'd sent him a message saying I'd done something stupid and was in block E on Blue Ward, expecting him to rock up with some chocolates and an apology. Instead, nothing.

Inside me, something fizzled out. I was done with being ashamed of my desperation, continually heartbroken by the fact that he would never care. I was done with waiting for him to lift me out of my greyness. The nurse was right, I'd have to lift myself and learn to fight.

That afternoon was lost in a blur of bad television – home makeover shows, programmes about antiques and *Friends* repeats, with a heavy bassline of pain and constant questioning drumming underneath it all.

If I wasn't Loyal Sam, and I wasn't Victim Kerri, who was I? Who could I be?

In my head I made a list.

I wanted to be bright.

I wanted to be bold.

I wanted to never give a shit about what other people thought again.

My nurse came back, joking about the hospital slop I was trying to eat, flashing a friendly smile as she leaned over and took my temperature. As she did, I noticed one particular badge standing out from the rest. The face of a woman, her dark hair tied up in a riot of flowers, her shoulders shrouded in brightly coloured cloth. But it was her stare that held my eye, bold and uncompromising below one big thick bristling monobrow. Angry, strong, unashamed.

'Oh, you've spotted Frida Kahlo,' the nurse said. 'I love her. She's brilliant.'

And I looked. And she was.

Chapter 26

Maxine

'Could you keep still please?' The beautician's voice is sounding a little tired because this is probably the twenty-eighth time she's said it. She's applying some luminous yellow gloop – which the public relations guy says is the ultimate acne-eliminating microbiome facial skincare – to my face while Mum films it. Of course, it looks silly – that's the whole point of my channel – and usually I'd be making faces and milking this moment for all the comedy value I could get. But I can't think, I can't focus; it takes all the effort I have not to jump out of the chair and run down the street.

I still can't believe that my friend has been lying to me. But there's no doubt about it.

She was never called Sam, apparently it was a nickname at school, Mandalor_Ian wrote. He had burrowed down into her defunct Facebook account, found a few people with the surname Taylor, including a great aunt in Australia who often commented on Sam's posts. He'd friended the aunt, who was pretty relaxed about who she linked up with, then searched through her history until he'd found references to a Kerri and an 'accident' in a thread with Malcolm Taylor, who turned out to be Kerri's dad. *I had a definite surname now, but the trail went cold for a while until I found out she'd changed her legal name from Kerri to Frida and she showed up on a London art college website. But this is interesting: a couple of days before Xav's death she begins following his PlayMii account again. She comments on one of his videos and they chat about old times. She even says she might stop by and see him at that final meet and greet on the day he died. Then suddenly here she is around town with Maxine.*

I only met Sam a couple of times at school, I have a crap memory for faces and the way she presents herself has changed so much. I guess I couldn't imagine how the shrinking grey figure I knew could transform into Frida – a vibrant, takes-no-prisoners ninja butterfly of a person. But I still feel so stupid. So ignorant, so trusting.

I think of the time we walked around Lewisham and I talked to her about school. We even went down her old street, past her old house and she still didn't say a thing.

But the worst thing of all, the thing that makes me sick with anger when I think about it, is that Ed has known for weeks. The first time they met, he acted strangely, the second time he tried to warn me, but after that – why did he take her side, keep her secret? And Leni must have realised too, at Panopticon, and said nothing.

I haven't just lost one friend, I've lost three.

Every time I think about it, I get hot, my heart hammering as I try to figure out how I feel. Anger mixes with fear, mixes with the horrible pulling-apart, whole-world-breaking feeling you get when a boyfriend cheats on you. Betrayal, that's what it is.

I think about the three of them, talking about me, keeping secrets, maybe even laughing about how stupid Maxine can't even see the obvious. *Stupid, stupid Maxine.*

The first thing I did after reading Mando's post was fire off some scorching messages to them all. Leni came back with some placatory *I'm sorry, I didn't know until Panopticon. She told me she was going to tell you.*

Ed's were longer, more complicated, but amounted to the same thing. She'd persuaded him to keep quiet. He felt sorry for her, she really wasn't so bad, yada yada.

And as for Frida, or Sam, or whatever she's really called . . . nothing.

Not a sorry, not an explanation, not even a second tick on the WhatsApp message. She's just dropped me out of her life, moved on without explanation.

Is it possible to miss someone and hate them at the same time?

'Please keep still,' the beautician says. 'I'm just going off to get the beads now.'

'Maxine,' Mum hisses. 'Are you asleep? You need to do your thing. We have to come back fighting, make some killer videos to sell this stationery.'

I roll my eyes.

'Yes, that's better. More like that.'

This week is the third week of August, known to everyone in our world as VCW, or VlogCon Week. Our chance to mingle with other creators, launch our crap stationery merch and meet and greet the people who made us what we are today – our loyal viewers. I'm supposed to be doing a live explainer on stage tomorrow, followed by a selfie-session the day after, then launching a competition to win a dead-rat pencil case. Mum and Paperfly are going on as if nothing has happened.

And then, as I lie there waiting for the beads, something just snaps. I'm sick of being ordered around, sick of people thinking they know better than me. And at that precise moment, I'm sick of Mum telling me how to run my channel.

'I don't want to sell stationery,' I say. 'The deal sucks, and you'd see it if you didn't have big pound signs in your eyes.'

'I do not,' she snaps back. 'Pricing is a complex art. I thought the Paperfly people knew what they were doing.'

'What they could get away with, you mean.'

'*Caramia*, we are halfway through this free facial which usually costs hundreds of pounds and we haven't filmed anything useable yet. Could we talk about this later?' Mum's face is taut with stress, harsh. I try to think of the last time we hugged when there weren't any cameras around. The last time we had a conversation about anything but the channel.

'Mum, maybe we shouldn't work on the channel together any more.'

'What?'

'Maybe . . . you're a bit fired?'

Oh, way to go Maxine – about as assertive as a wet lettuce. But still, I mean it. Carl can do all the managing. Maybe I can hire an assistant or an intern to help with the filming and stop me being late for everything. Someone who'll listen instead of telling me what to do.

Mum's jaw drops; her brown eyes flash with anger and hurt. 'You don't mean it. You couldn't do it alone.'

And there it is. I'm stupid. I'm helpless. Well, not any more.

'Just back off, Mum. Back off and watch me.'

Mum makes a small sound, a gasp of shock. Her eyes dart around the salon and I know she's raging but doesn't want to make a scene. 'You would be lost without me,' she snaps. 'Lost.'

Then she puts down the camera and walks away.

I want to run after her, let out all the anger I've been bottling up, but just then the beautician comes back and starts dotting green beads of something on to my face. My tears merge with the gloop and run down the side of my head. I really am alone now.

When I walk out of the salon my skin looks amazing, but my heart hurts.

I'm just drifting along the street, feeling the sun on my face, wondering what to do next, when I hear feet running behind me. I turn, panicked – but it's . . .

'Gus, isn't it?'

Ed's boyfriend is smiling and waving. 'Hi,' Gus says, slightly out of breath. He's cute. Really cute. 'Ed is waiting in Costa over there,' he says. 'He wants to speak to you. He says sorry. He says it's important.'

Ed is at a table at the corner, tucked away from the front of the shop. I sit down opposite him and don't say anything as Gus settles in next to him.

I should say: fuck off, Ed. I should say: you betrayed me and lied to me and I never want to see you again. But I see the ghost of a bruise around his eye, left over from the attack. Guilt takes control of my body and keeps me in my chair.

'I know, I get it, you're angry,' Ed says. 'That's why I sent Gus to get you – I knew you wouldn't tell him to eff off.'

'Thank you, English politeness,' Gus jokes, but I'm still not in the mood.

'How could you not tell me? You lied, Frida lied, Leni lied. I don't even get why.'

'She told me she'd tell you eventually, that she nearly told you that time you were at her place, but she was scared, she thought you'd probably freak out.'

'You *think?*'

Ed gives a long, pained sigh. 'Try to look at it from her perspective. She goes along to this meet-and-greet thing to talk to Xav for the first time in years – it's all very emotional so she ducks out and she ends up, by amazing coincidence, sitting next to you. You clearly don't recognise her – minus points for *that* by the way – and you get chatting. You get on. This poor girl hasn't had a proper friend in years, and before that her only mate was Xav, everyone's favourite emotional gaslighter. Now she's

237

found someone she gets on with, so she keeps telling herself it's OK, she's Frida now, Sam was never real anyway. That you never need to know. And then Xav gets killed and you're together when she finds out, and she has to pretend she doesn't know him, which half-kills her. I think after that she felt kind of trapped into going on with the deception.'

'So she explained all this to you, and you just accepted it? The coincidence of running into me? The fact she listened to me offloading all my Xav-related issues without saying a word? I even told her how guilty I felt about this kid that fell off the roof at school and she hugged me and DIDN'T SAY A THING.'

Ed shrugs. 'Yeah. I kept telling her she needed to tell you the truth but . . . you do know you've been a bit emotionally all-over-the-place lately?'

I gasp in outrage. *This coming from Mr Bitter and Angry?*

Ed has the good grace to look away from me, embarrassed. 'I suppose I'm more forgiving because she's actually been helping me. After I got out of hospital, she reached out and we talked. She's the only other victim of Xav I know. She was like me, wasted years loving him, trying to make him happy, going along with his plans, losing her identity and never getting anything back. It helped to talk to her. It helped me figure out who I am.'

I can see what he means. Ed's clothes and hair have changed, but it's more than that. He's still fit but not as toned, like he's not working out quite so much or so often. He seems relaxed, looser in the way he moves, less like he's trying to prove something.

I'm not ready to make peace, though I'm not ready to play nicey-nicey Maxine and accept I've been deceived, treated like a fool. So many times over the last few months, I've tackled my problems by asking, 'What would Frida do?' Well, the fake Frida I used to look up to would never stand for something like this.

'I'm sorry, Ed, but you can tell Frida I don't want to see her again. This is all just too . . . weird.'

Ed's eyes darken; I see fear on his face.

'That's it, though, Maxine – that's why I wanted to talk to you. It's Frida – she's vanished.'

Of course she has, I think. She's hiding because she's ashamed. But Ed explains that she hadn't responded to any of his texts after Panopticon, either. He'd been so worried that he'd been to her college only to find out she hadn't shown up for a few days. Her flatmates, who never really saw her anyway, said her bed hadn't been slept in.

'I'm worried, Max,' Ed said. 'I tried the police, but they say she's technically an adult and there's no sign of foul play, so there's nothing they can do. I thought maybe you might have heard something. Anything.'

There's a twist of worry inside me. Yes, of course I still care about her. It takes a while to switch that sort of thing off.

I think of all the sensible reasons why Frida might be ignoring us right now. Maybe she's just met someone amazing and is lying in bed somewhere in a haze of sexual bliss; maybe she's avoiding us because she's ashamed of lying; maybe . . . maybe . . . Oh shit.

Maybe The Face has realised who she is, and thinks she has the files.

Chapter 27

Frida

Becoming Frida was breathtakingly simple – and painfully complicated.

The outside, that was easy. I told Auntie my new name, and blocked Dad's number on my phone. I had to move on, cut out the past. If Dad wasn't going to get better, I couldn't let him hold me back any more. It was the only way I could survive.

Throwing out my tracksuits was especially satisfying. I scoured charity shops, jumble sales and market stalls for bright flashes of colour. I cut them and customised them. I matched and clashed. I grew my hair, I experimented (very badly) with make-up, I accessorised. In the mornings, I'd take time to pick things out; what to wear became an adventure.

I read voraciously about Frida Kahlo. She was eighteen when a bus accident nearly killed her – but she survived and started making brilliant, uncompromising art full of colour and life and reality. Her paintings of physical pain made my nose and wrist ache and the scars on my arms throb. Her paintings of life made me want to go out there and do everything, *see* everything. I didn't try to dress up as her – that would have been ridiculous – I was just inspired by her attitude, her love of life and colour, and the way she learned from her own pain. I forged my own personality, modelled on her. As Frida I walked differently. When people stared, I smiled, and when people stared too hard, I gave them the finger – but in an elegant, classy way – and watched them stutter and crumble. My colours were like armour. Sam could never have done this. Frida was badass.

But it's not so easy to change the inside, to uncurl my back from a lifetime of hunching, and uncurl whatever it was inside me that had been hiding for fifteen years.

A few days after the hospital let me go home, when I was still mostly-Sam, Leni showed up at my aunt's door.

'You look better than I thought you would,' she said, ignoring my fading bruises, bandaged nose and strapped-up arm and focusing on my colourful T-shirt. I ushered her into Auntie Fi's pristine front room and wondered if it was OK to let her sit on the Guest Chair.

'Nothing kicks you up the backside as much as a near-death experience.'

Leni looked different to me now. Her artfully patched jeans, silk waterfall jacket and niche Japanese sneakers looked contrived and artificial somehow. Her hair had changed again – it was pale pink now and I thought about how much effort it must take to keep dying it, how she spent hours of her life hunched over the sink with those horrible little rubbery gloves on, rubbing goo into her scalp. Then more hours straightening, moisturising, conditioning, de-frizzing. It shouldn't take so much hard work to be yourself.

Part of me was happy and excited to see her; another part sneered at me for my weakness, my servile happiness in being noticed.

Leni kept talking, a gush of words about how she couldn't believe they'd expelled me, how Mr Kline's classes are so much more boring without me, and what was I going to do? And what school was I going to go to now? And did I know she and Andy were now officially an item and that when you got to know him he was actually really sweet and he sent her the cutest little note last week. She asked about why I did it – wincing when I told her – and asked whether I'd been afraid, up there, clinging to the flagpole. She said how terrifying and how cool it was that I had fallen off a building.

'Do you mind me asking – how did you end up falling?'

'I don't know,' I answered, and for a moment, I was back on that roof, clinging on with my aching hands, cuts on my arms bleeding and throbbing, and something else, something dancing at the edge of my memory but too crazy to even think about seriously. 'I was so nearly safe, I thought I'd made it. I guess I just relaxed a second too early and lost my balance.'

She shook her head, waving her elegant white hands as if trying to push away the horrible thought.

'Do you fancy coming to the park this evening?' she said. 'No Xav, just me, Andy and Maxine. We're just going to get chips and hang out, but it might be fun.'

'No!' I practically shouted the word. She jumped back slightly in the Guest Chair, and one of Auntie's grey shiny cushions slid to the floor. I'd have to pick that up in a minute.

'I mean . . . I don't think it's good for me, hanging around Xav and his friends.'

She nodded, and I could tell from her expression that she hadn't expected me to say yes, that it had been a pity offer, something to make them all feel a bit less guilty about what they'd made me do. Why was she even here? Sure, she'd brought chocolates and a card, but maybe she'd just come for the gossip, so she could get closer to the drama, tell everyone at school about my bruises and my busted nose and the state of my mental health. She was dough, like all the others, using my trauma to make herself more interesting.

'Besides,' I added. 'You guys think you're so *fascinating*, but you're way too boring for me.'

Leni's eyes filled with hurt, anger. And maybe it wasn't the best thing to say, but it was the most Frida thing I could think of in that moment.

Up until that point, I'd believed I could still go back, blow everyone away with my new identity and force them to be impressed with me. But fuck that, they'd had their chance. I had to cut myself off from my old life.

After that came the hard part, the donkey work. Staying away from the stuff that was bad for me, pushing myself to change.

I threw away my phone. No, that's an exaggeration – I swapped my smartphone for an old Nokia of Auntie Fi's. I deleted most of my social media feeds, leaving just a picture of a gravestone to symbolise the 'death' of Sam. Then I logged out of everything. I made art. Masks. Lots and lots of masks of different shapes and sizes. I didn't even share them on Instagram, I just made them for me, displayed them on a shelf in my room.

My new school was a last chance saloon for troubled kids, but it was OK – we were allowed to wear our own clothes and tell the teachers to piss off, and best of all, people left me alone there. We all had our own shit to deal with. I had scars and a backstory and developed a mean mouth if people messed with me. I even made friends – a few, although I never really let people in, never let them get close. I didn't want to be hurt again.

About a year after my fall, I overheard one of the girls at my new school talking about her favourite PlayMii star.

'He's flipping hilarious. I tell you, there is nothing that guy won't say. And he's fit.' Her face flipped into a little pout of disappointment. 'Why are all the hottest ones gay?'

I looked over her shoulder, the blue and green PlayMii colours drawing me in, locking my gaze to the screen like they always had. It was Xav and Ed, doing something stupid with cling film again.

I closed my eyes, but I could still hear his laugh through the tinny phone speaker – a loud joyous cackle that made you want to laugh too.

'What are you smiling at?' the girl said. 'I thought you hated PlayMii.'

I touched my hands to my lips – I hadn't realised I was smiling at all. Quickly I turned away.

I knew the most important thing I could do for myself was stay away from Xav. But it's hard to avoid something like PlayMii, when everyone in the world is on it and talking about it. Xav's name would drop around me like casual little bombs. I'd go without for months and months, then dip into his channel, or Leni's, or Maxine's, just to check how they were doing, and every time I did, it was like dagger-sharp claws of resentment grasping at my insides. And in time I learned to acknowledge it, to accept it as part of who I am. Who I'll always be.

I didn't want what they had any more, but I didn't want them to have it, either. Was that so wrong?

Chapter 28

Maxine

When I get back from the cafe, Mum is in my room and there are four outfits laid out on the bed.

'We need to nail your look for VC,' she says. 'It needs to have leopard in it to match the stationery for when you do your presentation. Also, Carl says they've beefed up security tomorrow – there are mad people planning to protest outside the event. You know, that crazy theory that PlayMii somehow assassinated Xavier? That we are all part of some big conspiracy? Anyway, we need to be careful to distance ourselves from them without creating a backlash, and I think a rainbow pin on your hairband will send a strong message of respect.'

I stare at her. Behind her on the wall are my sticky notes with questions like *Who killed Xav? Who has the files?* Around her are all the teenage things I've dragged out of my boxes and thrown around the room in a frenzied attempt to turn back time. In front of her is her terrified daughter wondering if her best friend and betrayer has been attacked by a murderer. And she's talking about outfits. And stationery. And VlogCon.

I explode. And, oh God, it feels good to finally let myself scream.

'You're fired, Mum, I told you. GET OUT! GET OUT! GET OUT!'

I pick something up – I think it's a cushion – and throw it. It crashes into my make-up table, sending tiny bottles and jars flying to the floor. I pick up something else – Mr Dodo – and fling it again. It glances off Mum's head. Then I surge forward and throw the clothes; those three carefully chosen outfits go flying across the room.

'Maxine, calm down!'

'NO. You need to LISTEN.'

We didn't do this shouting teenager thing before, Mum and me. She swanned off to America and left me with Dad, and I took it. She swanned back and sent me to another school, and I took it. She barged into my PlayMii life and made a business out of it, and I took it. She picks my outfits, she talks for me in meetings, she thinks about how to 'play' things when one of my friends has been murdered. She films me and films me and films me. And I just take it. Adaptable Maxine. Docile Maxine. Stupid, easily led Maxine.

I realise that I'm screaming all this at her, my voice ragged and croaky, as I shove her towards the door and slam it in her face. I'm still shouting into the slab of wood.

'What about me? Not the channel, *me*. I don't want a fuck- ing CEO, I want a mother.'

My legs are weak. I drag myself back to the bed and pull the duvet over myself, my body shaking with sobs.

I'm not sure how long I lie there for just screaming and sobbing into my pillow. I can hear Mum storming about in the front room, swearing in Italian, probably throwing cush- ions – but eventually silence. I've just started to wonder if she's gone out when I hear my bedroom door open, her foot- steps on the hardwood floor. I tense myself, waiting for another argument and then I feel the mattress dip as she sits down next to me. I feel her arms around me through the bedcovers. I want to push her away, but my body doesn't have the energy, and the warmth of her arms feels good.

'Maxine,' she murmurs, just loud enough so I can hear. 'You were right. You were right about Paperfly, and you're right now. I had no idea you were struggling this much.'

'I'm not an idiot,' I say into the pillow, and she laughs.

I lift my head, shocked and angry and ready to fight again, but her expression is softer now.

'Of course you're not,' she says. 'You built this. You. All by yourself in your bedroom. You do stupid things to make millions of people laugh, but that doesn't make *you* stupid. I just thought if I took care of the business side of things, you'd be free to enjoy your life.'

I slump forward again, exhausted. She strokes my hair, but I push her hand away.

'But maybe . . .' she begins haltingly, 'maybe this is too much. If it's not fun any more, we can walk away. I'll get a proper job, you can finish your A levels, or train up to do something else. We can do it – if that's what you want. It's your life, Maxine.'

I stare up at her. Give up? Was that even possible? Shutting down the channel would change everything. No more daily stressing about what to wear, caking my face in make-up for a night in with Netflix, remembering to mention 'amazing brands' I'd discovered. No more worrying about saying or doing the wrong thing in public, about being cancelled. No more being recognised when I'm out buying heavy-flow tampons. No more raging tide of freebies, insincerity and expectations. The thought is exciting and scary, full of possibility. Who would I even be off camera?

Anyone I wanted to be.

But I'd still be me, still struggling to wrap my head around the way the world works, just without my fam around me to make me laugh, or make me look at things differently, without videos as an outlet for venting my frustration or my confusion. Would quitting solve anything?

When I speak, my voice is croaky and worn out. 'I'm not giving up.'

I'm not just talking about the channel and Paperfly. I'm not letting The Face get away with it, either. For a moment, I think about telling Mum everything. The words are cued up in my mouth, waiting to come out – about Frida, the emails from The Face, my search for the files. But then she smiles at me and strokes my hair and asks me what our next move is. I can hear the trust in her voice, the hope for a new start, and I just can't ruin it by telling her all the stupid things I've done to get into this situation. So I hug her, and we promise to work through the problem together.

Mum and I spend the next few hours hunched over our never-used dining table, discussing different ways to sort things out, writing an outline for the VC presentation, working out what to say to keep everyone happy. Fuelled by coffee and Pot Noodle, we cut and splice words, chop and change sentences, argue back and forth about whether to un-endorse the stationery – which might mean getting sued by Paperfly – or keep our contract and deal with the backlash from disappointed fans.

'Or maybe, somehow, we can do both,' Mum says.

I grin. 'Tell me more . . .'

Eventually we have thrashed out something that's not perfect, but that both of us can live with. Mum tosses the notepad down on the shiny glass surface and leans back in her chair.

'That's it,' she says. And then she smiles at me – a wicked, impish smile that reminds me of our popcorn-frenzy, dancing-round-the-kitchen days. 'Of course, you're going to ignore most of this and do your own thing, but that's OK. I trust you to do the right thing for the channel.'

Mum looks tired when she finally slinks off to bed, but I'm still wired, full of energy. I sit on the bed and stare at my wall. And stare. And stare.

I add things up in my head, and slowly I start to see a pattern.

And then I know. I know where Frida is. And I know exactly where the files are, too.

Chapter 29

Frida

DC Riley looked at me over his glasses. His weary gaze ran up and down, checking out my hyper-floral leggings, the big baggy tequila T-shirt, which was still slightly damp from my aerial yoga efforts that morning. My hair was a fright too, so I'd twisted it out of the way and wrapped it up in an old-lady scarf with a daffodil pattern on it. I could see the thought on his face: *Oh God, not another mad teenager.*

Normally, this sort of moment would appeal to my sense of humour – I'd go full-on-Frida, put my feet up on the desk and smile sweetly. But I was still in shock, unable to believe that Xav was gone. Still shaking from the effort of hiding my horror from Maxine, wrung out with grief. And then came the call from the police. Of course it did – I was an old friend of Xav's who had fallen out with him, then reconnected on the exact day he died. My hands were shaking so I sat on them, all attempts to be bold and brazen Frida disappearing. This shit was real.

I expected him to ask me outright for my alibi, but instead he asked me to talk about Xav, and how I felt about him. I was too numb, too tired to lie and deny, so I did exactly what he asked.

I told him that after my recovery I spent two years in Xav-rehab. I deleted him from my phone, tried not to think of him, taking it one day at a time like they do in AA. I did sensible things like apply for college, work on my masks, study some other boring subjects too, so I could get a proper job sometime. I hung out with ordinary people who weren't that interesting; I even dated a few boys, a couple of girls. But his name was always in the background, thrumming like white noise at the edges of my consciousness as his fame grew. And slowly the noise began to warp and increase – not just among my classmates but on mainstream news sites, the *Daily Mail* sidebar of shame, gossip magazines, adults. Over the years, I'd heard a lot of words used to describe Xav – charming, disruptive, hilarious, dangerous even. But now I was hearing a new one. *Problematic.*

It was bound to happen sooner or later. If you told Xav he couldn't say something, he'd say it louder. Tell him he has to behave a certain way and he'd do the opposite. An army of outraged people demanding his immediate cancellation was like energy to him, filling him with the burning, crackling need to do more, go further. More stunts, more outrage, more showing off.

I created a Google Alert for his name and woke up every morning to the pings of new emails and the half-amused, half-concerned feeling of *what's he done now?*

It was none of my business, of course. I already knew from Leni that I was on Xav's Dead To Me list, right between his dad and KSI. So he should be dead to *me*, too.

But still, I found myself accessing his channel, and what I saw filled me with worry.

The time he did a live unboxing of the contents of Ed's underwear drawer, laughing at the faded boxers and mismatched socks.

The next week, after Calvin Klein had sent over that free crate of tightie-whities for Ed, he made him model them for the camera, laughing and mocking his non-existent 'love handles'.

I saw Ed's face, gaunt and sleepless, as Xav lorded it over his gang of creepy friends who cracked up at every joke.

Worst of all was the fake-proposal stunt, where he made it look like he was going to propose to Ed – filling the room with balloons, hiring a string quartet, making a big speech about how sorry he was for being a dick and how Ed completed him – then giving him an onion ring instead.

The whole world thought he was turning into a monster. Only I understood. Fame was crushing him, pushing him nearer and nearer to self-destruction. He was out of control, in trouble.

I did something I swore I'd never do again. I signed into the PlayMii app under my old name and left a message on one of his less-popular uploads.

Hey Xav, I know I'm on the DTM list but do you need these? I sketched a picture of some yellow pants and uploaded it. He must have liked the sketch because he printed it out. It appears in his murder video.

Xav always ended his videos telling his fans that he read every single comment – even ones from haters – and he often replied. Especially to the ones from haters. He could have been lying; he could have been paying someone to look at his posts and insult the trolls so he didn't have to. That's what I would have done. But still, it was my only way of getting in touch with him and I had to try.

Twenty-four hours later, a comment appeared.

Yeah maybe. Are you coming to the meet and greet on Friday half-term? See you there? If you're lucky I'll do a selfie with you 😊 *Always happy to meet my loyal fans!*

A shameful spark of excitement lit up in me, but I slapped it down. I'd have to keep this under control if I was going to help him. He needed a friend, not another worshipper, and I needed to keep my sanity. But I also couldn't say no.

Sure, why not? I replied, fake nonchalant. *And sorry no selfies, not sure your massive head would fit in shot.* 😆

I wanted to say to him: *I've changed. I'm not your flunky any more*, but he'd have to figure that out for himself.

I spent Friday morning in my room, music cranked up to maximum and hardly able to keep in my gleeful excitement as I chose what to wear. I couldn't wait for Xav to see the real me. Frida. The woman who ignored expectations and condemnations, who fought to be her true self. I went to town even more than usual – picked my brightest Hawaiian shirt, knotted it over a full, Kahlo-ish flowered skirt that swished my legs as I walked. I slid on the resin bangles from Etsy that I'd saved for weeks to buy. I chose the pink ring because I liked the way it flashed on my pinkie finger when I made a gesture. And then the Chinese jade ring that got warm on my skin and clinked satisfyingly when I tapped it on my teeth. And then the skull one because it was my lucky ring and then the silver Claddagh and then . . . eventually I ran out of fingers. I did something ineffectual with eyeliner, shoved my book and phone into my tote bag, grabbed my coat and set off.

And bloody hell that place was *unreal*. As soon as you went in there was this surge of energy and excitement, of hundreds of people about to meet their heroes. It made me scared, short of breath. I couldn't take it.

As I wove my way through the people, a sudden whoop of excitement went up and the audience stood and raised their phones in the air, cameras primed. I looked up to see Maxine tottering out on to the stage, unsteady on her heels. At school I'd seen her as bold, mouthy and confident – probably because of how she'd swanned in and swept Leni off into a friendship, but here she looked smaller, more scared, desperate for the audience to like her. I felt a sudden rush of sympathy for her, and wondered how she was coping. But it wasn't her I'd come to see, so I rushed on to where Xav had arranged to meet me.

The shopping mall boiler room – how glamorous.

I'd only just let myself in when Xav came at me in a rush. I froze, panicking and wondering what the hell was going on, but then he was grabbing me, hugging me. I felt a tremble in his body that was almost like a sob, but I didn't hug him back, not properly. My arms stayed stiff and impersonal around his shoulders.

'I'm sorry I was an arse. I told myself if I just ghosted you, we could both move on when really I was just making it easier for myself. It was a dick move.' He pushed his hands through his hair in that Xav way of his. 'I've missed you, Samalam.'

I drew back from his embrace, surprised by my own self-discipline. Three years ago I'd have been a trembling mass of desire. *Maybe I really can handle this . . .*

'I go by Frida now,' I said, plonking myself down on a box of industrial-strength toilet cleaner, arranging the skirt over my knees.

'Well, you look good,' he said, and I gave him a dignified nod. My hands were shaking, so I clasped them together on my lap. I still wasn't immune to him – the attraction was there, like a magnet buried deep in my guts, pulling towards him. But I knew that when he said *good*, he didn't mean *goooooood*. I understood that now. And why waste love on someone who doesn't love you back?

'Enough of that,' I told him, waving my hand from side to side, seeing his eyes follow the rings. 'I know you, and something's going on. I've watched you do a string of really stupid things over the past few months and I've got a feeling you're not done.'

Xav stared at me, his brows furrowed, his expression serious – which meant he was definitely not serious. Slowly, a smile spread across his face. It was that same grin he'd had on that time we'd snuck into his dad's potting shed and set fire to his ashtray, the time we'd slipped porn mags into all the fishing journals at the newsagents. His wicked, dangerous, let's-destroy-everything smile.

'And you'd be right,' he said. 'I'm not done.' He laid it out then, these files he had, the way he'd collected dirt on pretty much everyone and wanted to burn down the whole hypo-critical, fake world of influencers. As I listened, I felt some-thing flicker to life in me – that need to destroy, to create havoc that I'd felt before. Only this time, it wasn't driven by anger or a need to prove myself, or even a desire to get close to Xav again. It was just the sheer, irresistible joy of breaking stuff that deserves to be broken.

'I'm sitting on something huge, too', he continued. 'Something that's going to blow your mind. I'll tell you later, when there's more time. Because it's ... not good.' For a moment he looked troubled, then he shrugged it off. 'So what do you think, old partner in crime? Are you in?'

'You realise you'll be trashing your career and burning bridges with all your friends?'

'Yup.'

'And you're OK with that?'

'A-O-fucking-K.'

'All right then, I'm in.'

Detective Riley glared at me.

'So, Xavier was planning to blackmail his fellow – ahem – "PlayMeeps"?'

I suppressed a giggle. I could tell that even saying the word PlayMeep was giving the detective physical pain.

'It's not blackmail,' I said. 'He never planned to threaten anybody or make them pay him. He was just going to make some facts public. He wasn't doing anything illegal; he just wanted to do a series of exposés like a newspaper would, although probably ruder.'

'And did he tell you where he kept these files?'

I shrugged and shook my head. 'Just that they were stored somewhere remotely. He said he accessed them via a secret passage, but I don't think he meant a literal one – it was probably something techy. Xav was good with computers.'

'And what was your role in all this?'

'Honestly? I think he wanted an audience and someone who'd still be speaking to him when it was all over. He was going to fill me in on the specifics later.'

'What else did you talk about after that?'

I shrugged. 'Old times, school stuff, gossip about Leni and Andy, an accident I had at school. We only really chatted for about fifteen minutes in the end, then he was off back to the green room and his little gang of groupies.'

I didn't think I needed to tell the detective what happened next.

I came out of that boiler room feeling weird and overwhelmed after seeing Xav again, and at first, I didn't feel like the old me. I didn't feel weak or pathetic or even a bit in love with him. Just happy, full of joy that I had my friend back. My brilliant friend.

My secret friend.

Who met me in the boiler room. In secret.

Come on, Frida, he has his reasons. He couldn't go blabbing about those files in public and he'd get mobbed if he'd met you in a cafe.

But still. I could feel the unease building in my belly.

I forced those old feelings back. *I'm over this. I'm better than this.*

I wandered through the grubby, samey corridors behind the scenes of the mall, until I found a fire exit, a sunny spot and some steps to sit on with my book. A chance to get back on an even keel after seeing Xav.

About twenty minutes later, the fire doors behind me banged open and shut again, and there was Maxine. And everything changed again.

Chapter 30

Maxine

I'm awake at first light, staring at a patch of sunlight making pretty shadows with the blobby designer lampshade on my ceiling, which now has homemade bunting hanging off it. I haven't slept much; I was too busy lying there making plans. I check my phone. Ed's responded, saying he'll come with me. Phew – I'm not going to be alone in this. I'm also going to need his technical skills.

It doesn't take me long to get dressed. By my calculation, I can get across to Lewisham then back home to change in time to leave for VC, so I shove on a pair of old cutdown tracky bottoms that I use as shorts and a faded plain T-shirt that I usually sleep in. I'm comfy. I'm good to go. I'm out of the door and in the back of the car before I realise that I haven't put any make-up on.

The day is already heating up when Ed slides into the seat next to me.

'Are you sure about this?' he says. 'I checked the other day and there was no answer.'

I feel a wave of uncertainty, but I nod because the alternative is too horrible. The alternative is that The Face has her.

The street looks every bit as dilapidated as the last time I walked down it, arm in arm with my lovely new friend. I remember now the way her hand tensed in the crook of my elbow as we rounded the corner, the way her head ducked down, shoulders hunched in a posture I'd never seen her in before, mouth clamped shut as I vented away about my south London days. At the time, I thought she was just echoing the tension I was feeling. Now I know that she was shrinking back into Sam's life, Sam's feelings. I kind of get why she hid it from me. I'm still angry, but I get it.

Here's her house. The front yard is scruffy; the wheelie-bins are crammed full of stuff – the recycling is full of old magazines and cardboard boxes, the other bin overflowing with odd scraps of wood, plastic and metal, and bin bags full of slimy kitchen waste warming in the morning sun. The smell makes me gag. I can see a light inside – at least some-one's up. It's 7 a.m. on a Saturday morning so that was never going to be guaranteed.

I press the bell, but Ed shakes his head. 'Doesn't work.' So I rattle the letterbox.

Inside, all is still. I crouch down and call through.

'Frida! Frida, it's Maxine. If someone's in there, can you open up? I just . . . I just want to know you're OK.'

A shadow moves in the doorway. It's dressed in dark brown clothes, so definitely not Frida. The door opens a crack and an old man pokes his head out.

No, he's not that old. He's just got one of those very, very tired faces, like he's been through a lot. And the moment he speaks, I recognise his voice. It's the guy from the funeral, the one who told me about the tiny coffin. And another desperately sad piece of Frida's puzzle slips into place.

'Kerri doesn't want to see anyone,' he says. 'But if you're Maxine, I think you should come in.'

He pulls the door open with difficulty and Ed and I step inside, into a hallway in chaos – the floor is covered in scraps of paper, bits of string. A dusty ball of bright yellow wool has unravelled and rolled across the floor.

I glance at the man and see his downcast eyes, a flicker of shame.

'We're having a clear-out,' is all he says, so we keep our expressions neutral and follow him.

The sitting room smells of stale curry and it's so stacked up with boxes, the bright sunlight from outside barely makes it in. In the half-light, through the stacks, I see her kneeling on the floor. She's wearing the flowered skirt again, and it fans out around her, blending in with the papers she's sorting through. One hand is just about to feed a page into a shredder when she looks up, sees me.

I don't know how to feel. Anger, betrayal, worry and fear, mixed with the spark of happiness I get when she looks up at me and smiles.

Then her face clouds. She's afraid of what I'm going to think, what I'm going to do.

And all the angry stuff I was going to say to her just floats away, just like that. I realise I don't want to scream at her or punish her. I just want to understand. And maybe, if it feels right, be friends again.

'Frida, you idiot.' My voice cracks as the words come out and I swallow hard. I am not going to cry, not now.

She laughs, a shy, nervous laugh as she gets to her feet. I can tell she's surprised – she was expecting to have to defend herself, to come out fighting. She shrugs, eyes full of regret as she speaks.

'I'm not the person you thought I was.'

'I think you are,' I say. 'I just didn't know the backstory.'

There's a hug, a strange, awkward Frida-like hug, and then we laugh at the weirdness, then Ed laughs too.

Frida's dad brings us tea, which, having glimpsed his kitchen, I am definitely not going to drink, and then it's time for answers. I have so many questions – about why she lied, how she changed so much since school, how she managed to get Ed so firmly on side. But my instinct is telling me to ask something else, and I'm learning to listen to it.

'Why did you run and hide after the party? Ed thought . . . well, we both thought something had happened to you. Something bad.'

'I didn't realise that social thing you talked about was going to be full of PlayMeeps – I thought it was just a bar review or something, but there were so many people . . .' She trails off. 'That's not true. Well, it's true in part. But I don't think you'll believe the real answer. I left because of the way Andy looked when he recognised me. I begged them both not to tell you, to let me tell you myself, same as I did with Ed, but there was something in his eyes – a cross between fear and panic and ... I don't know, something weird and threatening.'

I'm gaping, unable to respond. *Andy?* This must be some kind of mistake – Andy's about as threatening as a slap in the face with a teddy bear. But Frida's still talking.

'You see, I've been thinking a lot about the last time I saw Xav, about the questions he asked. He asked if I remembered much about the night I fell, kept asking what made me lose my grip. I could have fallen at any time – the school flagpole was rusty, I was clumsy and stupid and running on adrenaline. But I really thought I was safe and then there was this shadow, something in the corner of my eye and then I was just ... knocked off balance. At the time I thought I imagined it, but maybe there was someone with me on the roof that night.'

'You were pushed?' Ed's voice is faint with shock and disbelief.

'I don't know.' Frida's voice is filled with frustration. 'I mean, why would anyone do that to me? Sure, I'd been messing with you guys a bit, but they were only silly pranks.'

A stack of inexplicable incidents from school suddenly click into place. My phone. The bent wire in the mask. My shoes – *ew, my shoes!*

Frida's eyes flicker downwards. 'Not my proudest moment. Then at the party I smashed the Alex mask and there was this expression on his face, a look of fury and hatred. I didn't really take it on board at the time – I was too busy hating Xav – but it was really intense.'

'Come on, though. He wouldn't have pushed you off for that, surely?'

'But . . . I've been thinking of this over the past four days. What if he figured I was the one who took your phone and spread rumours about him and his ex? He was pretty obsessed with Leni by then. Maybe he was angry about that?'

Obsession. Ed and I lean back – we both feel how much that word makes sense. Those lovey-dovey barf-inducing videos they make together. The way he looks at her, touches her all the time, like he can't bear to be separate from her. We've always joked about how whipped Andy is, how completely enthralled he is by Leni, but what if it's the other way around – what if he's controlling her? I think of how Leni's been looking so tense and tired. *Has she been keeping his secret?*

I shake my head, shake the thought away. The idea that my friend is being abused, that Andy, dopey soppy Andy, could do something like that.

'I think Xav suspected it,' Frida goes on. 'He said a few things when we last met which made me think he had some kind of proof in those files of his. And so I ran, I ignored your messages, Ed, in case you told Andy where I was. I don't know why I came here but . . . I guess I feel safer with Dad, somehow.

'I know Andy didn't kill Xav, though,' she continues. 'He and Leni did that live stream that night, remember? They were at home the whole time.'

Ed groans. 'But you *can* fake a live stream, it's easy! Me and Xav used to do it all the time. You just need a bit of third-party software. You can even make it look more realistic by programming fake user comments to pop up on the feed for you to answer.'

I sink back on to the chair, silent. It hadn't even occurred to me to suspect Leni's live was fake. She was such a perfectionist, so upfront with her fans, and faking a live is seen as bad form. Or maybe this is why I never got as big as the rest of them – I'd just never want to lie like that. I guess I'm stupid after all. *So maybe I'm wrong about Andy, too.*

Frida's still talking, saying sorry for running out on me. I should be listening, but I'm not. My head is full of clashing, conflicting thoughts – the sheer horror that Andy could push Frida off the roof, then swan into school and carry on behaving like a normal person. It just wasn't possible. *But then . . . but then . . .*

Bits of the puzzle are clicking together in my brain now, dots connecting, faster and faster. *So this is what being smart feels like.*

I'm thinking about what Xav said to me that day. *Time to burn it all down.*

I'm thinking about what Ethan said. *He'd asked someone else to murder him, someone funnier.* What could be funnier than the boyfriend of his frenemy and rival PlayMeep, Leni_loves?

I'm thinking about the AlexMalex email address – why pick that name if it meant nothing? Andy loved being Alex, loved the security of that mask.

And I'm thinking, what if Andy pushed Frida and Xav had proof of what he had done?

Which leads me back to the burn files. Again. And the theory I had come up with in the early hours of this morning while I was trying to sleep.

'I know where the burn files are,' I say. Frida trails off, shocked, and I realise that she was in the middle of a big, elaborate and well-rehearsed apology for lying. I shrug it off like it's nothing. It *is* nothing; it doesn't matter. 'I've got them. They're on my computer.'

When we came into Frida's dad's place, I'd dropped my tote bag on a pile of old shoes by the door. Now I go back and get it, pulling my laptop out and starting it up. Frida and Ed follow me, jaws open in shock, while I talk.

'So, everyone knows that Xav was brilliant at computers, right?'

Frida and Ed both nod.

'Well, Xav always used to help me when I had computer issues and, after a while, because he was so busy being famous and successful, he set up this remote access thing so that he could nip in and tinker around with it, without me having to bring it round to him every time, which means . . .'

Ed's sitting bolt upright now, like a spark of insight has hit him between the eyes. 'He created a compromised DLL or system library that allows remote access via a shell! That way he just shells into the system whenever he wants to access the files!'

'Um, yeah, what he said,' Frida adds.

'That's right . . . I think?' I say. 'In English, I reckon he's just hidden the files in one of those weird system folders nobody ever looks in. I had a poke around last night but didn't know where to start. Ed, I was wondering . . .'

Ed is reaching forward and I hand him my laptop. There's a long, agonising few minutes of rapid keyboard tapping. Frida and I watch awkwardly while Ed mutters about .dll files, until . . .

'It's here, in WinSxS. He's just got rid of all the file extension letters and . . . I think he's used the initials of people's nicknames,' Ed says. 'There's tons of them, but they're all password protected.'

'Xavistheking,' we all say. We try a few different variations and eventually xav1sDk!ng works. And hey presto. Open sesame. There they are. The files Xav died for, the dirt on every single influencer who ever crossed him. There are so many videos in there, each labelled with a nickname. It's no wonder my computer was so slow and crap.

Ed looks up at me, his eyes serious.

'Maxine,' Ed says, 'there's one here marked MP.'

Maxi-Pad. I nod. I was expecting that. 'Might as well start with that one.'

We click, and there it is, his big, lovely, narcissistic face smiling at us all. Frida bites her lip. Ed's fingers tremble on the keyboard.

'Welcome, friends, to Wile E. Coyote TV. Which creator's career will we blow up with dynamite or drop off a cliff today?'

Frida's hand flies up to her mouth. 'He watched it,' she says. 'He *saw*.'

Whatever it is matters to her a lot. But I'm just staring now, as a thumbnail of me appears behind him on-screen. 'So, you think she's all air-headed sweetness and light? There's more to Maxine than meets the eye. Which of her supposedly close friends do you think she might be imitating here?' It cuts to the video of me, jumping around in a fright wig and terrible make-up, saying, 'Ooh I'm such a busy, successful, inspiring person, buy my new fifty shades of blue make-up palette . . .'

A splutter of laughter comes from Ed. 'She would have *killed* you.'

'Or Andy would,' says Frida.

And then we're back to now. To the weird, unbelievable reality.

Now is the right time to tell the whole story. To tell Ed and Frida about the emails from Alex Malex, that I was to blame for Ed's attack. But just as I'm looking for the words, my phone rings: old school, voice-call rings. Which means it's Mum.

'Where are you?' she says. 'It's ten a.m.! You've got to be onstage at VC in an hour.'

I go cold. '*Ohhhh shit.*'

Ed and Frida, who are trawling through the rest of the files together, look up at me.

'I have to get to VC.' It's the last thing I want to do, but thousands of people have bought tickets. They're expecting a witty chat, some crappy stationery and a chance to get a selfie with me, and if I don't show they will not be impressed. There is no acceptable excuse for missing VlogCon after promising you'll be there.

Frida's looking at me like I'm mad, but Ed knows the score. 'Do you have a change of clothes? Make-up?'

I shake my head. I can't believe I thought I'd be able to dash here and back and change before lunchtime. Classic Maxine.

'You can borrow this.' Frida holds out a stick of crusty mascara that looks like it's been at the bottom of her bag for months.

I shake my head, my fingers working fast on my phone, ordering a car. 'It's OK, I can make it. And when I'm there, I can talk to Leni, clear this whole thing up.'

'You can't,' Ed says, just as Frida blurts, 'It's not safe!'

'Seriously, call the cops,' Ed adds. 'And that's not something I'd say every day.'

But how can we be sure? Frida's vague recollection and my emails aren't going to convince anyone, and besides, I'm still not a hundred percent sure he's a killer. I need to see Leni's face when I ask her the question. Then I'll know. I get up and shove my laptop back into the tote bag with one hand, while ordering the car with the other.

'If you're going to be like that, we're coming with you,' Frida says.

And so that's how it is. The three of us cram into the sweltering car with me in the middle, the laptop burning hot on my bare knees as we search through the files.

'I can't find Andy's,' I say. 'He didn't really have that many nicknames for him so maybe he's filed it under Leni. Let's see . . . Lenster, Leni-Loony, Nellie the Elephant . . .'

'God, Xav was such a little shit, wasn't he?' Frida sighs. Her voice, even now, isn't entirely disapproving. It sets me off balance, this half-Frida, half-Sam reaction.

'Have you tried anime-niac?' Ed puts in.

'No.' I suddenly realise what to look for. 'It'll be Elesnore.' The nickname she hated most. And there it is: ELSNR.

Just as I'm about to click on it, the car lurches. The driver has slammed on the brakes.

'Sorry about that,' he says. 'Bloody hell, heatwaves always bring out the crazies!'

We look up and . . . whoa. We're about a hundred metres from the conference centre and the street is swarming with people, with *protesters*. They're sweating in the mid-morning heat, holding banners, shouting. Some of them look like the fans I meet on a day-to-day basis; others look like they're along for the ride, angry and looking for trouble. I notice one with a handmade banner that says XAV KILLED 4 LIKES; another holds a tatty piece of cardboard daubed with PLAYMII = MURDERERS; another JUSTICE 4 XAVVVVV. Police are moving through the crowd, sweating in high-vis and stab vests. I can hear shouts for justice, shouts about conspiracy, about the police messing things up. Anger fills the air, thick and choking in the heat.

'Oh, you're having a laugh! Why are they stretching cling film across the street?' the driver says, shaking his head in young-people-these-days disbelief.

Outside, a group of protesters argues with a police officer, who is trying to pull a length of cling film off a nearby lamp post to get the traffic moving again. The three of us watch, slack jawed.

'Who needs the burn files?' Frida says, her voice edged in awe. 'This is exactly the kind of mayhem Xav wanted.'

People are wild with grief and sadness, whipped up into a frenzy by conspiracy theories, scared creators like Jace D and secret groups like Facehunters. And me. Because maybe the FU contributed too. They need somebody to blame and, like Ola said, they followed the money.

'I don't think I can get you any closer than this,' the driver says. 'Not if you're in a hurry.'

We thank him and pile out, I fold the laptop back into my bag as I go, and we run through the heat and the crowds, pushing our way, fighting to stay together and keeping our heads down. I pull my sweat-frizzy hair out of its ponytail and forward over my face, hunching my shoulders. For the first time today I'm grateful I look a mess – hopefully nobody will recognise me.

For the past few years, since I've been appearing as a creator rather than attending as a fan, I've gone straight into the underground car park in a cab – quick, easy and discreet. But on foot, I have no idea how to make it to the VIP entrance. We brave the main hall, a sea of bodies pressed in together, waving tickets, weaving through queues, taking selfies with their friends. The hum and buzz of voices fills the air, electric with excitement.

And then, with stab of horror I see a crowd of people strutting through the doors wearing The Face masks. I suppose they think it's some kind of joke, performance art, some sick stunt. Security is already all over them, but still, my heart is slamming in my chest. There are just too many people; there's too much weirdness.

'This is *horrible*,' Frida breathes. I link my hand in hers, my other in Ed's, squeezing tight. We have to stay together.

Ed points at a door marked *office*. We could take shelter there, to get directions to the green room where Leni and the others will be waiting. Just as we move towards it, a voice shouts.

'It's Ed! Over there! Come on!' There's a change in the mood of the crowd. I feel, rather than see, the heads turn in our direction, feel their attention focused, laser-sharp, on us. We break into a run.

We don't look back, just run and dodge and push. We duck past a security officer, through the door, and shut it hard. Frida leans back on it, but luckily nobody tries to force it open.

We're breathless, panicked. They probably just wanted selfies and a chat, but the protests, The Face masks, the heat and the angry mood have spooked us. When we're finally calm enough to look around the room, we see a woman with short grey hair and half-moon glasses sitting behind the desk, sipping coffee, looking like she's seen it all before. I explain who we are, and she directs us down a corridor and to the left, to where the green room is.

No sooner am I through the VIP door than Mum is on me, grabbing me by the shoulders.

'Oh, Maxine, I was so worried.' She pulls me into a hug. I feel a stab of my old sulkiness – *doesn't she trust me?* But then she goes on. 'I knew you wouldn't miss this for no reason, so I thought you were in trouble.'

After a few minutes telling her I'm OK and listening to her panicky reaction to what I'm wearing, runners appear all around me with clipboards and schedules, overriding Mum's protest that I just need five minutes to change. I'm already late. I'm swept out of the door, fitted with a mic and pulled by the sheer force of the organisers' panic to the side of the stage.

And then, yet again, I'm out in front of glaring lights.

My flip-flops squeak on the stage floor as I walk to the middle. It's different this time. I'm not worried about the faces looking up at me, the ocean of phones swaying, filming my every move. I realise I've been scared of something bigger, something darker now for months, that has blown my every-day PlayMeep fears out of the water.

The crowd has gone quiet, expectant. There's a more serious vibe than there was last time I was on stage, and then I realise why. They're wondering why I'm standing in front of them in shorts, flip-flops and no make-up. I'm also still clinging to the grubby tote bag with my laptop in it, hugging it tight to my chest.

'I . . .' Now the panic comes. I can't remember a single word of the speech Mum and I worked out. It's just gone. There's a flicker from the screen behind me and I glance at it – a montage of Maxine moments, cut together with pictures of pens, pads and the rest of my tat. This is why I'm here. This is what I need to talk about. My grip on the laptop tightens; I can feel the sweat from my hand soaking into the bag. I have no defences, no leopard look to hide behind, no clever cuts or screen wipes to jazz up the performance. This is just me.

'So,' I say. 'Stationery. Hands up who wants me to talk about stationery?'

A forest of hands goes up in the air, a few excited whoops. A smattering of boos. I can still do it if I want, still get my mind back on track and try to flog some pencils and note-pads. But instead, another question comes out of my mouth.

'Hands up who wants me to talk about Xav?'

A murmur of approval. Even more hands go up. 'Xav is the King!' someone squeals from the back, and the crowd laughs nervously.

'OK. Now, hands up who wants me to tell them where the burn files are?'

This time, there's a roar, a scream that fills the room, and when it hits me, it forces me to take a step back. It should terrify me but somehow instead it gives me this connection, this energy that makes me brave. The Face can't get to me here. My friends and mum are safe, standing in the wings nearby. For the past few months, I've been holding back, scared of saying the wrong thing, upsetting the wrong people. I've been trying to sort this myself without trusting my own instincts. But that didn't work, did it? Not because I'm stupid, but because I was alone. We're Generation Z and we don't solve problems by sitting alone obsessing; we talk to our fam. We work it out together.

And so, I tell them. The whole freaking story, from the beginning. I tell them how I joined an online sleuthing group, how I found the Alex email address, how The Face tried to threaten me.

'So . . . it was my fault that Ed was attacked. The Face did it to show me he was serious.' I glance at the sidelines, see Ed's stricken expression. All the apologies in the world won't make this one better, but I say it anyway. 'I'm sorry, Ed.' I turn back to the crowd, so I don't have to see his shock and anger.

I don't tell them about suspecting Andy – it's too soon for that and I don't want to start a witch-hunt. But I talk about how, together with some good friends, we figured out where the files were and how to access them.

'So, basically, they've been on my computer all along.' I shrug, and climb up on to the high stool, just to be more comfortable. 'And now I have to decide. Do I give them to The Face? Give them to the police? Or just do what Xav wanted and put them out there for all to see? I know what you guys will want. You want the dirt, don't you?'

A roar of approval. The sound vibrates through the air; I can feel it vibrate up through the legs of the stool. I wait a moment for it to die down.

'But just think about this, though. We try to share our lives as much as we can. You've seen our nights out, our nights in, our underwear, our zits, what kind of toilet paper we buy. But every human needs secrets, silly mistakes we've made that we've tried to move on from. Sometimes it's an embarrassing outfit, or a badly-worded tweet, sometimes it's feelings that are perfectly natural, but which we're not proud of. Even your best friend is allowed to keep a little bit of themselves private from you, right?

'I'll tell you what my burn file is right now. It's a video of me mouthing off about Leni one time, when I was feeling jealous of her mega-success. It's stupid, I know it is, and I'm not proud of it, but it's also natural for people to feel like this sometimes and healthier if we keep some of those uglier feelings to ourselves.

'So, although I know it's what Xav wanted, I won't be making the files public, and I definitely won't be handing them over to the sick fuck that killed my friend. I'm going straight to the police as soon as I get off this stage and they can make the next move.'

For the first time, I glance to the side of the stage and see Mum staring at me, her hand clamped over her mouth in horror as she realises everything that I've been keeping from her, everything she's been too distracted to see.

The crowd is roaring and whooping as I clamber off my high stool. They're ecstatic – I guess you would be if you were expecting some waffle about overpriced stationery and got a murder-explainer instead. They're stamping their feet, screaming for more, but I have nothing left to give. My legs are two sticks of jelly, barely holding me upright as I stagger off stage.

I look around for Ed and Frida, but with a stab of sadness I realise they're gone. *Ed's angry ... I can hardly blame him.*

Mum and a random show-runner are holding me up now. Without them I'd be a puddle of exhaustion on the floor. My ears are still ringing from the roar of the crowd, which is stamping and chanting my name. *MaxINE . . . MaxINE . . .*

'I need space,' I manage to pant.

The runner speaks into her walkie-talkie, static talks back, and then she puts on a big fake beam of a smile. 'I've found the perfect place for you – it's the VIP room the queen used when she came here!'

She looks at me expectantly, like I'm going to say *oooh*, but I just nod vaguely at her, and she and Mum whisk me along the corridors. I don't even feel my legs moving. It's like I'm being pushed on smooth, caring rails.

The VIP room is tiny but carpeted and wallpapered – old-school luxury. There's even a comfy sofa and a little coffee table in the corner.

'Oooh,' Mum says drily. 'Look over there, the queen's en suite toilet!'

'Mum . . . I'm sorry, but can I be alone for a bit? Please? I just need a minute to breathe. I'll meet you in the green room.'

She looks horrified, about to protest, but she can see I'm serious. Once she's made sure I'm not going to faint, she retreats. 'Take as long as you like,' she says. 'We'll call the police as soon as you're ready.'

I nod. I'm incapable of speech, all out of words. She hesitates at the doorway and then leaves.

I go into the queen's toilet, lock the door and sit down on the closed seat.

And breathe.

Breathe.

Feel the air going into my nose, feel it come out again.

Remember what Leni said? All that mindfulness stuff really does work if you do it right. But now, of course, I'm thinking about Leni, and then Andy, and then my heart is thud-thud-thudding again. There's something else about our theory, something I'm missing that makes me think we haven't quite got the whole story, but my head is too full, my brain shouting too many panicky messages at me to think clearly.

I pull the laptop out of the bag again and flip it open. The burn files folder is still open on the screen. I find Leni's video and click play.

Chapter 31

Ed

I take the can and down its contents, sticky sweet cough medicine with bubbles. I don't care what it tastes like; I just want the can to be empty. Now I crush it in my hand, squeezing it down to a twisted wad of metal, digging into my hand. I throw it across the floor, where it skitters under a chair, and I look for another one. Frida gazes at me coolly and without judgement.

The reason that Frida and I get on so well now is that she gets the anger side of things. When Xav and I split up, everyone else wanted me to play the victim – poor boy, broken child, controlled by an egomaniac, had his heart broken on a live stream. It's easier to root for someone who acts the martyr, who turns the other cheek. But Frida understood the need to fight back. She told me the lengths she used to go to to vent her frustration at the way Xav made her feel. And she gets it now, too, because Maxine lied to us both.

We're in the packed green room, hiding behind a giant cardboard cut-out of Jace D and downing cans of Caveman, the free energy drinks provided by the sponsor. I'm not satisfied by crushing cans – I want to smash something bigger, something louder.

'I know, me too,' Frida says. 'Right now, the only thing stopping me from putting shit in her shoes again is the fact that I lied too. It's like the two betrayals have cancelled each other out.'

'Fucking hell, Frida. She ... she was *talking to him*. To that *thing*.' My words gush out, spinning the wheres and the whys and the WTFs.

Frida repeats the same words over and over: 'She should have told us. Why didn't she tell us?'

Because of her I was in hospital on morphine, having baby-head hallucinations, torn up with confusion. Because of her some bastard threw me down on a bed and punched me, and kept punching.

It's then I remember the detail, the memory of Xav's signature scent wafting over me with each blow. It had come at me like a ghost, confused me, slowed my reactions. It was designed to throw me off, to make me less likely to realise I knew my attacker. Because I wasn't just attacked by some bastard, I was beaten by a guy I'd been to school with, someone I'd called a friend, who I trusted.

A guy who had also been terrorising Maxine, controlling her.

I feel sick.

I sense Frida tensing by my side and look up. The atmosphere in the room has changed. Before, it had been buzzing, alive with dozens of influencers and execs laughing, striking poses and throwing stuff, all jacked up on excitement, nerves and unlimited supplies of Caveman. Now it's fallen silent.

Everyone is watching the live feed of Maxine's talk, which is being beamed out through the event's official PlayMii channel on to wall-mounted screens. Over everyone's heads I can just about see this tiny, isolated little figure in tatty shorts, holding a laptop over her head in defiance.

But that's not what Frida's staring at. She's looking past the crowd to the doorway. She's looking at *him*.

Andy and Leni are standing near the entrance to the green room, gazing at the screen like everyone else. Their hands are intertwined as usual, but I can see how tight his grip is on her; his knuckles are white. He turns to look down at her, an expression of utter panic in his eyes.

We both start to move forward, then hesitate at the same time, but I can tell by the snarl on Frida's face that she's spoiling for a fight as much as I am.

Andy is whispering something to Leni now, his face fierce, twisted with rage. Leni shrinks back a little and, although I can't see her face, I realise Maxine's theory must be right – Andy is a monster, just like Xav's dad – controlling and brutal.

As one, Frida and I step back behind the cardboard cut-out. I'm shaking. By now I can't tell whether it's anger or fear. Frida is almost jumping up and down, her body humming with pent-up energy and rage.

'I'm going to walk over there and punch him in the nuts,' she snarls. 'I don't give a shit about his taekwondo or whatever. I'll do it.'

'Wait.' I grab her arm, can't believe I'm the one saying it. 'Let's think first. Maxine's coming off stage now. As soon as she rocks up in here, he's going to be on her, trying to get that laptop. That's why he's waiting by the door. But he doesn't know we know about him. As soon as she gets here, we can run interference, keep him away from her until the cops get here.'

'And then I kick him in the balls.'

'Then you can kick him in the balls. I will personally hold him down for you.'

By this time, the live feed has ended, and cut to a much less interesting panel discussion on cookery. The Caveman-fuelled crowed is moving around now, buzzing with caffeine and gossip and shock. A couple of quick-thinking PlayMeeps are already recording their reactions – either claiming total extreme surprise or total extreme lack of surprise, saying they expected it, saying they always thought Maxine was mixed up in it somehow. PlayMeeps do love to be ahead of the curve. Frida calls the police – although it might take them a while to get in here as the protests outside are getting more intense. Through the green-room windows, we can hear the shouting getting louder.

Frida and I push through the confusion towards the door, hoping to get to Maxine before Andy does, but when we emerge, there's still no sign of her.

'She should be here by now.' Frida's voice is uneasy. 'Maybe she's talking to the police already . . .' But then her voice trails off.

Shit.

Frida says it before I have a chance to. 'He's gone. Andy. He's gone to find her.'

Chapter 32

Maxine

I click on ELSNR and, as I do, I notice the date. It was added to the folder less than a week before Xav died.

Wile E. Coyote TV starts up again and, this time, Xav isn't goofing around in the first shot. His voice is serious, normal, as if he's just talking to a person sitting opposite him rather than a PlayMii audience.

'I've been friends with Leni_loves and her boyfriend Andy since school. We made our first videos together, we've traded PlayMii tips and insults, and even though we've had beef the past few years, it was never serious. I love those guys, and I wish them well.

'Or at least, I did. Until I learned what Andy has done . . .'

Up until this point, I'd been hoping Xav would start talking about something else, some old problematic quote he's dug up from before Andy knew better, but the seriousness, the anger in his eyes – I haven't seen him like that before. Everything Ed, Frida and I have put together is true.

The screen cuts to a grainy CCTV video and, for a moment, I don't know what I'm looking at. A darkened rooftop, a rusted flagpole jutting out. *It's the top of our old school, where some of the kids used to go to smoke.* And there, a hooded figure climbing over the edge. *Oh, Frida.*

Xav's voiceover kicks in:'This is a friend of mine, from long ago, who was about to do something splendidly, magnificently crazy.'

Despite my shock, my mouth twists into a little smile. Those two were as bad as each other – it's so obvious why they were friends.

But then there's a second figure, creeping in from the side. Hooded in black, just like Frida was. With a surge of recognition, I see the movement, the soft, graceful tread of someone trained in martial arts. The figure glances over their shoulder and for an instant I see a face. It's quick, but probably enough for police to freeze-frame and magnify. I don't need to. I know it's Andy.

Another creak of the door pulls my attention away from the screen. Footsteps across the floor just outside. I slam the volume on mute instinctively, and wait for the person to say something, to tap on the door. But there's nothing.

Looking down, I see the shadow of two feet through the crack under the door.

'Hello?' My voice echoes off the expensive tiles.'Mum?'

'It's me, Leni.' Her voice sounds scared, trembling. I get to my feet. My hand lingers on the lock, but I hesitate.

'Are you all right in there, Max?' she asks. 'I heard your speech. I can't believe all this was happening to you – I'm so sorry you couldn't tell me. Max?'

I still hesitate. Maybe she doesn't know. Or maybe she's too scared of Andy to step out of line.

'Come on, Len.' It's Andy's voice, last heard doing impressions of Taylor Swift with a mouthful of tofu chow mein. Now he sounds harsh and mocking. 'She's worked it out. That's why she's hiding in there. Let's be honest, we owe it to her not to pretend. Maxine, we can open that door by unscrewing the lock from the outside. You might as well just come out now. We're not planning to stab you or anything.'

We. Not I. *We.* It's true: Leni knows.

Leni knows and she's standing by him.

I can't think about that now. Can't let myself feel the betrayal. They want the video, they'll stop at nothing to get it and here I am, helpless, trapped in this cubicle.

But . . .

A thought occurs to me, the beginning of a plan. I crouch down on the floor and my fingers fly over the computer keys. I'm not thinking about the consequences of what I'm doing, but my hands are trembling and the blood is pounding in my head. Deep down I can hear Mum's voice, saying words like 'stupid' and 'irresponsible' and 'dangerous'. I can also hear Frida chanting: 'Do it! Do it!'

Time. I need time. I hear the scrape of the lock and the door flies open, pushing me back further into the cubicle, trapping me there. I click on one last button, then snap the lid on my laptop shut and cradle it to my chest. It hums there, quietly, still doing its thing. It had better bloody hurry up.

Andy looks down at me and laughs – a hoarse, dry *hah* I've never heard from him before. He enjoys this. He enjoys looking down on me, seeing me scared. A grin flashes on his face.

'Yep, she's got it,' he calls over his shoulder. He reaches in and pulls the laptop out of my weak, feeble hands.

'Sorry about this, Maxine. We didn't have much choice after your presentation earlier. The police will be expecting you to hand the files in, so we need to swap ours out before you do that. I've got a bit of software that will purge it completely from your laptop, leaving no trace.'

I struggle to my feet, my legs still weak and shaky, my body now so full of fight or flight adrenaline that I'm dizzy with it. In the VIP room outside, Leni stands near the door with one perfectly manicured hand on the lock.

Today, Leni's hair is the colour of fire – red, orange and gold ombré, and her silk slip dress is blood-crimson. Her nails are sharp with steel-coloured tips. Gone is the wide-eyed Bambi from school, the startled anime girl, the mermaid in blue water. But her elfin face shines with fear and worry, and she rushes towards me.

'Oh Maxine,' she says. I freeze in horror as she throws her arms around me, folding me into that familiar cloud of products and scent. 'I wanted to tell you, I really wanted to. It's been so horrible.'

I still can't understand what's going on, but I whisper in her ear: 'Leni, is he making you do this? I can help you.'

She pulls back from me; an expression of confusion flits across her face. 'What do you mean, is he making me?'

Andy bursts out a shout of laughter. 'I bloody wish,' he says, as if we're sitting back at their flat making couples in-jokes. 'Can't make this woman do anything she doesn't want to.'

It's then that the creeping, horrifying truth hits me.

'It was . . . both of you.'

I'm in shock, numb as Leni takes me by the hand, leads me to the sofa and coffee table. Andy places my laptop on the table in front of me and taps it expectantly.

The little white light on it blinks slowly. *Is it done?*

Leni sighs and runs her fingers through her hair, her nails flashing through the red. For a moment, it looks strangely crooked, and then I realise she's been wearing a wig. Of course she bloody has – nobody can change their hair colour that often without destroying it.

It makes me remember something – that niggling detail I was worrying about earlier . The person I saw at Xav's flat . . . A figure in black with close-cut hair, too small to be a man . . .

'It was you sneaking around at Xav's!' I say.

'I'm sorry I scared you.' She looks regretful. 'I got your text saying you were going there before coming to us and I panicked. I'd given Xav one of my Crimson Rush palettes and I got this mad idea in my head that if you saw it you'd figure out I'd been there. I rushed over and let myself in, thinking I'd be in and out before you even arrived – how could I guess that *you'd* get there early? Maxine, I didn't mean for any of this to happen.'

I remembered the flash of red in the figure's hand that day. I'd thought it was a phone but it could easily have been a small make-up set – and maybe if I'd ever unboxed my own sample I'd have realised. But now I'm busy adding things up in my mind, getting used to a whole new reality. 'It was you who sent me all those emails, all those threats. And you killed him. You . . . you killed Xav.'

It's crazy, but there's still a part of me that thinks maybe she's got a logical explanation for this. Some kind of accident, a game that got out of hand . . .

She echoes my thoughts with a sigh. 'Things just got out of hand. It's Xav, he just . . .' She turns to me and her eyes are almost pleading, and I realise something: she wants to explain, she wants me to understand why she did this. Like everyone else I meet, she *wants* to tell me her secrets.

'I'm listening,' I say.

Andy fidgets impatiently by the door. 'Oh come on, Leni, we haven't got time for this.'

She raises a gleaming hand and he stops. Just stops. And I realise I had the dynamic of this relationship right the first time. Leni is the one in charge.

'I just want to fix things between us,' she says, a pleading look in her eyes. 'I just want you to understand. Here, take your phone – send a message to your mum and Ed saying you're with some fans and you'll see them soon. Come on, it's been so long since we've had a chance to talk properly.'

Andy hands me my phone and I tap out a message. They're watching me – there's no way I can include some kind code for *rescue me*. But there's one way I can send a signal that Leni might not notice.

Tied up talking to bloody fans again, I write. *See you later.*

I wait to see if Leni can see the significance of what I've put, the subtle distress signal buried in a one-line message in

290

the words *bloody fans*, something I would never write. She bites her lip.

'What about the exclamation marks?' Leni asks.

She hasn't noticed. Leni really isn't the person I thought she was. I only hope that Frida and Ed know me better.

I dutifully add some exclamations, and an eye-roll emoji for good measure.

Then she settles back, feeling more comfortable, and begins to speak.

Chapter 33

Leni

Remember how the Alex Malex mask was so stuffy? And how it stank of PVA glue? You had to keep your head still, dead in the centre of it, or you couldn't see out of the eyeholes and it wobbled around on your shoulders when you made the slightest move. I know Andy loved that thing, but it was a pain in the arse.

And do you remember how I nearly had a panic attack making that greatest fears video? I just stood there, with Xav barking at me. 'Wake up, Nelly, what are you afraid of? No-make-up selfies? Chipping a nail? If your life is so damn easy, just make something up, just bullshit.'

Just bullshit. This was it, the flaw in my relationship with Xav woven into every video we made together, every conversation we had, right from the start. I wanted perfection and grace, videos people could aspire to – whether it was eye-popping stunts or flawless skin. Xav wanted chaos, bloopers, issues oozing out of us in a public display of weakness. On the first video we made, you stumbled during your twabbing thing – remember, Maxine? It looked crap and I wanted to cut it, but Xav point-blank refused.

'Nobody's perfect, so why should we pretend to be?' he'd said.

But if we weren't trying for perfection, trying to be better than the millions of other bored teens making videos in their bedrooms on Sunday afternoons, then how would we ever get anywhere? How would we ever break away from this ordinary, dreary life, become something different? It was all right for Mr Charisma to coast on his personal charm, but some of us had to try harder.

'Earth to Leni? Are you OK?' your voice cut in then. I couldn't see you through the eyeholes but you sounded anxious and concerned. 'You don't have to reveal your greatest fear if you don't want to.'

'Yes, she does, Maxamillion, otherwise the whole thing won't work.'

My greatest fear. The words were there, in my mouth waiting to burst out, but I couldn't say it, couldn't reveal my flaws to a bunch of almost-strangers and possible future rivals. I couldn't share the what-ifs that woke me up at 3 a.m., breathless with terror. The thoughts that even at that moment were bubbling up and threatening to overwhelm me.

I whispered it quietly, in the privacy of the mask. It was the first, the only time I ever said it, because saying something out loud makes it more real.

'I am afraid that I am nothing.'

The words made me clammy with panic; tears began to prickle my eyes. Because it was true – I wasn't interesting. Not one bit. I didn't have a Story. Not like Xav, who hid his bruises beneath a rainbow flag. Not like Ed, who endured sneering racism with a side-order of homophobia from class-mates, teachers, randoms in the street. Even you had your sad little Harry Potter cupboard. But if someone was to write the origin story of Eleanore Grange-Fuller you'd find a straight, white, average-looking, middle-class girl with loving, supportive parents and vaguely nice eyes. No body issues, no mental-health issues. Enough cash around to buy make-up hauls and a good phone, but not enough to make me remark-able for being rich, like Andy.

You'd find nothing.

And so, I lived happily ever after, without all the messy bits in between that make us real. Check my privilege. My privi-lege was a prison. My privilege kept me down.

I was, as Xav so often told me, dough. Soft and bland. Uncooked.

A stab of panic twisted in my mind. *What if Xav's right? What if I'm too ordinary ever to be anything? What if I'll just get a nice job and find a nice man and settle down around the corner from here, just like Mum and Dad want me to. What if nobody ever really sees me?*

The mask was stifling me – I pushed it off my head, took a gulp of clean, fresh air.

'Norma . . .' Xav began, and despite the fact he was using a hated nickname, I could hear a note of concern in his voice. Ugh. I couldn't show weakness; he'd just use it against me later – at least that's what I'd have done. I carefully put the mask down (we were all still treating that bloody mask like it was a delicate work of art) and walked off.

I got around the corner and was just at the door of Hal's Kebab, ready to ruin perfection with chips, when I heard footsteps coming after me. Heavy, running-boy footsteps.

Andy. My soppy knight in shining armour, a simpering look of concern on his face. His hand touched my shoulder lightly and my body immediately responded, hot and tingling where his fingers touched. Ugh. I hated this instinctive pull towards him. The last thing I needed was a nice, rich, blandly handsome boyfriend to make my life even happier and easier. To tempt me to settle down, and settle for less.

'What?' I snapped.

'Xav is a moron,' he said. 'And you can storm off all you like, it'll never hurt him. He likes it. I think he gets high on people's anger. But there are still ways.'

Then I saw he was holding something in his hand – Xav's grey school jumper. He took hold of one of the seams and ripped.

I snorted. What a pathetic thing to do. 'What was that for? Surely Xav won't care if his jumper is torn?'

'No but . . . put it this way. You want to punch him in the face, right?'

Yes, I did.

'Well, now his dad will do it for you.'

I stared at Andy as slowly the enormity of what he'd done sank in, and everything shifted. I was appalled. I was *fascinated*. The beige, *meh* rich kid morphed before my eyes into something wild and different. A tiny spark flared deep in my soul. I touched his hands and this time I let myself feel the heat in my fingers from the contact. It spread out through my body, a feeling like molten silver.

'You did that for me?'

'Yes.'

Different feelings whirled around in me. It was strange, and scary and wrong, but powerful – addictive, even. It made me feel like . . . more than just nothing.

That's when it began, I suppose. The game which took over our lives. We called it Don't Cross Me and the rules were simple. Firstly: if someone hurt Andy, I would take revenge, and if someone hurt me, it was up to Andy. Second: the revenge had to be as twisted and out of proportion as possible. We were selective – it didn't happen every day. But when Mr Walker tried to get Andy to drop French, I sent the head an anonymous but very convincing note saying Walker was touching up the students. It didn't go far, but he was suspended for a few weeks while they looked into it, which was quite satisfying. When Aimee Palmer called me a bug-eyed weirdo, Andy set up a fake Insta account, chatted her up for weeks, arranged a date and stood her up.

We spent a lot of time planning, choosing our targets carefully. But our most hated figure of all was the troll.

When the comments started appearing under our videos, everyone else seemed to shrug them off. Of course that's the right thing to do – we all have to put up with online hate – but there was something about them, something so sneaky and dedicated and painfully personal, that I just couldn't tolerate. This troll had gone to the trouble of setting up multiple accounts (although all the comments appeared at the same time, with the same misspellings, calling us 'priviliged'). The comments were clever, funny and spot-on and started getting quite a few likes. And it bugged me.

That same person stole your phone – remember, Maxine? Those messages nearly destroyed my relationship with Andy. He was devastated that I'd talked to you about having doubts and I felt completely humiliated and exposed. But I also realised the messages misspelled the same words as the troll's posts. It had to be the same person.

I interrogated the girl who gave you your phone back, who just said 'some boy' gave it to her. That surprised me – writing snide comments about me and Andy didn't seem like a very boyish thing to do.

Oh, Andy and I talked for hours about what we were going to do to that troll, each plan more elaborate and far-fetched than the last. And then, on the day of the flashmob video, when Xav was being particularly infuriating, I saw her. Xav's sad little friend, hovering around the edges of the crowd, idly kicking stones with her trainer in her tired and tatty gender-neutral school uniform.

Some boy.

Up until then, when I thought about Sam, I'd always felt sorry for her – dumped by Xav as soon as they got out of primary school, no friends, no discernible personality. We'd watched videos together a couple of times in geography when I was really bored, and I'd felt a lot less dull compared to her. I'd liked her – sort of. But this was unforgivable. It had to be stopped.

'Let's not be clumsy on this one,' I told Andy. 'We'll bide our time, gather information.'

And so I got close to her again, tried to find out why she'd done it, to come up with a plan. But then she stormed out of Andy's party, wrenching the mask out of his hands and smashing it. Andy loved that mask, loved the status of being Alex Malex. He was raging.

Then a few days later he turned up under my window, breathless, his eyes wild, the street lamps lighting up his triumphant grin.

'Holy shit,' he whispered. 'I just pushed Sam off the school roof.'

I slammed the window shut, heart pounding. *Oh God, oh God. Andy, you absolute fuckwit.* I mean, I wanted a good origin story, but prison was taking it a bit too far.

I opened the window again. 'Did anybody see you?'

When he got into my bedroom he was red-faced, panting, his eyes glittering. I think he was expecting gratitude, or even some action from thankful little me, but we didn't have time for that. We needed a plan.

'You total idiot! What made you do it?'

'I couldn't resist. She put something online about going off to do a stunt that was going to blow Alex Malex out of the water, so I followed her. I started off just hiding in a bush and filming her, thinking it would make a great takedown video, but then she went and climbed up the fire escape on to the roof, so I followed her up there too and there she was, nearly falling off the frickin' flagpole. When I crept up close to get a better shot she started to turn round and I panicked – I kind of lunged forward and nudged her foot off-balance ... and she just ... went. I don't think she saw me, I don't think she even felt it. It was actually kind of easy.'

I rolled my eyes. Easy to do was one thing. Easy to get away with was something else.

That next week was hell for us.

Luckily Sam survived, so no murder charge. But Andy had to tell his dad what he'd done so he could pull strings to get rid of the CCTV footage, which meant he was grounded for eternity and his mum still blames me, even now. And of course Alex Malex was over and we all came a hair's breadth from being permanently excluded.

But there was no knock on the door. No sombre-faced police officer asking difficult questions. Because it turned out Sam really had felt nothing, seen nothing. When I saw her, she even looked strangely stronger than before. I wondered if Andy had actually done her a favour.

Slowly, we started to breathe again, and to laugh. It became the standing joke between us – that time Andy took Don't Cross Me a little bit too far.

So you see, Maxine, I never meant for any of this to happen. I really didn't. And we moved on. Until Xav forced us to bring our little game back.

Chapter 34

Maxine and Leni

Maxine

Leni looks at me, studying my face. There is a line between her usually flawless brows, a slash of anxiety.

'You don't get it,' she says, squeezing her eyes tight shut. 'I thought you of all people . . .'

I've done a lot of pretending in my time – faking enthusiasm for stationery, plastering a smile on my face when I haven't slept for days. It's not something I like doing but right now my life depends on it. I try to keep my face straight, try not to let the shock at my friend's words show. The way she sees the world – it's all about her. All the lovely compassionate things she's said about Xav since he died, it's all about getting *her* more attention, giving *her* public profile more depth. But underneath all the pretence, she's right. She's just *nothing*. I grip my hands tight together in front of me, glance at the laptop on the table, its light still pulsing. I hope it's done its job.

'I'm trying to . . .' I say. 'This is a lot.'

'I know, right?' Leni says. 'It's been a lot. Too much. And that's even before all the stuff with Xav. Because Xav always kept on about it, you know?'

'About Frida's fall?'

Leni shakes her head. 'No, about me being boring, *ordinary*. You know Xav, he finds a weak spot and just keeps jabbing his finger in. Jab, jab jab. My videos were *a snorefest*. My editing style was *basic*. My look was *trying too hard*. My nicknames became Ele*snore* or Ele*norm*. Remember when my Silver Shimmer palette came out? He did that whole video taking out all the silvers, painting them on his face until he turned grey, "as dull as Leni's personality", as he put it. He had no idea that I'd been through all this. He still thought of me as this silly sheltered girl with no life experience. Andy tried to talk to him about it once, but by then, Xav was going into full meltdown – he wouldn't listen to reason. And I think –' she glances at Andy'– I think that's when Andy might have said something that made Xav suspicious.'

'Come on, Leni, we need to get this done,' Andy says. 'The police are probably looking for her.'

Get this done. The words make the skin on the back of my neck prickle. Was he just talking about getting my computer password or were they planning to hurt me?

'I need to understand.' I'm fighting to keep the horror out of my voice. 'I d-don't want to lose our friendship.'

A smile flickers at the corners of her mouth. I've said the right thing.

'Tell me,' I say.

Leni

I don't know if I mentioned this before, but Andy and I went through a kind of a weird time at the end of last year. We were living together, working together, just cooped up, 24–7. We talked about nothing but the channel, what was going to make good content, how we needed to push numbers. I know Andy won't mind me saying this but there was about a month when the only time we touched each other was in front of the camera. I kept thinking and thinking about it because it just didn't compute. We'd been so tight, so connected. We'd been through so much together.

By then Don't Cross Me had become just a fantasy game, something we'd talk about lying in bed at night, trading make-believe revenge in the dark. We had too much to lose to play for real.

Most of our revenge fantasies were about Xav. I was barely talking to him by then, and when he dumped Ed, I realised it was the perfect opportunity for me to take the high ground, cut him off for good and maybe position myself as a spokesperson against emotional abuse. I made some strong content, and remember when I cut Xav dead at the Vloggie Awards? That photo got amazing numbers.

So I was really surprised when he came up to me later on backstage looking worried – I'd never seen Xav look worried before. He leaned in close to me, gripping my arm.

'Look, I know you hate me and I get that, but I've found out something that's more important than all that,' he said. 'It's about Andy and Sam. It sounds dramatic but I'm worried you're in danger. Don't tell Andy – please, *please* don't tell Andy. Just come and see me so I can explain it to you alone.'

Then his face lit up with a wicked grin as an idea occurred

to him. 'Actually, don't just come chat to me, come *murder* me!'

He laid it out then, his whole absurd plan about faking his death. He wanted the whole world to believe it; that's why he didn't want any messages on his phone or an email trail to give it away. If I'd been listening properly, I've had told him what a load of rubbish his plan was, how he'd end up being prosecuted for wasting police time, but I wasn't. Because all I could think of was, *he knows. He knows about Sam.*

And then my mind started whirring, working with the only advantage we had. *He thinks I don't know.*

I was shaking when I got home – not with fear but with that kind of desperate, nervous energy I feel whenever I need to get going on something, need to plan. I burst in the front door to find Andy fresh from his Kendo session, his skin slick with sweat, glowing with freshly charged strength and power. As I told him, his eyes glittered. We found ourselves smiling at each other and suddenly things weren't so stale any more. Not when everything we'd worked for was being threatened.

He'd have killed Xav for me that very night, I knew it. But we couldn't mess this up. We couldn't act hastily as he'd done with Sam. Besides, it was my turn. And I had already been invited in. You look shocked, Maxine, and I know you could never have done something like this; you don't have it in you. To be honest, I wasn't sure I had what it takes, either. But sometimes, in order to grow, you have to step out of your comfort zone.

I kept my options open. I packed a knife in my bag that night, I made a fake live-stream video with Andy, I put on my dark wig and brown contact lenses I usually wore to avoid getting hassled in the street. Just as Xav instructed, I crept in through the utility room window and up the fire escape stairs, where Xav had turned the camera off. But I still kept thinking I wasn't going to do it.

Xav opened the door and laughed. 'Wow, you've finally gone completely normcore!'

'Piss off, Xav,' I snapped back, and a funny expression came over his face. He looked . . . *ashamed*.

'Shit, it's like I can't help myself,' he said. 'I'm sorry.'

Xav apologising – the shock of that pushed my anger down a little and for the next ten minutes or so we played nice. I sat with him on his sculptural leather sofa. I made small talk, exchanged gossip. That's when I gave him the Crimson Rush sample, still wanting to impress him, somehow. Pathetic, really.

My anger subsided. I began to think this whole situation was something we had imagined. Andy and I could work on him, shut him up, somehow. I could put up with his constant jibes and mocking. There was still a way back.

Xav leaned in towards me. So close I could smell the Problematic on him. He reached out and touched my hand. The contact was so shocking I nearly jumped back.

'Look, Lenster, I've been doing a lot of soul searching lately and I want to clear the air. All that time ago, when we did the Greatest Fears video . . . I heard you. The voice changer app recorded you saying your real greatest fear and ... I suppose I used it against you. I know, I know, I'm a complete and utter shit. I'm working on myself.'

I couldn't respond. I was too busy fighting this torrent of rage and frustration at what he'd just said. He'd weaponised my weakness and attacked me over and over, and now, after this one glib apology, he kind of shrugged off the subject, as if his bullying hadn't chipped away at my confidence for *years*.

'There's something more important I need to tell you,' he said. 'I'm worried about you. Andy isn't the person you think he is.'

Xav explained that he'd been having some big feels after the fallout with Ed. Realised that maybe he'd gone a bit too far. Maybe he'd hurt a few too many people, starting with his oldest, most loyal friend, poor sad Sam.

'I started to add up some of the things Andy said over the years,' he said. 'Stuff about you standing by him when he made his "little mistake" that nearly got us expelled. I started trying to find out what really happened.'

Xav had gone into detective mode, ended up tracking down our old caretaker's widow and charming her into letting him go through her late husband's things. The old Boomer always felt guilty about it, apparently, hung on to an ancient piece of security footage without knowing what to do with it.

'Andy must have lied to you about what happened. He's ... he's sick. I don't know the word for it. To do something like this and call it a little mistake! He's fooled you, but don't let him take you in any longer.'

I listened, chewing the inside of my cheek harder and harder with the effort not to speak out, not to tell him I wasn't the naive idiot he thought I was. That I had power, that I had power over *him*, in the form of a knife, sitting in my bag.

I thanked him – I bloody *thanked* him for warning me. I said he'd given me a lot to think about, and then asked him where the footage was. 'Can I see it for myself?'

'Not now, it's hidden somewhere.' He waved his hand vaguely over at the gaming and filming room.

'And what are you planning to do with it?'

Xav winked. 'We'll just see what happens after I die! But I'll hold it back a little while, give you a chance to distance yourself. Your brand can survive this, Leni. Carl will help. You'll be OK.'

My first instinct then was to beg. To burst into tears, plead with Xav not to do this, tell him that Andy was sorry. *Please don't make me split up with my boyfriend, I love him.*

Fuck that, though. I would not humiliate myself any more in front of this idiot. This *fool*. He clearly couldn't read my expression because a second later he jumped to his feet, bouncing with that trademark Xav energy.

'You all right? Good,' he said. 'Let's do this. I'll get the props.' As an afterthought, he picked up the Crimson Rush and tucked it away on his shelf with all his other freebies, like it didn't matter.

I still wasn't going to do it, though. I left my knife in the bag, took the fake one he gave me, stood in the kitchen waiting for my cue, and then . . .

I don't know, something changed. I was sick of Xav dominating my life – jibing from the sidelines, threatening my career, putting me down. I stopped thinking. I dropped the trick knife, grabbed one out of Xav's knife block and just . . . did it.

It felt weird. Real. Messy. Fake blood and real blood mingling. You don't see the half of it on that video. It was horrible, so sticky. I had no idea what I was doing but it's almost like the knife knew the way. Xav's body bucked and pushed against me, then went limp and became something that wasn't Xav any more.

I shut down the camera. He was gone, and so was my anger at him. Now I just felt so desperately sad that he'd kept pushing, that it had ended this way. 'Oh Xav, you poor fool,' I said softly, closing his eyes.

My right glove was sticky, my heart beat faster and faster, and for the first time, I realised what Xav had been getting at. I'd never done anything crazy before, never let myself make a mistake, taken a step I couldn't take back. Life up until now had been pale, easy – a shadow.

Priorities, Leni. I had to concentrate on the practicalities. I scoured the place for USB drives, shoved them all in my bag. I copied Xav's files, wiped most of them from his hard drive. I grabbed his phone – although I threw it in the river later, freaked out by the idea the police could track it.

All the while the video was sitting there onscreen.

At first, I meant to delete it, but I needed to watch it first, to see what I'd done. It was real, raw. Most importantly, because the shot was so tightly set up (thank you, Xav), you couldn't see much of me at all. Just my arms and the mask. Watching it again, seeing Xav's eyes widen with fright, the comment about his hair breaking the tension slightly, then the mask looming in . . .

It was just an amazing, *amazing* video. It was perfect, first-take.

Now I finally understood why Andy had pushed Sam, why Sam had climbed on that flagpole, why people do stupid, crazy things all the time. It's because, in the moment, you just *have* to. And maybe I could use Xav's death; it could be the making of me, a chance to show the world there was more to me than make-up. That I have *lived*, I have *suffered*. To show the world that I'm not nothing. I never was.

I clicked upload.

Maxine

My mind is racing. It's taking all my self-control not to scream or run or rage. I'm angry, but also sad and heartbroken at her cold description of Xav's death and ashamed at the fact that I've never seen through her before. But above all else my brain is screaming at me to get out of there. To survive.

I can see the way Andy is eyeing me, assessing what kind of threat I pose. I think I know the rules now. As long as I haven't crossed them, I'm safe.

But I *have* crossed them. If they find out what I've just done, there's no way I'm leaving this room alive.

'God, Leni, I had no idea you were under so much pressure,' I said, trying to keep my voice even. 'Why didn't you ask me outright to look for the files for you? You know I would have done it. You didn't have to threaten me.'

I want to add, *You didn't need to attack Ed*, but Andy is staring at me intently now, searching my voice for criticism, for crossing.

'I'm just saying, I'd have done it, no questions asked,' I add.

Leni shakes her head. 'But you *did* keep asking questions,' she says. 'Like the funeral – I'd have been happy to tell you we'd bought those flowers, it just seemed fitting to send a bouquet from Alex. But you went all detective on us instead, and Andy ... Andy thought it might be fun to shake you and the others up a little. He enjoyed leaving little messages dotted all over the internet to tease the conspiracy theorists – it's been nice to do some trolling of our own for a change.'

'Are you going to kill me now?' My voice squeaks and trembles, giving me away.

Leni looks horrified. 'God, Maxine, no. You're my *friend*. Even if you tell the police all this – and you *won't* because we're *friends* – there's no evidence without that video. The police have already checked us out – they weren't fooled by the fake-live of course, that was just for fans. But Carl swore he was with us that night. Anything to protect his last big money-making client. So, without the video, we're good.'

'I'm going to need your password, Maxine,' Andy says. He's still between me and the door; his whole body looks poised, ready to crush me if I make a wrong move. I don't think he's fooled by my fake understanding, not for a second.

'OK,' I stammer. 'But I want you to let me go now. Unlock the door, Andy. I'll stand by it and the second you're in, I'm gone. D-deal?'

They exchange one of their telepathic-couple-looks and nod. 'Deal.'

Andy turns the lock and I position myself by the door, muscles tensed, trying to hide my instinctive need to run. I tell them my password, and Andy steps aside.

'OK, I'm in,' Leni says.

I put my hand on the door, turn the handle, and feel a rush of hope and relief as it opens. I force my legs to move, to walk, not run. To play calm as I leave the room. *Please, please, laptop be slow.*

I'm in the corridor now. *Keep going. Keep moving. Faster now. Faster . . .* I break into a run. At the end of the corridor there's light, there are people, I can hear the buzz of their conversation, shouts of laughter, the crackle of a security guard's radio. I'll be safe there in public. I just need to reach it before they see . . .

But then it comes, a scream from Leni, a roar of primal rage from Andy.

His footsteps thunder down the corridor behind me. He's not thinking straight, lost sight of common sense after what he's just seen, what I've just done to them.

Up ahead, I see a passer-by pause to check her phone. Her expression changes and I'm sure she's looking at it: Xav's burn files video that I uploaded to the VlogCon channel when I was hiding in the toilet cubicle. They'll all have seen it by now.

A sharp pain in my shoulder, a hand wrenching me back and I lose my balance. My head hits the floor hard and I turn to see Andy's face, twisted with rage as his weight crashes down on me, forcing the breath out of my lungs. His fist slams into my face; pain blooms, pain like I've never felt before. Real. Harsh. Screaming through my head until I can't think about anything else. And then I feel his hands close around my throat, hot and strangely gentle. They start to squeeze. I scrabble at his wrists, trying to push him away with the heel of my hand. It's like pushing against stone. He's not moving, just tightening his grip around my neck. My whole body is pinned to the ground; his face is a blur as I close my eyes against it . . .

And then . . .

And then . . .

And then . . .

Chapter 35

Maxine

And then there's another roar of rage. I don't know where it's coming from, I barely recognise it as human, but suddenly Andy's weight is pulled off me. I roll over on to my side, coughing, curling into a ball. The instinct to keep myself safe is stronger than my need to know what's going on. And so, I just hear it – Leni's wails, the sound of trainers scrabbling on the floor, a struggle.

There's another sound, an otherworldly, horrendous shriek that goes on and on. I don't want to turn over, don't want to see.

I feel a hand on my shoulder.

'Are you OK?' The voice is Ed's, taut with worry. 'Can you sit up?'

I can't answer, just give a croak, and roll back over, pain blooming in my side from where I hit the floor.

Then I see it. Andy, prone on the floor, pinned down. Frida sits on his chest, fists clenched into tight, brightly ringed balls of fury as they strike out again, again.

It's like all the anger she ever felt – being ignored at school, rejected by Xav, desperately sad at home – all that fury is pouring out on Andy's face right now. Andy should be stronger than her, he should be able to push her off easily, but he's just prone, helpless in the face of her raw rage.

I look around for Leni, but she's gone.

'Frida,' I croak.

Ed's hand settles back on my shoulder as if to tell me, *Stay there*. There's a world of care in that gesture, a hope that he's forgiven me for the secrets I kept, for what happened to him. Ed gets up and pulls Frida away effortlessly, drawing her into his arms. Her face is red-raw, a mess of snot and tears, but she doesn't fight any more, just sobs in his arms in great heaves, like she's never cried before.

Andy is struggling to his feet, his face cut to ribbons by Frida's rings, when the police come.

Police station tea is even hotter and sweeter than Ethan's. Someone drapes a blanket over my shoulders – it's still baking outside, but I am shivering. Detective Riley looks even more tired than before, his pudgy fingers running through his thinning hair. He tells me at length what I have done wrong – not showing him the video messages or the Alex email, not telling him as soon as I found the files. But after my interview, when the tape is turned off, he sighs.

'Miss Grange-Fuller and Mr Duncan were under suspicion, evidence was being gathered, but we didn't have enough to arrest them. If we'd had those emails . . .'

I slump down in my seat, flooded with guilt again, and his tone softens slightly. 'No point having regrets, Miss Fernando.

If I've learned anything in this game, it's that people make some funny old decisions when they're under pressure.'

I feel disorientated, almost drunk as I stumble out of my interview. Down the corridor another door opens and Frida comes out, looking every bit as drained as me. In the foyer, Ed is slumped on a plastic chair playing a game on his phone. We don't discuss it, just get in an Uber and head to my place, hole up in my room full of teenage relics and whodunnit wallcharts. A room that feel like home to me now, because they're here.

Mum distributes snacks – not cake pops or branded iced cookies that look good on camera, but big bowls of Lidl crisps and plain old chocolate Hobnobs. My phone has been beeping like mad with Facehunters updates and, when I get a moment, I'll go on there, apologise for using my fake ID and thank them for helping when I was at my lowest. I genuinely love those guys. Even Ola.

But right now, there's something else I need to watch – the footage of what happened to Leni afterwards. There's a lot of it online – it's VC, so everyone who was there filmed it – and there are lots of viewpoints to choose from. But the most viewed one, the one all the news sites have gone with, shows a girl in the main hall where all the merch stalls are. At first she's just recording her shock at having witnessed Xav's video on the big screens. Then there's a flash of scarlet in the background.

'Isn't that . . .?' the girl says. Then she realises it couldn't be. It couldn't be Leni because the figure she has seen has close-cropped hair, is wearing a grey hoodie, the most un-Leni item of clothing in the world. But then, the figure pulls the hood further up with one hand and we see a shimmer of steel fingernails. The girl turns to her friend.

'It *is* her. Hey look, Ally, it's her! It's Leni_Loves!'

Another voice shrieks, outraged, as if this is her greatest crime, 'Oh my days, she's been wearing *wigs!*'

The sound from the crowd as it surges forward is otherworldly. As one they are screeching her name in anger, in shock. Leni presses up against the wall, looking frantically around her, but there's nowhere to go, thousands of fans crowding in on her, holding her down, taking her picture. She sinks to the floor, hugs her knees. The girl holding the camera is being jostled back by the rest of the crowd now but it means you can see dozens of arms holding cameras, pointing them directly at Leni's face. She stares in panic, her wide eyes gazing at them. Her lips are moving but I can't work out what she's saying – something like *don't* and *it's not true . . .*

Eventually Leni pushes back against the wall, squeezing her eyes shut with shame and fear. She stays there, curled into a ball with the people around her shouting accusations: *Did you know? How could you not know?*

What would have happened if they'd known for sure she was The Face, or if the police, still in their riot gear from outside, hadn't pushed their way through the crowd at that moment?

'Bloody hell,' I say. My brain still hasn't finished adjusting to the reality of who Leni is, of what she's done, and there's a part of me that's still shocked by how brutal the scene looks, the sheer naked anger of fans who realise they've been lied to on an epic scale.

'She deserves it,' Ed says.

Frida stays quiet, looks at her bare hands. The police confiscated all the rings as evidence. She's hoping there won't be an assault charge, but they won't confirm it yet. But despite this, since her attack on Andy, it's like something's settled in her. That anger, that delight in mayhem has shrunk down. Like me, she's probably trying to figure out how she feels now. Who she is, when she's not raging or scared. That's OK, though – Frida's good at reinvention.

And now that we've talked and talked until our throats are sore, and watched every video from every angle, what is left for us to do?

'We were on season five, weren't we?' Ed says finally.

'Season five. The twerking episode. Perfect.'

Frida groans. 'Ugh. *Glee*. This is going to be so pathetically cringe, isn't it?' But she settles down on the bed next to Ed; we pull the covers up and watch.

Chapter 36

Frida, six months on

There is no point bringing flowers to Xav's grave. No point at all. It's been six months and still you can't see the headstone for red roses, rainbow teddy bears, bows and assorted tat. The air around smells of rotten vegetation. Xav would have sneered at it all for its tackiness, but still love the fact that it's there. That people still remember him even now.

The love stones are the sweetest. The ground in front of his grave is covered with a sea of colourful pebbles painted with the names of lovers – boys, girls, non-binary, pansexual, asexual and just plain friendship – all kinds of love are here. I'm still not sure if Xav himself ever knew how to love, if he'd have figured it out had he got the chance, but this is what he has come to mean to people and, if it helps them, then I like it.

Maxine links arms with me and the contact feels safe, reassuring, bringing me back to the present. A time when Xav is here, in the ground. When I'm working on my relationship with Dad. Trying to be patient and help him. When Ed is carving out a new life as an A-level student with a hot barman boyfriend and when Leni and Andy are in prison awaiting trial for murder, conspiracy to murder and various charges surrounding the attack on me. I saw a photo of Leni at an early hearing – hair still shorn, violet eyes sparkling. She didn't look beaten, not at all. And although she can't make videos in jail, subscriptions to her channel have doubled and her make-up palettes are changing hands for hundreds of pounds online. People are so weird.

We walk the last few metres to the graveside together, and then I break away, kneel in the wet grass, brush some dead flowers away from his name.

Xavier Bailey

Taken too soon

For once, Xav's dad has picked the right words, chosen the truth. What would he have done, what would he have been if Leni hadn't killed him? Would he have walked away from PlayMii like he'd planned and made a difference in the world? Would he have been my friend again? Maybe, in another universe, we made it to Indonesia to save the wrinkly orange dudes.

I glance over at Maxine and see that her lips are pressed together, tight and thin. She's twisting a tissue between her hard-bitten fingers, but she won't cry. Maxine's not dough any more; there's steel in her now, and wisdom – although her videos are every bit as silly as they've ever been. I notice today she's wearing jeans and a plain puffy jacket, and no leopard print. I don't think I've seen her wear it for weeks. I guess sometimes reinventing yourself means *not* having a signature look.

No more secrets, that's the rule between us now. If we've got a problem, we share it. But there are some things I still don't feel ready to talk about.

Ed and I weren't looking at the VC PlayMii channel when the video went live. We were too busy freaking out – Maxine's text about 'bloody fans' had sent us into even more of a panic, as we knew she'd never, ever say that. So, we were scrambling around, phoning the police, desperately searching for Maxine in the crowds at the conference centre.

But still, when the video went live, we knew something momentous had happened. The reaction rippled through the crowds and, suddenly, there it was on the big screen over the stage. A security video of two figures on a rooftop, one clinging to a flagpole, the other one leaning forward, while Xav's voice, from beyond the grave, explains to the audience what they're seeing.

And for a few moments, I was frozen to the spot, just staring, the world whirling around me, setting itself into a new alignment, a new way of thinking. I really was pushed, Andy really did attack me. But behind that knowledge was something bigger, more important, than mere attempted murder.

Xav had moved heaven and earth to get that security footage, and he'd done it for me. Xav was sorry. Xav cared. And because he cared about me, Leni killed him. Every time I think about it, I get a burst of joy, with a hard chaser of guilt. It's my fault he's here, in this grave, instead of creating mayhem in the world.

I can feel it building up in me now – the anger, that healthy, warm rage I've always had inside me, every injustice in the world pouring down into my belly creating a righteous fire. But Maxine senses it as I tense up. She looks at me and smiles, and it just . . . goes away.

'Ready?' Maxine says, passing me a flagpole we made out of a piece of garden bamboo.

'Ready,' I say, reaching into the basket-bag on my shoulder.

It was hard to find a pair of yellow pants that were every bit as disgusting and awful as the ones Xav and I had used as our emblem, the ones I had destroyed. But eBay is a strange and mysterious thing, and somewhere amidst the second-hand The Face masks, overpriced Leni_Loves palettes and knock-off ITS_XAVVVVV T-shirts, there they were, in all their mustard-coloured polyester glory.

Gently, I hook them on to the pole and they flap gently, pleasingly in the breeze, and I whisper goodbye to Mister Frodo, from Sam.

Saying goodbye is easier now, because for the first time in my life I have a friend, a proper, honest-to-goodness friend. Someone who knows when I'm about to blow up and swoops in, defusing the bomb. Someone who texts me all night with gossip and stupid jokes, even though she's going to see me first thing in the morning for sunrise aerial yoga. Someone who meets me for milkshake, then makes me laugh until strawberry smoothie comes out of my nose – and doesn't look horrified when it does.

I'm still not sure how to do it, how to draw the line between friendship and all-consuming love. But I'm working on it. And, anyway, I know Maxine won't disappoint me. She won't let me down or break my heart like Xav.

I really don't know what I'd do if she did.

If you've been affected by any of the issues raised in this book, please visit:
https://www.youngminds.org.uk/

Acknowledgements

Still reading? Thank you so much! Thank you to every reader for giving this book your time and your eyeballs. And also thank you to every book blogger, Bookstagrammer, Booktokker, Booktuber and print reviewer who has championed my first book, *The Girl Who . . .* , and *Dead Lucky*, too. You do what you do for the love of books and the lift you give us is astonishing.

Writing about influencers was always going to be a challenge – the pressures and weirdnesses of putting your whole self online have always fascinated me but, let's face it, Gen Z readers are always going to know more about the world of YouTube, Instagram and TikTok than me. So I'm so grateful to the influencers I've spoken to over the last year who have helped me keep the PlayMeeps' voices real and especially to Jake Edwards, whose help and guidance was invaluable. If I've made the odd gaffe, it's very much my fault, not theirs. The same goes for Louise Mitchell, who gave me insight into police procedures around investigating major crimes. Lou, I'm sorry that Detective Riley is such a dinosaur, I'll try to include a more on-the-ball copper next time.

None of this would have been possible without my brilliant agent Lina Langlee and her colleague Julie Fergusson, who helped and supported me through the early stages, and talked me through a fair few crises. My editor Olivia Hutchings has been so brilliant at picking through my tangled web, gently undoing the knots and tying the loose ends together. Likewise, thanks to Stephanie Melrose and Francesca Banks for their ninja publicity work and Madeleine Hall for hand-holding me through some of the social media stuff I really should have already known about. And on the subject of social media, big thanks to fellow author and Instagram dreamweaver AJ West.

It took me a long time to understand that writing isn't a solitary occupation at all, that you can't write your best book without help and support from others. Lauren Henderson, who looked at my first book and encouraged me to keep going. Radhika Holmström and Miriam Sattar Holmström – you were all so helpful. A big shout-out to my online group Writers International, which is bursting with talented authors, the wonderful, welcoming Good Ship group, The D20 and D21 author groups and the Witches who keep me grounded. Dawn Smith and Tiffany Sherlock deserve a special mention for being utterly amazing, as does Whelkvis, our muse.

And finally my family. Richard, who gave me time, space and encouragement to write and my children Rufus and Elena, who didn't. Mum and Paul, Dad and Sandra, Lucia, Rob and Sya – I love you all more than Maxine loves leopard print, more than Leni loves make-up, more than Xav loves himself. And that's saying something.